a *Songbird* novel

True Love

MELISSA PEARL

NOTE FROM THE AUTHOR

Rock 'n' roll has always been one of my favorite genres. I love feeling a heavy beat thrum through my veins, and I love blasting the music so loud it's the only thing to exist in that moment.

Nessa is kind of like the girl I wanted to be as a teenager, but I never had the courage. I love that she plays the drums. I love her quiet "stick it" attitude, and I love her faithful loyalty to Jimmy. Writing this love story was a total privilege. Chaos has been in the Songbird world since its inception, and it's been so cool finally getting to write Jimmy and Nessa's journey. Music is what brought them together and makes them the kind of couple they are.

There is so much we can learn from music of any kind. I love the emotion it creates within me—a sense of joy, excitement, peace, sadness, inspiration…music speaks in a way that nothing else can.

I hope you are inspired by this soundtrack and experience all the emotions I did while writing this story.

xx
Melissa

TRUE LOVE SOUNDTRACK

(Please note: The songs listed below are not always the original versions, but the ones I chose to listen to while constructing this book. The songs are listed in the order they appear.)

UNKISS ME
Performed by Maroon 5

I MISS YOU
Performed by Blink-182

WHEN WE STAND TOGETHER
Performed by Nickelback

WELCOME TO MY LIFE
Performed by Simple Plan

BRAND NEW DAY
Performed by Forty Foot Echo

THE ART OF LOSING
Performed by American Hi-Fi

HANGING BY A MOMENT
Performed by Lifehouse

CALYPSO
Performed by Spiderbait

CARPE DIEM
Performed by Green Day

TROUBLE
Performed by Pink

RUN
Performed by Pink

GOING UNDER
Performed by Evanescence

F**KIN' PERFECT
Performed by Pink

FALL TO PIECES
Performed by Avril Lavigne

TEENAGE DIRTBAG
Performed by Wheatus

TRUE LOVE
Performed by Pink, Lily Allen

SIGHT OF THE SUN
Performed by Fun

ROCK N ROLL
Performed by Avril Lavigne

COME ON, LET'S GO
Performed by Girl in a Coma

ONE DAY
Performed by Simple Plan

SHE IS BEAUTIFUL
Performed by Children of Bodom

MIRROR
Performed by BarlowGirl

LUCKY
Performed by Jason Mraz, Colbie Caillat

I'M GONNA BE (500 MILES)
Performed by The Proclaimers

FIGHT SONG
Performed by Rachel Platten

To enhance your reading experience, you can
listen along to the playlist for TRUE LOVE on
Spotify.
https://open.spotify.com/user/12146962946/pl
aylist/0vSC9L5du2ztsNbqTMQZZM

For two totally amazing women...

Pink
&
Bethany Hamilton

You are very different women, but your strength, tenacity, and die-hard attitude have inspired me. You have become people women around the world can look up to. Thank you for never giving in and letting life's circumstances beat you.

ONE

NESSA

It's so easy to look back on your life and wonder, "What if?"

What if he'd never heard me playing the drums in the music suite that day? What if we hadn't won *Shock Wave* and scored a deal with Torrence Records?

What if I'd never let him kiss me?

The motorcycle rumbled beneath me, sending vibrations shooting down my legs as I sat at the empty crossroads in the middle of America and wondered.

It was an overcast day, but the sun was burning

off the clouds, and it would soon heat up. I was in no hurry for that to happen. The morning air was cool and refreshing, a light breeze ruffling tendrils of dark hair across my leather jacket. The road was a silent, black snake winding through the countryside, and I was a lone rider trying to decide which way to turn. After an early morning shower, the asphalt was slick, and the first rays of sun were creating an eerie steam on the surface. I stared at it until the wisps of steam turned into a fuzzy mirage.

I had to make a choice.

Gripping the handlebars, I held my breath as I considered each option.

Left meant returning to Jimmy—the leader of our band, Chaos, and the guy who broke my heart.

Right meant...well, I wasn't sure what right meant. I couldn't return to my childhood home in Mississippi, and Chicago without Rosie or Chaos held no appeal.

"Unkiss Me" by Maroon 5 swirled in my brain. It'd been torturing me nonstop since the day I threw my drumsticks at Jimmy and split.

If only he could unkiss me.

If only we could take back what we'd done, but the past was sealed and no amount of wishing would change that. I'd been playing out of my league the whole time...I should have known I'd lose. Guys like Jimmy Baker didn't fall for girls like me.

I looked left, my heart tugging me back to my boys, the only family I still had, but I couldn't. The idea of facing Jimmy was too much.

Images of his gorgeous face warping and turning to ash danced in the front of my mind, like some morbid horror movie I couldn't get away from. I sat in a bar last night, in the sleepy little town of Payton, and I don't know what possessed me, but the bartender and I burned photos of the people who'd broken us. Jimmy's straight nose and bright blue eyes bubbled and twisted, his pouty lips that tasted so damn good started to split and melt away...just like I needed them to. I thought it would help me, but I'd been fighting tears ever since.

I stared down the long, empty road. If I turned that way, I'd be heading back to the life I'd been wanting for years, except it had been tainted.

Gunning the engine, I released the clutch and turned right. Guilt singed me as I rode through the early morning light, further away from my responsibilities. I'd signed a contract a few weeks ago, promising Torrence Records I'd play the drums for Chaos, record an album, and then tour the country. But after what went down, I had to get out. I'd been on my Triumph Speedmaster for nearly two weeks, cruising the highways and backroads of the magnificent USA. It was an escape ploy, and I'd have to face up to my commitments eventually, but a few more days away wouldn't hurt anybody.

Rosie always used to say that time healed most things, and I only needed a little more.

At least that's what I told myself as I jerked off the main road and headed down a winding route that looked untouched. I was cruising the edge of a hill, an open plain to my right and a steep embankment rising on my left. I glanced across the lane and smiled at the random, gray rocks jutting out from the hill. It was like God had been playing marbles with the angels and they'd forgotten to pack away their toys. The thought made me chuckle.

I opened up the throttle a little more, enjoying the roar of the Speedmaster's engine. The second I laid eyes on the charcoal bike, I'd had to make it mine. I'd pictured myself cruising the roads, the scenery flashing past me as I lost myself in the rush. It was the first thing I purchased with my grandmother's inheritance money. The lawyer lets me have it in small bursts, like a yearly allowance. My grandma knew me all too well. She'd set everything up just the way I needed it to be.

That deep sadness I pretended didn't linger in the pit of my belly swirled up my throat, making it hard to swallow. I pressed my lips together and blinked, slapping down the visor on my helmet and accelerating up the hill.

I crested the rise at speed, and my stomach lurched as I grappled the brakes. A pick-up truck lay upside-down, angling across both lanes and leaving me nowhere to go. I glimpsed the unconscious driver with his blood-spattered face. He was dangling upside-down in his seat, but I had no time to do anything about it. The slick road protested against the sudden jerk of my squealing tires, and I slammed into the driver's door. The impact sent me flying, the weightless sensation coming to a bitter end as I circled over the truck and smashed into the implacable asphalt. I landed on my back, a loud pop echoing in my head as my helmet struck the ground. I whimpered and fought for air, my body protesting against the pain.

A flash of black caught my eye, and I flinched. My bike careened up the steep embankment before hurtling toward me. Its heavy weight clamped down on my arm and snatched my fingers into the burning-hot engine.

I screamed—a feral, unchecked sound that tore out of my throat before the blinding agony cut off my senses and left me panting on the road.

There were no sounds around me. The motorcycle engine cut off after the crash, and all that remained was a chilling hush. The skin on my elbows and left hip burned from the way I'd landed. My clothes must have been torn, because a cool breeze stung my grazes.

I lay like a helpless starfish on the road. My arm was trapped, and I was too afraid to move in case I'd broken something. I didn't even want to lift the visor on my helmet.

A hawk swooped above me, gliding on the wind currents and then disappearing into the ever-brightening sky. All I could do was lie there, caught in an unfathomable nightmare...and like some sick joke, the only thing I could think about was damn Jimmy Baker and the way his photograph warped and faded as I tried to let him go.

TWO

JIMMY

I couldn't let her go.

I don't know what the hell had come over me, but that night with Nessa had changed everything.

Slumping back onto the couch, I stared at the drum kit in our practice area, picturing her sitting on that stool and smashing the hell out of the skins. A smile would light her face and she'd poke the tip of her tongue out between her rosebud lips. Her pale brown eyes would sparkle with the sheer joy of drumming. If only I'd realized all those times we played together how I'd really felt about her.

But she was gone.

I swallowed, the noise sounding loud and thick in my ears. Snatching my phone off the cushion beside me, I opened iTunes and searched for something to break the tormenting silence. If Nessa was there, she'd be thumping around upstairs in her room. Music would blast from her sound system—Avril Lavigne or Pink, most likely. I smiled as I imagined her dancing around the house in her ripped jeans, the little stud in her nose glinting as she threw back her head and belted out the lyrics.

She'd moved into the guest house about a week after we'd moved into our new pad in LA. We'd been all set up and living together in the main house when she'd walked in on Flick and some random girl doing it in the shower.

She'd had a fit, packed her bags and relocated into the guest house at the back of the property. We'd all laughed pretty hard, but I'd actually been kinda sad, which was why I insisted the practice area remained in the living room of the guest house. Nessa didn't complain, and it gave me the perfect excuse to see her whenever I wanted. If only I'd understood my real motivation. I'd thought it was all about the music, when in reality, it'd been all about her.

I punched my thumb onto "I Miss You" by Blink-182. The beat kicked in quickly, and I leaned my head against the sofa. Gazing up at the ceiling, my mind rushed back to the last time I'd seen my best friend.

The Torrence Records recording studio blew my mind. The entire band stood there in stunned silence, our mouths falling open as we gazed around the square space with its padded walls. The pristine equipment glinted under the overhead lights, and we all started chuckling like kids in a candy store. Flick's eyes were bright, the look on his face reminding me of a love-struck teen.

I laid my guitar case down on the floor and smiled at Nessa. She gave me a long, steady look then turned for the drum kit. I sighed. She hadn't smiled at me once since our fight in the guest house. I had to wonder if she'd ever smile at me again. I thought time would heal it, but nine days later and she was still being pigheaded.

"Okay, guys, what do you think?" Marcus strolled in, his face practically beaming. He had to be one of the nicest guys I'd ever met, and I couldn't believe we'd lucked out with him as our manager. Torrence Records assigned him to us the day after we won Shock Wave, and he'd been dealing with everything. Today was our first recording session for our very first single.

Holy shit! Our first official single!

We'd shared our stuff on the YouTube channel we started in high school, and when we entered Shock Wave our following went through the roof, but we'd never made a proper recording like this. Shock Wave had helped us get our covers onto iTunes, but we'd never had a hit on the radio, we'd never made a whole album, and we'd never gone on a nationwide tour. This was it. This was everything we'd been working for since the ninth grade.

A glee I couldn't describe skittered through me as I

stepped up to the mic and laughed into it.

"This is so freaking cool," Ralphie chuckled, pulling out his bass guitar and lifting the strap over his head.

"I thought you guys might like it." Marcus slid his hands into his pockets. He was silently laughing at our excitement; I could tell by the glint in his hazel eyes. His sandy-brown hair had been styled to look scruffy, and he ran his fingers over the messy spikes before turning to Nessa.

"The kit okay?"

"Yeah, it'll be fine," she mumbled, taking a seat on the stool and pulling out her beloved drumsticks. She had about ten pairs, but she'd brought her favorite today—the ones with the small nicks that she'd colored over with black ink. The musical tattoo on her middle finger caught my eye like it always did as she wrapped her petite hands around the sticks and gave the snare a little tap. She banged the bass drum pedal and adjusted her perky little butt on the seat.

An image of my hands running over the curve of her ass flashed in my brain. My fingers trailed up her soft skin, tracing the tattoo on her left hip before I gripped her to me and…

I closed my eyes against the memory, wishing for the millionth time that it had never happened. Yet in a weird way, I didn't regret it, either. She'd been perfection, like nothing I'd ever known…and it scared the living shit out of me.

Nessa caught me staring at her and gave me a pointed look. I turned my back on it then grabbed my guitar and checked the tuning. Garrett, the sound guy, interrupted my tweaking.

"*Alright, dudes and dudette.*" His surfer drawl made me grin. It was so far removed from my Chicago upbringing that even after seven months in LA, I still wasn't used to it. "*Nessy, babe, give me a beat and we'll test out the levels.*"

Nessa did a quick roll on the snare then launched into an epic solo. She was so damn sexy on those drums, her long hair flying as she threw her head back and smashed the cymbals. In spite of her awesome sound, I'd seen her play better. She seemed a little off that day. Who was I kidding? She'd been off all week. Her eyes were closed, and I waited for that small smile to light her face, but it never came.

Her eyes snapped open as she finished and I grinned at her, but she just stared at me, deadpan.

I rolled my eyes and turned away. She needed to get over it. I was protecting us, not trying to hurt her. My throat constricted, reminding me I was a lying scumbag.

Flick and Ralphie did their sound checks, and then it was my turn. My fingers danced over the strings as I let rip and tried to expel some of my frustrations with a kick-ass solo. It worked a little, but as soon as I'd finished I could feel the hate vibes Nessa was shooting into my back. Her brown eyes, usually so soft and sweet, were dark and disgruntled when I turned to face her.

I cleared my throat. "*Okay, are we ready to try this?*"

Marcus stepped out of the room and stood behind the glass. He was looking pretty pleased with our warm-up solos. I could tell he was hyped about what Chaos could do for Torrence Records. He was twenty-three—the youngest manager at Torrence—and we were his first gig with the company. He needed us to do well. Like hell we were going to disappoint him.

"Okay, Ness, count us in." I nodded at her.

She banged her sticks together and brought us in with a beat, but it was stiff and robotic. I flicked her a quick glare, which she scowled at. We couldn't screw up. She'd ruin everything if she let her emotions railroad our first recording session.

In spite of my annoyance, I came in with my riff, Ralphie quickly joining me on the second beat. At least he sounded good. We weren't singing that session, but I mouthed the words as I played, making sure I stayed in time. Marcus delivered the song to us two days after we won Shock Wave, and we'd been practicing all week.

We got to the end of the second verse, and Nessa was supposed to launch into a quick solo that would build us into the second chorus, but she missed her cue.

We all stuttered to a stop, and I spun to face her.

"What's up?"

She glared at me then shrugged. "Nothing. Let's just do it again."

"We can't screw this up, you know that, right?" I stepped toward her, lowering my voice.

"Yes, I know that," she gritted out, digging the drumsticks into the holes of her ripped jeans.

"Then figure it out," I snapped. "When you come in for recording time like this, you leave your shit at the door."

Her eyes flashed wide, her skin turning hot pink. "Well, I don't have your expertise for being callous, so you can shove your advice up your ass."

I gripped the neck of my guitar as I leaned toward her and hissed, "Don't do this now. You'll fuck up *everything."*

Nessa's expression could have torn me to shreds. Her eyes bored into me, daring me to expose what we'd done, and how I'd handled it, to everyone in the room.

I glanced over my shoulder, hoping Flick and Ralphie couldn't hear me as I muttered, "Seriously, you need to get over that. We have more important things at stake here. This is huge, don't be the wrecking ball."

Her eyes glassed over with a fine sheen of tears, making me feel like total shit.

I looked down with a sigh. "Listen — "

"Fuck you, Jimmy." She pointed with her drumstick. "Go stand over there and do what you're supposed to. I'll do my thing, you do yours. That's the way you want it, right?"

Marcus opened the door and popped his head in. "Is everything okay in here?"

"Yeah." I spun around with a reassuring smile. "Nessa was just struggling with the beat a little. We haven't practiced this song as much as we should have."

"Are you kidding me right now?" Flick snapped. "We've been working our asses off."

I rolled my eyes, willing Flick to shut the hell up. I was dealing with it.

"O-kay." Marcus gave us a curious look. "Let's take it from the top. Studio time's expensive. We don't want to waste it."

I gave him a tight smile and nodded before turning back to Nessa. "You got this?"

She gave me another one of her off-putting stares and clicked her sticks together. She did a little better the next time. Her anger added power to her playing, but she was still off. It wasn't going to work if she didn't get it together. Her beat was the glue for this song, and we'd all fall apart if she didn't deliver.

Her small solo went okay, but she didn't crescendo like she needed to for the final chorus. My guitar let out an irate twang, and I jerked back to face her.

"Seriously. What is your problem today?"

She shook her head and looked to the others. "Sorry, guys. I'm just not feelin' it."

"No worries, Nester, you'll figure it out." Ralphie winked at her, and she gave him a closed-mouth grin, the cute one that makes her cheeks puff out.

My insides twisted, and I was tempted to drop to my knees and apologize for what I'd done, but I couldn't.

Instead, I played the asshole card and gave her an emphatic look. "I don't give a shit if you're pissed at me. None of that matters right now. Chaos is about the music, nothing more."

"The music," she muttered, lurching off the stool. "That's it? That's all we're about?"

Humiliation scorched me. I was so aware of everyone's eyes on us. I didn't need the sound techs and Marcus thinking we were just a bunch of nineteen-year-old punks trying to make it big in a world we didn't belong in. Heat worked its way up my neck, and I clenched my jaw.

"Stop embarrassing us and sit your ass back down. We can talk about this later." I spat out the words like I was some militant parent.

Nessa stood her ground and glared at me. "But we won't, because you're emotionally retarded! Chaos is not just about the music, and if that's all you think of us, then you can go to Hell!" She hurled her drumsticks at me and kicked her stool out of the way before fleeing the room.

I raised my arm to stop from being hit in the head, bashing the sticks to the ground when they connected with my forearm. "Nessa!"

Marcus tried to stop her, but she shoved him out of the way and ran. I was tempted to follow her but figured a public showdown on the street was the last thing we needed. Anger thrummed through me so thick and strong, I was worried what I might do to her if she was within reach. I'd never hit her, although the idea of grabbing her by the shoulders and giving her a damn good shake was tempting.

Lifting my guitar off with a heavy sigh, I turned back to the guys and gave them a sad smile.

"What the hell is going down with you two?" Flick glared at me.

"Nothing." I shook my head then scratched my gray beanie. "She's probably PMSing or something."

Ralphie grunted and glared at me. He'd always been protective of Nessa and never let me get away with putting her down. I mumbled an apology and dug the toe of my Vans into the dark-gray carpet.

Flick stomped toward me, his black Doc Martens landing right beside my feet. "Whatever it is, go and make it right or you'll screw it up for all of us."

I tried.

I apologized profusely to Marcus, who was really good about it, and then I took my shamefaced ass back to the house to find Nessa.

She wasn't there.

I searched every room, trying to fool myself into believing that the haphazard way her drawers hung open, clothes spilling out of them and trailing along the floor, didn't mean she'd dashed home, grabbed the essentials and split.

But she had.

It'd been two weeks. We'd tried calling her a thousand times, but she wouldn't respond to any of us. It was my fault, and I couldn't even make it right.

The lyrics for "I Miss You" soaked into me, leaving me hollow. I wanted her back. Chaos was nothing without her. *I* was nothing without her.

If only I hadn't been so fucking scared to believe it.

THREE

NESSA

The clouds slowly melted away, and the sun began to shine. The black surface I lay on continued to heat up, making me a sausage in a frying pan. The smell of burned rubber wafted in the cool breeze that continued to whistle around me. I wrinkled my nose, fighting the emetic terror trying to eat me alive.

I had no idea how much time had passed. It could have been ten minutes or three hours. My body radiated with different aches and pains as my senses did an inventory to figure out how much damage had been done. The only thing that remained completely numb was my hand.

I turned my head a little, peering through the visor at my trapped arm. My gut told me it was bad, and I didn't want to wrap my brain around the implications. Tears burned my eyes, but I snapped them shut, not wanting to give in to them.

My mind was a scrambled mess, jumping from Jimmy's warped photograph to our final fight. The look on his face as he raised his arm against my sticks and that feeling of pushing Marcus aside before storming out of the room still festered strong within me. I thought I'd be able to move past what Jimmy did. I kept my mouth shut and practiced with the band, pretending my insides weren't crumbling, but walking into the recording studio unnerved me. It forced me to ask myself how long I could keep playing pretend. And then, when Jimmy said we were nothing more than the music, I couldn't take it. I couldn't sit there and act like my heart wasn't breaking. So, I split…like I always did.

"Run," I whispered.

That was my tendency. Get away from the hurt before it could destroy me. It'd worked in the past, sort of, although this was only the second time I'd physically escaped. The first time hadn't ended well, either.

"You'll never learn," I grumbled words that had been shouted at me numerous times in the past.

My left shoulder began to cramp, a small protest against being trapped. I wanted to reach over and give it a rub, but I was still too afraid to move, worried my back was broken. I had no idea. I could wriggle my toes within my boots, so I guessed that was a good sign, but who the hell was I kidding?

Good sign?

What good could possibly come from this?

My lips trembled and my chin bunched as I fought back the sob rising up my body. I was about to start whimpering and give in to a low, pitiful wail when a faint rumbling caught my ear.

I sucked in a quick breath, straining for more. The sound grew closer, the low rumble becoming the distinct sound of an engine. I shut my eyes, praying they'd see the truck in time.

My heart thundered then seized for a second when I heard the squeal of brakes. From what I could tell, the car jerked to the side of the road, and then came the sound of a slamming door and pounding feet.

I opened my mouth to call out, but I had no voice, so I lay there like a mute fool listening to boots scraping on asphalt, a softly muttered curse, the clink and crunch of shattered glass.

I tried for sound again, this time managing a faint moan. I wanted to raise my arm, but fear kept it locked to the ground. I scraped the road with my right hand, the black surface scorching the pads of my fingers.

"See me," I whispered.

A quick intake of breath and scampering of feet gave me hope. Soon, a tall man with sandy blond hair and a face like Thor knelt down beside me. His hair was tied back in a low ponytail and a lock had broken free, framing the left side of his chiseled face. He tucked it back with quivering fingers, his blue eyes wide with concern.

"Are you okay?" His voice trembled, and he shook my right shoulder.

My body acted limp as he rattled me with his burly hand.

I couldn't speak. My heart was still pounding with a mixture of relief and terror. I'd been found. I was going to make it. But then I thought of my numb hand, and an overpowering dread cut off my air supply.

His face blanched, and he yanked at the zipper of my jacket, poking his fingers into my neck. He closed his eyes and dipped his chin.

Did he think I was dead or something?

"Help me," I whispered.

He jolted, staring down at me and blinking rapidly. His face bunched with worry as he lifted my visor.

Bright sunlight hit me, and I squinted against the glare.

"No." The man expelled the word on a heavy breath. "Please, no." He stared down at my face squished inside the helmet and looked ready to break down and cry.

"Please, help me." I licked my lower lip. "Help me." And finally, the whimper I'd been holding back broke free. My chest heaved and shuddered. There was no point fighting it anymore; help had arrived, and I could let go. The feeble walls that had been holding me together began to splinter.

"It's okay. I'll help you, Nessa."

I glanced at him, my forehead wrinkling as I tried to figure out how he knew my name...and then it came to me.

"Josh?" The bartender. The guy who'd served me Coke and brought out my southern twang. I hardly ever spoke like that anymore, but the second I'd heard his voice, I'd slipped back into my old ways. He'd made me comfortable, let me open up about everything...and then burned pictures with me.

He gazed down at my face with a sweet smile. "Hey, Nessa. Don't you worry, now. I'm right here to help you."

I blinked and he gave me another comforting smile before jumping up and gripping the bottom of my motorbike. Fear skittered through me, tinged with relief. I didn't want to be trapped anymore, but...

With a grunt, he hefted it up, trying to free my arm, but all it did was yank on my mangled fingers. A sharp pain tore through my nerves, forcing a savage scream out of me. White-hot agony spotted my vision. I needed the numb back. I needed the numb!

My loud cries made him lower the bike in wide-eyed horror.

"I'm sorry. I don't think I should be moving that without help." His voice shook as he knelt down beside me again and dialed 911.

I closed my eyes, numbness returning as the blood supply to my arm was once again cut off by the heavy motorcycle. I kept my eyes shut while

Josh spoke to the operator, only opening them to answer a question or two about allergies and medication.

Help was on the way.

That part felt good, made it easier to breathe, but I couldn't stop thinking about my hand and the excruciating pain I'd endured when Josh tried to free me. What did it mean?

"My hand," I whimpered.

"It's going to be okay." Josh kept saying that, like his own little mantra, as we waited for the ambulance to arrive.

I guess it helped a little, but it couldn't erase the truth. I saw the look in his eyes as he tried to reassure me, the pale pastiness of his skin. My hand was a mangled wreck.

The thought was a boulder on my chest, making the air in my lungs hard to squeeze out. I blinked at the scorching tears in my eyes and ground my teeth together.

I couldn't lose my hand.

Playing the drums got me through everything. They surrounded me, keeping me safely hidden, and let me pound the crap out of them until I was spent...relieved.

How was I supposed to survive if I couldn't play anymore?

FOUR

JIMMY

The guest house door clicked open, and I leaned forward to see Marcus saunter into our practice space. His shiny shoes tapped on the white tiles before he reached the carpet and the staccato sound disappeared. As usual, he greeted me with an easy, friendly smile, extending his hand. I gave it a quick shake, noting the tension in his hazel gaze. It'd been there since Nessa split the recording studio and hadn't returned.

"How's it going, man?" He sat on the adjacent couch, flicking his jacket back and leaning his elbows against his knees.

I shrugged and grunted, nestling against the cushions.

"You look, well…" Marcus scratched the back of his head and glanced at the dark-blue carpet.

"Like shit," Flick mumbled, his thick boots stomping over the tiles. Ralphie trailed behind him, scratching at his trimmed goatee. I gazed at my friends as they slumped onto the two-seater in the carpeted area. They were as different as heavy metal and boy-band pop. Flick was a taut, lean guy who lived in skinny jeans, Doc Marten boots, and was hardly ever without his beloved beanie. His sharp features and dark-brown eyes gave him a menacing look. It didn't help that he wasn't much of a smiler, but the guy was all talent. He could basically play any instrument he wanted, and when it came to composing, he was a freaking genius.

Ralphie, on the other hand, was a tall, broad ball of fluff. He wore baggy jeans that hung so low, his boxers, or butt crack, were on full display whenever he bent over. He always wore Converse and checkered shirts, and no matter what he was doing, he had a lazy smile on his face. He was the most unflappable person in the universe.

Ralphie kicked out his leg and shot me a glum smile. "When was the last time you slept?"

I covered my face and groaned.

Marcus sighed. "Listen, guys, I know this is hard, but it's been two weeks, and our grace period is officially over."

My head shot up, and I glared at Marcus. "What the fuck is that supposed to mean?"

The stubble on his chin made a scratchy sound as he rubbed at it. He was obviously reluctant to share his news.

"I've spent the last two hours in a meeting with exec. They're not willing to kick around waiting anymore. Torrence Records is a big label. They've made commitments, invested money. You all signed a contract, and you have to uphold it."

"We can't right now. We have no drummer," I spat.

Marcus looked across at Flick and Ralphie then finally turned to me. "I've found you a new one."

I shook my head, but Marcus kept going.

"His name's Jace. He's twenty-two, he's had a lot of experience, and he's got a very similar vibe to—"

"No." I said the word emphatically, like he was a defiant toddler and I was his parent telling him off.

"Jimmy…"

"He's not Nessa!" I shouted.

"Yeah, well, she's not an option right now." Marcus lurched out of his seat, pacing to the drum kit and back again. "I know you guys don't want to hear this, but we have no idea if she's ever coming back."

The words were like arrow fire, piercing my chest and making it damn hard to breathe.

Marcus lowered his voice. "I really hate saying this to you, but if you're not willing to move forward with this new guy we found you, then the deal's off. No album, no tour, nothing."

I glanced at Flick. His nostrils flared and his dark gaze was thunderous as he looked at me. I knew what he really meant. He was scared shitless I'd refuse and that everything we'd been working so hard for would turn to dust.

The idea of doing this without Nessa was unfathomable. She and I had started this whole thing. We'd dreamed of this since ninth grade…and I'd gone and fucked it all up.

"Shit," I muttered, scrubbing a hand over my face. "So, we have no more time then?"

Marcus gave me a sad smile. "Jace is coming around this afternoon to play with you guys. We'll get a feel for if he works, and then we'll go from there. He can't sing like Ness, but he's a really good drummer and we can figure out other harmonies. It won't change the sound of Chaos too much."

I glared at him, hating the idea with every fiber of my being.

He met my anger with an intense gaze that wouldn't let up. I slammed back onto the couch and thumped the cushion with my fist.

"Jimmy, you have to give him a fair chance." Marcus pointed at me, but then his shoulders slumped. "I'm sorry, okay. I really am. I wish we weren't in this position. You guys are a tight unit, and it's going to be really hard to let someone new in, but you're just going to have to get over it and ask yourselves, how bad do you want this?"

He took a second to gaze at each of us before pulling out his keys. "I'll see you this afternoon."

His shoes were deafening as he made a quick

retreat out of the guest house. I closed my eyes and released a heavy sigh as the door swung open then clicked shut. Our manager's departure was followed with a stagnant silence that smothered all of us.

"Fuck," I muttered, digging my elbows into my knees.

"This sucks." Ralphie looked pale and restless. "We can't do this without my little Nester."

"We have to, you assholes. We don't have a choice!" Flick sprung off the couch then thumped into the kitchen. The bottles in the refrigerator door rattled against each other as he yanked it open and pulled out a beer. Popping the cap, he tossed it back in three swigs before throwing the bottle into the sink. It smashed against the stainless steel side, the shattering glass making me flinch.

I breathed out through my nose, the weight of responsibility feeling too heavy to bear. I didn't know how it happened. Maybe it was because I started the band, but these guys had somehow made me their leader. It was nothing official, just an unspoken understanding between us. I never put my foot down or any shit like that, but I seemed to have final say.

Flick leaned against the counter, his sharp cheekbones protruding as he clenched his jaw.

"Why did she have to split?" He glared at me. "What did you do to her?"

"Nothing." I looked away from his dark intensity, still not willing to admit my shame. I didn't want them knowing what Nessa and I got up to the night we won *Shock Wave*...and how I'd handled the aftermath. Flick was damn observant, though. It was probably only a matter of time, but I wanted to keep it under wraps for as long as I could.

"Look, it doesn't even matter why." Ralphie's deep voice cut through the awkward tension. "What matters is that she's safe and okay, which hopefully she is." He licked his bottom lip then scratched his goatee. "But Flick's right, we have to keep going. Nessa might not want to be a part of it right now, but she'll figure it out like she always does." He shrugged. "And then she'll come back." He nodded, as if trying to make himself believe it. "When that happens, there'll be a place for her, but not if we quit."

His pale gray gaze landed on me, and all I could do was nod in agreement. I glanced at Flick, who moved toward the practice area. The chain on the side of his jeans swished against the black denim. Stopping by his guitar, he lifted it off the stand and put the strap over his shoulder. He turned on his amp and strummed the strings, picking up the chorus of "When We Stand Together" by Nickelback. With a sigh, Ralphie stood and grabbed his bass. He picked up the bass line easily, and before I could stop myself, I sang the end of the chorus. I kept up the tune, reaching for my guitar while staring at the empty drum kit. We sounded dead without her. We needed a beat, something to keep us all together, or we'd disintegrate. I couldn't keep hiding from the truth.

Nessa leaving may have been my fault, but it was her choice. No matter where she was or what she was up to, I had to let it go. Chaos deserved to live on, with or without her.

FIVE

NESSA

Someone had pumped cement into my ears, and it was setting into a hard, unbreakable mass. My head weighed a million pounds, and I didn't know if I'd ever be able to lift it off my pillow again. Wincing, I slowly opened my eyes and took in the pale-yellow walls with the white trim. A pea-green curtain with little white squares on it hung around one half of my bed.

I frowned. *Where the hell am I?*

Rubbing my eyes, I scrubbed a hand over my face and noted the IV drip in the back of my hand. I went to brush my fingers over it, and that's when I registered the white stump on my left arm.

A stump—a swollen, bandaged ending to my arm.

No hand. No fingers...just a stump.

I sucked in a ragged breath, my jaw locking as I fought to expel the air. I let out a weird gasping sound, and the air finally flew free on a sob. My right hand trembled as I reached for the thick bandage, gently running the pads of my fingers over the wrapping. My arm stopped just where my watch would usually sit. There was no lump at the end of my wrist, no bones or muscle or tissue extending out to create a hand that could hold a drumstick.

My face bunched, my lips pulling into a taut line as I tried to wrap my brain around the new reality.

"Hi." A soft, sweet drawl I didn't recognize caught my attention. "I'm Doctor Kennedy."

I glanced at the woman. She was in green scrubs and had a stethoscope draped around her neck. Her short hair was tied back in a stubby little ponytail. She looked tired but was smiling at me like she actually cared.

"How are you feelin'?" She rested her hand against the railing of the bed.

"What'd you do with my hand?"

Her expression crested with sadness before settling on a resigned smile. "Your fingers were damaged beyond repair. We examined the bones and tissue very carefully before making our decision, but in the end, we really had no choice but to remove the hand. Is it hurting right now?"

I stared down at it, brushing my fingers over the numb stump and shaking my head.

"Well, make sure you keep us posted on that. You've got a morphine drip right here." She pointed to the clear IV tubing going into my vein then pulled something from behind my shoulder and placed it in my right hand. I gazed at the dark-gray plastic with the black button on the top. "If the pain starts to bother you, just click the button once, and it will administer a little more into your bloodstream."

I rubbed my thumb lightly over the button then looked back up at her, trying to soak it all in.

"Thankfully, the rest of your body only has minor scrapes and bruising. There were no other broken bones and only minimal road burn on your hip and elbow. You'll be sore for a few days, but you're young and healthy. Your body is already working to repair itself, and you'll be back to normal in no time."

I lifted my stump, struggling for air as I looked at her incredulously.

Her lips crested with a sorrowful smile. "You will adjust. It may be hard, but it's not going to stop you from doing the things you want. We're going to get you all the help and care you need to recover."

A tear slipped out the corner of my eye, trailing down my cheek as I leaned my head back against the pillows and gazed up at the fluorescent lights.

"Do you have any family we can call? We found contact information for a Rosemary Hart in

Chicago, but she's…"

"Gone," I whispered. The pain in my belly surged, rushing at me like a charging bull. Great big horns gouged into me, reopening a gaping wound inside, one I'd been trying to ignore for nearly two years. I clamped my teeth together and forced air in through my nose.

"Do you have anyone else we can call? Your parents, maybe?"

I shook my head. "I don't want you calling them."

They couldn't know. My situation was only proof that they'd been right about me all along. I could picture their smug, knowing smiles. *"Well, what did you expect, Vanessa? If you'd just done what we'd said, you wouldn't be here. This is called justice, plain and simple."* My mother's bitter voice echoed in my mind. I thought I'd run far enough away to never hear it again, but there it was screeching in my ear like poorly played bagpipes.

The doctor swallowed. It was a loud gulp that made me glance her way. "I know this is an extremely difficult situation for you right now, but you're going to need all the support you can get."

"I don't have anyone," I muttered.

A month before, I would have said Chaos in a heartbeat, but the idea of facing them in that moment was too much. I didn't want them to see my missing hand. I didn't want their sympathy or pained expressions. Ralphie would give me that sad, compassionate smile of his, and I'd be undone. No, all I wanted was to disappear and pretend like none of it was happening.

I shut my eyes and turned my head away from the doctor, willing her to leave the room quickly. Finally, her shoes squeaked on the shiny floor and the door swung open. The noises of hospital life wafted in briefly—a wave of shuffling and conversation, but then the door clicked shut and I was left in my own silence…a deafening sound that had once tried to break me and threatened to do so again.

SIX

JIMMY

My finger tapped on my pants as I waited for the new guy to walk in the door. I saw him coming down the path. He was decked out in ripped jeans and a fitted Ramones T-shirt, and his black and white checkered Converse looked well worn. His hair was down to his chin and kind of scrappy—a rich brown color that reminded me of Nessa's.

He walked in the door and raised a large hand in greeting. He had fat lips that stretched into a broad smile, displaying a set of straight white teeth. His dark eyebrows rose as he took us all in.

"So, guys, this is Jace." Marcus slapped him on

the back and grinned up at him. He looked like a shrimp beside the tall, muscular drummer.

"How's it going?" Jace had a deep voice like Ralphie, but it had a languid quality to it. Everything about the guy seemed unhurried and relaxed. How the hell was he supposed to play the drums? We were a rock band, not a jazz ensemble.

Although we *had* been asked to play at a wedding for two jazz freaks—Cole and Ella. Cole was a friend of my brother's. He'd been the one to get us a little exposure when we first started out as a band. We'd played at his uncle's bar in Chicago numerous times. In fact, we'd also helped him win his girl back when he serenaded her with "500 Miles" by the Proclaimers in the middle of a college campus. It'd been freaking epic.

I sniffed out a laugh as I remembered the initial conversation. We'd all be stunned silent. Chaos to play at their wedding? It was the most bizarre choice ever. They laughed at our confusion and swore it was a no-brainer. Chaos was the only band they wanted. "Put your own spin on the music we love. We trust you," Ella had said.

We'd been working it out the week of the *Shock Wave* final. Nessa had been so honored and near giddy with excitement as she came up with one idea after another. I still had the scrap of paper with our proposed playlist in my back pocket. For some weird reason, I was compelled to keep it with me. The plan had been to win *Shock Wave* then spend our spare time prepping for the wedding, set for late October. We hadn't worked on any of the songs since Nessa split.

The depressing thought faded in my mind as I became increasingly aware of the awkward silence hovering in the room. Much to my surprise, it was Flick who broke it.

"Well, you gonna show us what you can do?" He gave Jace a pointed look.

The new guy chuckled and eased around Marcus, loping over to the kit and adjusting it to fit him. His legs were twice the length of Nessa's. My chest restricted as he raised the stool and moved the drums around. I gripped the back of my neck, willing myself not to yell, "Don't touch anything! That belongs to Ness!"

I clenched my jaw and swallowed. Marcus stood beside me and grinned when Jace pulled the sticks from his back pocket then tapped them together. He started with a simple beat that quickly became complicated.

Much to my dismay, he was fucking awesome. The guy could play, and he looked damn good doing it. The girls would go wild for him. An uncertain jealousy ripped through me. I'd always been the sexy one in the band. Girls fawned over me and I'd relished it, until…

I cleared my throat and raised my thumb to stop him. "Yeah, sounds good."

"Thanks, man." Jace raised his dimpled chin at me. "Do you want to play something together?"

"Uh, yeah, sure. Yeah." I nodded, reluctantly reaching for my guitar and flicking the strap over my head. I'd never played with another drummer before. Flick had sometimes jumped onto the kit and messed around, but Nessa had always been our girl, and it felt weird not having her there.

"Let's, um, go with, uh..." I looked to Flick.

"How about you start working on some of the stuff for your album," Marcus suggested. "Jace knows the songs." His phone started ringing. He pulled it out of his pocket and walked for the door, leaving us to practice as a foursome.

I turned back to Jace and tried to smile at him but couldn't. Poor guy, it wasn't his fault. Ralphie hadn't said a word since he'd walked in, just kept looking at Jace with this morose frown. Flick was a little more open about it all, but he'd always been motivated by the music...which I was, too.

I reminded myself of that before pulling back my shoulders and giving the strings a quick strum.

"Let's start with 'Agility'," I muttered. It was the single we had tried recording a couple of weeks ago. I figured it was the best one to start with, even though it burned like a mother having to play it again. I hadn't gone near the song since Nessa left.

We stumbled our way through the first round, but Jace played it like a pro. He didn't miss a beat, and the second time through, we nailed it pretty cleanly. I couldn't help a smile. It was good to be in sync again. Flick felt it, too. He offered up one of his occasional grins, and it gave me the boost I needed to suggest the next song.

Two hours later, we were dripping with sweat and having the time of our lives. Gelling with Jace had not been hard. The guy had skills. I wouldn't say he was better than Nessa, but he'd have to be a close second. Ralphie was kicking it on bass, and Flick jumped from keys to guitar with his usual nonchalance.

Marcus walked in as we started up "Agility" again. I decided to end the practice how we'd started it, and the guys liked the idea. I played my intro and stepped up to the mic. I was about to sing the first line when I caught sight of Marcus's expression.

He looked ashen, like he'd just been punched in the stomach then told his dog had died.

I slapped my fingers over the guitar strings and raised a fist to shut the band up. The music petered out, Jace being the last to pick up on my cue.

"What?" I scowled at our manager, my stomach pinching as I waited for the bad news. Had Torrence fucking pulled out on us? They couldn't do that. We had a contract.

"It's, uh…" Marcus rubbed the back of his neck, his shell-shocked gaze trained on mine. "It's Nessa," he ended in a whisper.

My heart lurched in my chest, and I froze on the spot. I never wanted to hear her name said in a broken whisper like that again. The look on Marcus's face shredded my guts.

"Where is she?" Ralphie asked, his voice deep with concern.

"Arkansas," Marcus murmured. His eyes were still on me, etched with horrified sadness.

She's dead. My Nessa is dead.

The air in my lungs turned to liquid nitrogen.

"What the fuck is she doing there?" Flick's temper always showed when he was scared. That only made it worse. Flick's reaction confirmed I wasn't imagining the look on Marcus's face.

Our manager swallowed then let out a long sigh. "She's been in a motorcycle accident."

My grip on the neck of my guitar tightened, and my jaw worked to the side as I fought for the strength to ask, "Is she still alive?" I could barely whisper the words.

"Yes," Marcus assured me with a quick nod. "But she's..." His forehead wrinkled, his lips dipping into a sorrowful frown.

"But what!" I shouted.

Marcus flinched then grimaced. "I'm sorry, man, but...she's lost her hand. She...they had to amputate."

My ears started ringing. I missed Flick's muttered shock and was only vaguely aware of Ralphie slumping to the floor beside me. A loud twang came out of his amp.

I couldn't move for a second. Shock froze my core and I stopped breathing. Nessa had lost her hand. That couldn't be possible. She...that...it couldn't.

I pictured her lying alone in some hospital bed and waking up to find her hand missing. Her cute little face would crease with horror and then despair, her big brown eyes would fill with tears, and there'd be no one there to comfort her.

The thought worked like an electric shock on my body, and I gulped in a lungful of air.

"I gotta go." I swallowed the boulder in my throat and sucked in another breath.

With a calm I didn't expect, I lifted my guitar over my head and gently placed it on the stand.

"I gotta go," I mumbled again. "I gotta go to Arkansas." I stumbled over to Marcus and fisted the front of his shirt. "Tell me where she is."

His expression was agonized, but he eventually told me the details. I released him and stumbled out of the house, pulling the phone from my back pocket and dialing my brother. Troy was the only person I ever wanted with me in a crisis. And this was a fucking big crisis.

SEVEN

NESSA

Sleep had been impossible to capture. I couldn't get comfortable. No matter how I shuffled, my body groaned and complained. It didn't help that every time I shut my eyes, I relived the accident— the squeal of tires, the crunch of my landing, the agony of my fingers getting mangled in the engine. My eyes would snap open, and I'd awaken in a darkened room. The faint light from the IV monitor would cast a soft glow across my bed, enough for me to make out the ugly stump resting on a stack of pillows beside me.

Josh had arrived an hour before midnight and

helped ease my restlessness with his calm, smooth voice. He looked troubled but wouldn't tell me why, and I didn't have it in me to ask. I had my own shit to deal with.

I was caught in a weird dream when I first heard Jimmy's voice in the hallway. My bike was cruising that beautiful road along the hillside. I crested the rise, about to encounter the upturned truck, when I heard him shouting. The dream began to fade, and instead of a mangled truck housing a bloodied driver, I saw Jimmy. He was standing in the middle of the road with his guitar, shirtless and looking sexy as hell. But he was yelling at me. I couldn't figure out what he was saying.

I murmured his name, trying to interrupt him, but it did no good.

"Hey, Nessa, it's okay." Josh's voice spoke over the top of Jimmy's.

I winced, confused by the dual realities.

"You don't have to see him if you don't want to." Josh's voice was soft and deep, taking a few moments to register.

"Jimmy." I whispered his name again then opened my eyes and found Josh hovering above me. He had black bags under his eyes and a weary smile on his face.

My forehead wrinkled. "He's here?"

"Yeah, he came as soon as he heard. He's currently fighting with the nurse to get down here." Josh pointed over his shoulder, and I heard Jimmy's voice loud and clear.

"You think I give a rat's ass about policy!"

Typical. He'd probably been in the hospital less than five minutes, and he'd already gotten into a fight. My stomach quivered with a soft chuckle, but my smile was fleeting.

Jimmy was here.

Josh gently brushed a lock of hair off my cheek. "Do you want to see him?"

"No," I croaked, "and yes." My eyes filled with instant tears, and I bit my lips together. "I don't know," I whispered. "I don't want him to be the only person I need right now, but he is."

Damn it!

My nose began to tingle as tears built in my eyes. They were going to fall.

Josh leaned over me and placed a sweet kiss on my forehead. "I'll go get him."

He stepped out of the room and left me to compose myself. Jimmy was going to appear at any moment. I sniffed and lifted my hand to rub my eyes, but all I had was a stump. I grimaced and laid it back down on the pillows, tugging the bed covers up to hide it. With my good hand, I scrubbed my face again and ran my fingers through my hair. I probably looked a mess, and I shouldn't have cared at all, but I did.

Quick footsteps neared my door.

I spotted Jimmy's hand before anything else. His long fingers wrapped around the wood to push it open…and an unwelcome memory flooded my mind.

The sticks felt good in my hands as I banged the drum skins with as much force as I could. I had my earplugs in and "Welcome To My Life" by Simple Plan was blasting. The song encapsulated everything I was feeling after what I'd witnessed the night before. It was my go-to song when I was in a really dark and shitty place. They understood me like no one else could.

Two nights earlier, Jimmy and I had slept together, and it had been the best sex I'd ever had. I never expected him to make a move on me. He was Jimmy Baker, and I was just his lil' buddy, Nessa. I'd never had the courage to let my feelings show. But then he'd kissed me, enveloped me, *and I hadn't been able to hold back.*

Throughout the filming of Shock Wave, *we'd become even closer than we already were. I figured when he came on to me, he was finally starting to feel all the things I did. My unwavering love had won him over. Like a clueless idiot, I'd dreamed of happily ever after while he was probably thinking, "Sweet. Another notch on my belt."*

I could have won first prize for world's biggest fool. Like I'd ever be anyone's happily ever after. I should have known better.

When I woke up the next morning to find him gone, I didn't want to believe the certainty swirling in my brain. I tried to convince myself that he'd left the bed while I was still asleep because he didn't want to wake me, and then I started thinking he was just avoiding eye contact the next day because he didn't want the guys to know...but that night, he'd proved my fears right.

He'd always been a player. I'd desperately hoped after our magic that I'd somehow changed him, but I was full of shit.

The second chorus kicked in. I smashed those drums like my life depended on it…and then I saw his hand on the door, his long fingers curving around the white frame as he pushed it open then loped into the guest house with a tight smile on his face.

I stopped playing and glared at him while yanking the buds out of my ears.

He jerked still when he noted my expression, his smile quickly dying.

"How was your night?" I dropped my sticks on the floor and rose from my stool.

"Oh, you know, the usual." He shrugged, walking into the kitchen and pulling open the fridge. He grabbed a can of Coke then pointed at it. "You want one?"

I moved around the drum kit and walked to the edge of the kitchen, crossing my arms and throwing him the blackest look I could muster.

Slapping the door shut, he rolled his eyes and walked to the counter, spinning around and resting his butt against it. "Aw, come on, Ness. Don't be like that."

I looked away from him, clenching my jaw and swallowing. Part of me wanted to flee up the stairs and lock myself in my room, but I needed to know. I needed him to look me in the eye and say it.

"So, our night meant nothing to you?"

The can paused halfway to his lips, and he tipped his head. "Our night?"

Damn, I should have kept the drumsticks in my hand. He needed one shoved up his nose, the jackass.

Jimmy gave me a bashful smile. "You mean the night we won Shock Wave. *Well, you know…it was a* celebration. Just a little fun."

"It wasn't just that," I whispered, remembering the way he'd held me. It was impossible to hide my emotion. I wanted to bury it deep and not give him the satisfaction of seeing one tear, but my eyes were burning, and it took everything in me not to let loose the sobs quivering in my belly. "Why are you doing this?"

"Ness, come on." He placed his can on the counter and walked toward me. "You know it would never work out with us. It would complicate everything. I don't know what you're expecting of me right now."

I glanced up at him, my lips parting.

He gave me his sexy half-smile, gliding his hands into his pockets like he was the coolest guy on the planet. I wished he wasn't. I wanted him to trip and fall or do something dorky, but he just continually oozed this smoking-hot charm that I couldn't resist.

"I'm not a 'fall in love' kinda guy. You know that about me. If you didn't want casual, you should have stopped it from going too far."

"How?" I practically squeaked. "I've been in love with you since the ninth grade. You finally come on to me, and I'm supposed to push you away? I couldn't have said no if I'd wanted to."

He just stared at me then, like I'd slapped him in the face or something. "You've been in love with me since ninth grade?"

My cheeks grew hot, and I stepped away from him. "It doesn't matter now. You're never going to love me, are you?"

He swallowed and looked to the floor. "Not the way you want me to."

My chest grew tight, like there was a fist inside it, squeezing my heart until I thought I might pass out. I stumbled back, and Jimmy lurched forward to steady me.

I batted his hand away and hissed, "Screw you, Jimmy," before fleeing to my room.

Jimmy's face appeared—his gorgeous, straight nose and those bewitching blue eyes. I gazed at his mouth, remembering what it tasted like and how it felt on my skin...but then it morphed into a hard line, and all I could see was him standing in that kitchen telling me he'd never love me.

"Hey," he whispered, his gaze drinking me in like he was seeing me for the first time. His face glowed with a look I didn't recognize.

"What are you doing here?" My voice sounded flat and wooden as I asked the stupidest question ever.

His forehead wrinkled, and he stopped by the end of the bed, shoving his hands into his pockets. He was wearing my favorite pair of jeans, the ones that hugged his ass, yet sat low enough on the hip that when he was shirtless, I could see all of his tornado tattoo. It started on his right hipbone and spun musical notes up to his rib cage—*Peace in Chaos* was written around it. Rosie had designed it, and that made it the most precious tattoo on his body.

I swallowed and closed my eyes against the image of him naked on the bed. I'd run my tongue over every inch of ink that marked him. From the pulse on his wrist, to the musical score covering his left arm, to the swirling guitar decorating most of his back.

"How are you feeling?" His soft tone drew my eyes open.

He looked pretty damn agonized, like he hadn't slept all night. I glanced at his nails; they were chewed to the nub. He saw me staring at them and curled his fingers to hide the evidence of his worrying.

"I've felt better," I mumbled, looking back down at the blanket.

"Is your hand hurt—?"

"Seriously, Jimmy, why are you here? I didn't ask you to come." I had to interrupt him. I didn't want to talk about my damn hand...or serious lack of it. I hated that he knew. I didn't want him to see me that way. I'd never felt more ugly in my life, and in spite of the fact I should have hated Jimmy Baker, my heart still kicked a beat when he walked into the room. My insides still sizzled with an attraction that had been haunting me since I was fourteen years old.

Jimmy's forearms flexed as he gripped the end of my bed and stared down at me. "Marcus got the call, and as soon as I heard, I had to come. I thought you might need me."

I couldn't look him in the eye, so I trained my gaze on the lucky guitar pick he wore around his neck. I'd given it to him after we won the school talent quest. He never took it off. That should have meant something, but it didn't—not in that moment.

I should have been touched that he'd dropped everything to come see me, but I couldn't muster the emotion. It was overrun by the deafening sound of him admitting we'd never be anything more than band members...and I couldn't even be that anymore.

I licked the corner of my mouth and stared at him; the hurt and despair radiating through me was almost too much to bear. I didn't know why he'd come, but I did know he had the capability to destroy me. I already felt broken. I had no idea how I was going to pull myself together again, but I didn't need Jimmy's help.

I pressed my lips together and looked down at my right hand. My fingers were trembling as I picked at a loose cotton thread and whispered, "You thought wrong. I'm fine, Jimmy. I don't need you."

EIGHT

JIMMY

Her words stung like a bitch. I shrugged my shoulders and went for nonplussed, but inside, I was raging. She did need me, damn it. She just didn't want to admit it.

I didn't say anything. I was worried if I opened my mouth, some more bullshit would come flying out and I'd only make things worse. Instead, I just looked at her.

She laid her head back and closed her eyes, so I stood at the end of the bed and watched her fall asleep. Her skin was so pale, and her hair was almost black under the dull lights. It'd only been two weeks since I'd seen her, but it felt like months. I ran my gaze down her pert little body, tucked beneath the hospital bedding, and as it traveled back up her fine curves, I caught sight of her left arm hiding under the sheets.

I hesitated for a moment, dread restricting my airways, but then crept around the edge of the bed. Leaning over her, I listened to the even sound of her breathing and figured she was asleep. I cautiously lifted the blanket. My stomach lurched. A short, white stub lay on a pile of pillows. The skin above the thick bandaging was red and swollen, and for a moment, I couldn't make that mangled appendage Nessa's arm. It couldn't be real...but it was.

Tears were set on scorching my eyeballs to ash, so I blinked rapidly to clear them and lowered the blanket back in place.

My jaw quivered as I tried to clamp it shut, and in the end, I had to bite my knuckle to stop from screaming. It was my fault. She took off because of me. She should have been safe in LA with us, not driving some random road in the middle of fucking nowhere.

Guilt singed my insides, making me crumple into the chair beside her.

No hand.

She had no left hand.

I dug my fingers into my hair and leaned back, my teeth grinding together until it hurt. Yanking my phone out of my back pocket, I sought the solace of music. It was the only thing that ever really calmed me. I didn't care what it was—I just needed a beat, a melody, something to stop the inferno within. My fingers trembled as I clipped the earplug lead into my phone then shoved the buds in my ears. I pressed 'shuffle play.'

"Brand New Day" by Forty Foot Echo drifted into my brain, and my face scrunched tight as the words punched me in the chest. I gazed at Nessa with her porcelain skin, so beautiful and exquisite. I'd been blind the whole time. A fucking idiot.

In spite of how much the song hurt me, it inspired me at the same time. I did want to change. I wanted to become the man she needed me to be. But I had no idea how.

"You doing okay?" Troy's deep voice made me jump. He stood in the door, big and powerful as always. I'd been the runt in our family. He took after Dad...at least in appearance, whereas I'd come out the spitting image of my mother—fine-boned with long, skinny fingers and a lanky body that I worked damn hard to keep ripped. I pulled the buds from my ears and dropped the phone in my lap.

"No." My voice shook, and I whacked my head against the back of my chair. "No, I'm not okay."

Troy gave me a sympathetic smile before approaching the bed. His boots tapped lightly on the floor, but they sounded loud in the quiet room. He ran his fingers along the thick plastic edge of the hospital bed and stared down at Nessa. He winced when he spotted the shape of her stump beneath the blanket. "This is going be a really hard pill for her to swallow."

"It's not fair," I murmured.

"Life never is." Troy shrugged.

I glared at him, hating the way he always put such a simple spin on things. He took everything in his stride, facing it with a relaxed calm that bugged the shit out of me.

"I can't believe I let this happen." I stared at the morphine drip sticking out of her right hand until the clear plastic blurred into a fuzzy line.

Troy moved over to me and flicked my shoulder with the back of his thick fingers. "This isn't your fault. She had an accident."

"She shouldn't have been out here, man. I drove her away," I croaked, gripping the arms of the hospital chair.

Troy sighed and stepped away. Planting his feet, he stared down at me with a look only Troy Baker could give. That pale blue scrutiny could always uncover the truth. When we were kids, he was the only one who could see through my lies. He was older than me by six years, but we'd always been close. We'd had to be.

"There's more than what you told me on the plane, isn't there?" he muttered, obviously preparing himself for another dose of my bullshit.

I eyed the white buttons on his checkered shirt and cringed. Guilt was an iron mallet bashing me over the head as I let out a heavy sigh and finally admitted what no one else knew. "The night after we slept together, I was losing it. I mean, being with her was like…nothing I'd ever experienced."

Troy rolled his eyes. "Yeah, well that's what happens when you have sex with someone you actually care about."

I shook my head. "It freaked me out, man."

Scratching the back of his head, Troy pursed his lips. "You didn't just tell her this wouldn't work out, did you?"

My expression crumpled. "She got under my skin. I mean, I had to put her off, make her hate me for a little bit so we could move on and be friends again. I needed to make my point loud and clear." I swallowed back the bile surging up my throat. It was an effort to get through the truth. I'd never hated myself more. "The next night, I made sure she saw me leave the club with these two hotties. I wanted her to know I'd be getting some. I wanted her to see." The last words came out as a broken whisper.

"Well, there's nothing like a threesome to really make your point," Troy muttered darkly. "Did you go through with it?"

I shot him a look that gave away my night of drunken debauchery. Rabbits would have been jealous. I grimaced while Troy let out a disgusted groan.

"Seriously, Jimmy, how the hell do you get so many women when you know so little about them?"

I grunted and looked back at Nessa, remembering how hollow I'd felt as I shuffled home in the early hours of the morning, regret like shackles on my wrists and ankles. "I only want one now."

"Are you sure?" he snapped.

Spinning around, I aimed a fierce glare at my brother. "Yes."

His expression was unrelenting as he pointed at Nessa. "Because if you really want her, then you're going to be working damn hard and you have to be all in. She's going to have enough to deal with. She doesn't need your bullshit on top of it all."

I huffed out a sharp breath. "I'm in."

His lips dipped into a skeptical frown, and I knew what he was about to say.

"Dad would see it differently."

I clenched my fists, my nostrils flaring as Troy brought up the one issue that got us fighting.

"You've idolized him your whole life and always taken his advice, but he's wrong, Jimmy...and as shitty as this whole situation is, maybe this is the wake-up call you've been needing."

"She lost her hand," I gritted out. Tears blurred my vision. "Why should she have to pay for *my* wake-up call?"

Troy sighed. "I don't understand how it all works, man. I just know Dad is full of shit and you have to stop trying to be like him."

I swallowed, blinking rapidly to clear my eyes. "I know." I nodded. "I'm starting to see what you mean."

Troy's eyebrows rose at my words. I'd never spoken that way before. Dad and his playboy ways had always been my aspiration. The guy was rich, happy, and free; what could be better than that? Romance was for sappy losers who weren't good-looking enough to score the hotties. I used to pride myself on saying shit like that. I can't believe Nessa had loved me for so long when I'd strutted around being such a dick, but she had. She'd stuck it out until I'd made her think we'd never have a future together...until I'd let her see how much of a heartless bastard I could really be.

I squeezed my eyes shut and clenched my jaw. My knee started bobbing as that sick bile swirled inside me again. I hated myself for what I'd done, and I wasn't even sure how to make it right.

I just knew I had to try.

NINE

NESSA

I spent another week at that hospital in Arkansas before they finally released me, and I was forced back to LA. I didn't have much choice. There was no one else who could help me, and even though I didn't want to admit it, I couldn't do it on my own. Rosie might have left me money to live on, but I was a handless nineteen-year-old who'd just crashed her way out of a job…and a normal life.

I wasn't stupid. The nurses and physical therapist at the hospital had been amazing, teaching me how to do stuff and quietly going about assisting me with everything in a way that didn't make me feel like a cripple. But then I'd go to do something simple, like button my jeans or lace up my boots, and I'd realize that I actually was one, and nothing would ever be the same again.

Dread simmered in my stomach, a constant warning of what I had yet to face. I couldn't speak on the flight back, I was a numb mute throughout LAX, and I could barely utter two words as Troy drove us back to the house. Jimmy had called ahead. Nina, our housekeeper, had made up my old room, and the guys were ordered to be on their best behavior.

I couldn't help a small smile as Jimmy barked into the phone, double-checking that Flick and Ralphie weren't entertaining any chicks we didn't know. It was damn ironic coming from him.

Troy pulled onto our street, and I spotted the swarm of reporters and photographers hovering outside the main gate. They were like bugs—a vibrating clump desperate to snap a shot of the wounded drummer.

I quickly unlatched my seatbelt and dropped to the floor, squishing in behind Troy's seat. Jimmy glanced over his shoulder, his eyebrows rising with surprise, but then his blue gaze flooded with understanding. I looked away from him and dipped my head, praying Troy would drive through the swarm quickly.

As soon as the car approached, entertainment reporters and paparazzi surrounded the car. Torrence Records had issued a statement saying the

Chaos drummer had been injured in a motorcycle accident but wanted to reassure the fans that things would still be going ahead as planned, although a new drummer may take her place.

It nearly killed me when Jimmy told me about Jace. I couldn't wrap my brain around it at first. I guess I was the one who took off, though, right? What the hell else did I expect them to do? Jimmy didn't put it like that, but I could read between the lines. I'd really screwed myself over, and all I wanted was to blame Jimmy.

Troy revved the engine, and the crowd was forced to part. I covered my head with my right hand and kept my chin down. I'm sure a couple of ballsy photographers snapped some shots of the top of my head. There would no doubt be pictures of me circulating the Internet by the end of the day. At least they hadn't seen my stump. I nursed it against my stomach until Troy pulled his station wagon to a stop and opened the back door for me.

"You're safe now. They won't come onto the property." His large hand rubbed the back of my leather jacket, my long locks rustling against the fabric.

I expelled the breath I'd been holding and struggled out of my spot. Troy caught me with his hand before I assed over onto the concrete driveway. I glanced down the driveway, at the gate, and saw the determined swarm still desperate for a peek.

"They'll get over it. A new story will pull them away soon enough," Troy murmured in my ear.

I grunted and turned for the house, grateful for the long hair hiding my face. The smell of fresh lawn clippings drew my attention, and I glanced at the lush lawn in front of the house. The whole property was gorgeous and maintained by the world's oldest and friendliest gardener. He'd recently trimmed the thick hedge lining the edge of the yard, and he'd probably pruned the trees bordering the backyard, as well. I'd only been gone three weeks, yet it'd felt like a year.

I drew in a shaky breath and looked at the white house with its perfect, straight lines and modern details. It had been a pretty sweet find, which Jimmy's dad arranged for us when we first moved to LA. He was an investment banker and basically sneezed cash out his nose. In spite of his sporadic involvement in his sons' lives, he was always there with the money when they needed it. I guess it was his way of saying he loved them, but I'd learned from experience not to bring that up around Troy.

The main house was a two-story four-bedder with an open kitchen and living area that took up most of the bottom floor. Everything was white and pristine, with huge glass windows letting in copious amounts of Californian sunlight. Thanks to Nina—the cleaning magician—the house maintained its sparkle...in spite of our thoughtless effort. She puttered away in the background, an unnoticeable fairy who worked like a Trojan and hated any kind of credit.

Jimmy sidled up beside me as we approached the front entrance. His hand rested on my lower back, but I stepped out of his reach as he opened the door.

For the first time ever, music wasn't blaring from the sound system. I gave Jimmy a confused frown and he shrugged. He looked just as baffled as me.

"We're back!" he shouted from the entrance while Troy trailed behind us, carrying my beat-up backpack. He trotted down the two wide steps then placed it on the tiled kitchen floor beside the black marble island. I stared out at the open living area. The midnight-blue carpet was covered with beanbags and PS4 equipment. Controls, *Rock Band 4* instruments, and wires were a tangled mess on the floor in front of the massive flat-screen TV mounted to the wall. The black glass coffee table had stacks of pages on one end and a pile of empty glasses and bottles on the other. Flick must have been writing something new; his acoustic guitar was propped against the end of the long leather couch. My gaze traveled to the glass doors. Across the lawn sat my guest house. The concrete path cut through the grass and curved once before stopping at the white door I used to love stepping through. Behind it was an oasis of instruments, and upstairs was my little haven—Nessa Land. I wanted to go back there, but for now, I was stuck living in the main house. Everyone had insisted on it. Even the physical therapist had told me I'd need the support. She'd set up a contact in LA to visit me on a regular basis and had booked me an appointment with an occupational therapist who would be by once a week to teach me how to cope with a one-handed lifestyle.

I cringed at the idea but was distracted by the thumping of feet upstairs.

"Hey, hey!" Ralphie loped down first, jumping off the final two stairs and running toward me with a bear hug at the ready. He lifted me off my feet and squeezed the living crap out of me.

"Hey, be careful with her," Jimmy snapped, stepping forward to intervene.

Ralphie ignored him.

"Good to have you back, Nester." His goatee tickled my neck, and I had to pound him on the back to let me down. He chuckled and dropped me to my feet then planted a sloppy kiss on my cheek.

"Gross." I chuckled and wiped off his slime. He just grinned and lightly punched me in the shoulder. I went to do a left-cross, our usual MO, but I no longer had a fist, just a pathetic stump.

Ralphie glimpsed it and his smile faltered. I swallowed and tucked my arm behind my back, feeling like a freak show. He rolled his eyes and snatched it up, forcing me to whack him the way I used to.

"I said be careful." Jimmy shoved Ralphie with a thunderous scowl.

"She's not made of glass, dude." Ralphie pulled a face that made me snicker. He'd been like my big brother for years, and there was no way he'd let me get away with treating myself like porcelain.

He lightly tapped the end of my stump with the palm of his hand before letting me go. "Hurt?"

"Phantom pains, but they come and go. Don't worry, you'll know if you've really hurt me, because I'll kick your ass."

Ralphie chuckled and was forced to step back as Flick pushed him aside and wrapped me in a tender hug. His arms glided around my waist before he splayed his hands against my back. I rested my chin on his shoulder. I wanted to say something, but my throat was too swollen.

With a loud sniff, Flick suddenly let me go and held me at arm's length. He wouldn't want me to see the sheen of tears in his eyes, so I looked to the floor until he grunted and muttered, "Well, at least I have shot at finally beating you in *Mortal Kombat* now."

"Oh, shut up, you asshole." I shoved his chest and laughed.

He grinned, wiping his lower lip with his thumb and giving me a wink. But he couldn't hide his sadness. He was heartbroken for me...all these guys were, because they knew how vitally important hands were to a musician.

Still not willing to face that fact, I dropped my gaze to the tiles and shouldered my way past Flick.

"I'm, um, I…" Rubbing my forehead, I forced a smile and said, "I'm tired, so I'm gonna go upstairs and get some rest. Thanks for the ride, Troy."

"Of course," he murmured, his face etched with a compassionate smile that threatened to unravel me. They were all looking at me like that. It was pretty hard to stomach, so I turned and walked up the stairs.

My old room was neat and tidy. The sunlight cast a bright and cheerful glow around the space, so I walked to the curtains and pulled them across, one at a time—everything was going to take longer. Plopping onto my bed, I looked down at my boots and slowly went about unlacing them. I couldn't decide if it was a good thing or not that taking my clothes off was a hell of a lot easier than putting them on.

I stripped down to my T-shirt and crawled under the covers. Tucking my right arm beneath my pillow, I stared at the red glow created by the bright curtains as they tried to block out the sun for me.

I guess I should have been grateful that only my hand was taken. The rest of my body had healed pretty well, and all that remained were some road burn scars that would take their own sweet time to disappear. I probably should have been thanking my lucky stars that I was right-handed and still capable of doing so much.

But in that moment, I couldn't muster one ounce of gratitude, so I closed my eyes and begged oblivion to take me away from my nightmare.

TEN

JIMMY

Nessa had been holed up in her room for two weeks when I couldn't take it anymore. I'd tried to leave her alone. After doing a little research online about amputees and talking to the occupational therapist that Nessa refused to come down and see, I'd learned that she was grieving like someone who'd just lost a loved one.

I read up on the stages of grief and was trying hard to let her work through them in her own time. I guessed she was suffering from major denial, because if she ever did show herself to use the bathroom or get food, she'd mutter something about being fine then give me a pissy look if I tried to press her.

So I'd backed off, given her space, worked my ass off at the gym, practiced with the band until my throat was hoarse, and headed to the recording studio when Marcus made me. I arranged it so Nina would be around when I wasn't. Nessa couldn't be left alone. I didn't care what she said. She wasn't fine. She was fragile, and my worry for her was eating me alive. I couldn't help wondering if Dad did have a valid point. Committing yourself to someone was damn hard work.

Sucking in a breath, I shunted the thought from my mind. When Nessa was gone, I felt like my insides had been scraped raw. I never wanted to feel that hollow again, so I trudged up the stairs and steeled myself for what would no doubt be a battle.

I tapped on her bedroom door. "Hey, Ness, it's me. Can I come in?"

I got no answer so I pressed my ear against the wood. I couldn't hear much. Pursing my lips, I crossed my arms and glared at the door handle, wondering if I should barge in. The guys were downstairs playing *Mortal Kombat X*. Music blared out of the stereo, and I figured it was as good a day as any for Nessa to get her ass out of bed and rejoin the world. She couldn't wallow forever.

Knocking a little harder, I wrapped my other hand around the doorknob and pushed the door open.

"Ness?" My nose wrinkled as I stepped into the

red-tinged room. The curtains were drawn tight, but they didn't stop the midday sun from breaking through. It smelled musty and stale, like the last wisps of fresh air gave up hope days ago and decided to flee for safety.

I eyed the lump in the bed as I walked toward the windows. All I could see was a crumpled duvet with a shock of dark, tousled hair poking out the top. Nessa didn't move while I strode to the curtains and snapped them open. The mound in the bed started then burrowed even further under the covers. Flicking up the window latches, I pushed the large glass pane open as wide as it would go and stuck my head out to gulp in some clean air.

I was a guy and I knew how to make a room stink, but hers was above and beyond.

Enough was enough. With my jaw set, I spun back to face her. "Ness, you gotta get up."

"Piss off," came her muffled reply.

I rolled my eyes and stomped over to the bed. Grabbing a handful of duvet, I went to flick it back, but it jerked to a stop before I could. I grunted and tugged a little harder, wrestling with the stubborn girl to get the damn cover off.

"Let go!" I yelled.

"*You* let go!" she shouted, kicking out her legs and nearly scoring a fast one right in my balls. I jumped back in the nick of time and ripped the duvet from her hands. It went flying over my shoulder and landed on the bookshelf behind me, knocking a stack of books onto the floor.

I spun around and glared down at Nessa, who was giving me the best evil eye I'd ever seen. I met her scowl with a raised chin and planted my hands on my hips, just the way my fifth grade teacher, Miss Grouse, used to. "You cannot spend the rest of your life in bed."

"It's *my* life," she snapped. "I can do what the hell I want with it. Now, give me the covers."

"No." I raised my eyebrows and tipped my head. "You stink. You need a shower, fresh air, and some decent food." I frowned when I spotted the chocolate bar wrappers and empty boxes of Junior Mints crumpled around her pillow.

She growled in her throat, her upper lip curling. With her hair so wild and her eyes so dark, she looked like a rabid dog ready to attack.

I crossed my arms but didn't retreat. I didn't give a shit if she thought I was being mean. For once in my life, I felt one hundred percent justified in my behavior.

"The physical therapist is arriving in an hour to see you, and you need to be ready for her this time. Now get your ass up, or I will strip you naked myself and wrestle you into that shower. I don't care how much you fight me." I leaned forward with a smirk. "I'm winning this round."

"Get the fuck out of my room," she snarled.

"I'll start the shower for you then, shall I?" I gave her a pleasant smile and ambled out the door, pretending her venom didn't sting. I'd seen Nessa in foul moods before, but she was never that dark.

I started the shower and waited until the spray

was the perfect temperature before heading back into Nessa's room. She was attempting to straighten the duvet back over her body. My heart hitched as I watched her left stump flick the cover over her legs. The bandages had been taken off, and she was left with a neat scar. The surgeon had done an amazing job, but it still hurt to look at it.

I couldn't let it get to me, though. Clenching my jaw, I stormed into the room muttering, "No you don't." Yanking off the covers before she could fight me, I picked her up and threw her over my shoulder. She kicked and screamed, bashing my back with her right fist and trying to take out my balls again with her flailing legs. I gritted my teeth and marched her to the bathroom.

Plonking her on the floor, I grabbed her shoulders while she screamed in my face, "You're an asshole! Get off me!"

I let her go and stepped away, my nostrils flaring. "Do I need to undress you?"

With an irate glare, she flipped me off.

I stared down at the cute little bass clef-treble clef tattoo on her raised middle finger and smirked. "Well, at least we know there's nothing wrong with your right hand."

She grunted and pushed me out of the room. I turned to ask her if she'd like me to get her some lunch, but she slammed the door in my face before I could.

With a soft chuckle, I pressed my ear against the wood until I was pretty sure she'd stepped under the hot spray.

Satisfied, I headed downstairs feeling triumphant.

I loped into the living area and scored two curious looks from Flick and Ralphie.

"She's in the shower," I murmured.

"Uh-huh." They both nodded at me then shared a look I didn't want to decipher. They'd be idiots if they hadn't worked out that something big went down with Nessa and me, but I wasn't about to spell it out for them.

Shuffling into the kitchen, I got to work cooking pancakes for her. I wasn't the world's best chef, but I could make some mean blueberry flapjacks.

Thirty minutes later, "Art of Losing" by American Hi-Fi was pumping through the sound system, Flick and Ralphie were ribbing each other senseless as they started their final battle on the PS4, and I had a neat stack of pancakes sitting on the kitchen counter.

Nessa appeared in the kitchen, quiet enough to startle the crap out of me. I jumped and placed my hand on my heart before giving her a tight smile that quickly became genuine. She looked better. Her hair was wet and brushed, hanging over her shoulders and coming down past her breasts. Droplets of water dripped from the ends, marking her baggy white T-shirt. Her emerald nose stud was back in her left nostril, which I thought was a good sign. She was wearing black yoga pants and her feet were bare. I grinned down at her cute little toes as they wiggled on the cool marble tiles.

"Hungry?" I asked, sliding the plate of pancakes

toward her.

Her lips twitched and she gave me a morose stare before glancing over her shoulder. The guys were oblivious, but her gaze trained straight on their hands and the way they flicked and pressed the controls while they laughed at each other. She swallowed and ran her fingers down her arm, gently squeezing her stump before looking up to the speaker on the wall.

I closed my eyes and cringed. "Art of Losing" was one of her favorite songs to play because of the kick-ass beat. I could picture the smile on her face whenever she used to play the song. She'd come in with her rat-tat—boom-ba-boom—rat-ta-tat—boom-ba-boom, and then I'd strum my riff. We'd grin at each other, and the song would be away.

Damn it, I should have thought.

I scrabbled for the remote, desperate to turn off the music.

"Leave it," she muttered, pulling herself onto the barstool and stealing a pancake off the top of the stack.

"You want syrup?"

She shook her head and nibbled at the food, looking too tired and sad to even bother eating.

My heart squeezed as I watched her. She was so dejected and forlorn. I wanted to snap her out of it. I wanted my Nessa back. I had no idea what to say to make her return, so instead I shoved my hands in my pockets and watched her eat.

She refused to even glance at me, which got awkward fast, and it was actually a huge relief when the doorbell rang and the physical therapist walked in.

She was bright and breezy, taking Nessa into the formal dining room off the living area and running through some exercises with her. I wanted to watch, but Nessa told me to piss off as soon as my head appeared in the doorway.

I did as I was told and paced around the kitchen, cleaning every surface until it sparkled. Ralphie came in at one point to get a drink and gave me the weirdest look I'd ever seen.

"Shut up," I barked while scrubbing the sink.

"Sorry, man, I've just never seen you cleaning before."

"I need to do something," I muttered.

Ralphie snickered and ambled back to the beanbag, shaking his head as he plopped onto it.

The sink was freaking spotless by the time I was done, the sun reflecting off the curved corner so brightly it was blinding.

After the therapist left, Nessa took off to her room again. I chased her up there, determined not to let her dive back beneath the sheets and pretend the world didn't exist. I had my mental armor on and was ready for any kind of argument she'd throw at me.

But I wasn't ready for what I saw when I walked through her bedroom door.

ELEVEN

NESSA

"What are you doing?" Jimmy snapped.

I flinched at his harsh tone but kept my head down. Shoving the handful of clothes into my bag, I drove them the rest of the way with my fist before spinning back to collect my jewelry off the dresser.

Jimmy stood in my path, blocking me from collecting the rest of my stuff, and asked again, "*What* are you doing?"

His blue eyes were fierce, staring down at me with a bright intensity that I found unnerving and irritatingly sexy at the same time.

I scowled and dug my elbow into his stomach as

I tried to shove past him. "What does it look like I'm doing?"

He wouldn't budge so I spun around and scrambled over the bed behind him, landing on my feet with a thud and bumping into the dresser.

He lurched forward to catch me but stopped when he saw I wasn't about to topple over. The anxiety radiating off him was palpable, but he tucked it into hiding behind a sharp frown. "You're not leaving. I won't let you."

I sighed and wrapped my fingers around my rings and necklaces. Shuffling past him, I dropped my handful on top of my pile of clothes then attempted to zip my bag shut. It was damn impossible, so I ended up clutching the handles together and shoving it under my arm.

I walked for the door and was once again blocked by the world's most stubborn jackass.

"Move." My eyebrows rose. I tried for my most emphatic look, but it was no match for Jimmy's glare.

He shook his head while I rolled my eyes and groaned. "I'm not going far. I'm just moving to the guest house."

Relief washed over his face, but it didn't dull his anger. "Why?"

"Because I don't want to live with a bunch of stinky boys." I shouldered past him.

"You think *we* stink?" Jimmy muttered, following me down the hallway. "You were in your room this morning, right?"

I glared at him over my shoulder but nearly lost

my frown when I spotted the cute teasing look on his face. Damn it, why did he have to be so adorable?

"Ness, you can't leave."

"I'm not having you march into my room again and man-handle me into the bathroom. I want my own space." I clomped down the stairs, Jimmy hot on my heels.

"But you can't! You can't live on your own. How are you going to manage that?"

I stopped short on the bottom step and spun around to face him. He nearly barreled into me but grabbed the handrail and jerked to a stop just in time. He stood one step above me, gazing down with a pleading look that was bound to undo me. It was just another reason for me to leave. I wouldn't let myself give in to his magic again.

"I'll manage," I croaked.

In all honesty, I had no idea how. The physical therapy session freaking hurt, and I didn't know how I was supposed to move forward with my life. She promised me I'd be able to, and if I'd be willing to meet with the occupational therapist, then we could really make progress. But for some reason, I couldn't face it. I just wanted to be by myself and figure it out in my own way.

I swallowed and skipped down the last two steps, heading for the glass doors.

"Where you going?" Flick asked as I bustled past them.

"Moving back to the guest house," I spat.

"Are you sure?" Ralphie stood, hitching up his

loose jeans.

I went to reach for the door handle and suddenly realized I couldn't turn it with my left hand. Dropping the bag on the floor, I looked over my shoulder and gave them all a tight smile, attempting to hide my thundering heart rate. "I'm sure." I only barely managed the words before yanking the door open with my right hand, snatching up my stuff, and storming down the concrete path.

I half-expected Jimmy to chase me and throw me over his shoulder again, but no one followed. I dropped my stuff then pushed open the guest house door and dragged my bag in behind me.

Inhaling a deep breath, I sought that peaceful feeling I always had when I walked into that place, but I couldn't find it. I kicked the bag with the toe of my unlaced Converse and gazed at my little oasis.

The instruments were set up the way they always were, although my kit looked different. The stool sat higher. And the drums weren't at the exact angles I was used to. My stomach roiled, and I stomped down the two steps ready to fix it, but my feet jerked to a stop at the edge of the carpeted area. A sharp fear held me still. I hadn't touched a kit since the day I left LA. I hadn't even picked up a pair of sticks, and now I couldn't. Not the way I used to.

I stumbled away from the equipment and fell against the kitchen counter, knocking off two empty Coke cans. They pinged onto the floor, bouncing a couple of times before rolling to a stop beneath the pantry door. Running my finger along the white Formica counter, I gazed at the empty pizza boxes stacked on top of each other. The guys must have been jamming pretty late into the night. I'd have to expect them on a regular basis, and I was prepared for that. The real reason I wanted to return was upstairs. Grabbing my bag, I tromped up the stairs and walked into my old room, a small smile touching my lips.

It was a wooden A-frame space, supposed to be upstairs storage, but I'd turned it into Nessa Land. With the help of frost cloth and fairy lights, I'd transformed the space into a magical haven that no one but me was allowed into. Not even Jimmy had been in there. The night we hooked up, we spent most of it having sex on the couch by my drum kit, and then we stumbled into the downstairs bedroom for the rest of the night. It had been a wild ride and not easily forgotten. Memories pierced me, different images flashing through my mind as I relived his touch, his taste, his moans of ecstasy as he lost himself inside me.

I skimmed the edges of my room, taking in the framed pictures of Rosie and me, plus my plethora of trinkets scattered over every flat surface— stickers, graffiti pens, loose change, my first set of drumsticks, one of Jimmy's picks, a stack of friendship bracelets Ralphie's sister made me when she was going through her creative stage, the skull ring Flick had bought me at some county fair a couple of years back. As it always did, my gaze returned to the picture of Rosie and me, taken about a week before she died. She looked so bright and full of energy, her hazel eyes sparkling at the camera as we tried to take a 'sexy selfie.' Our duck faces were idiotic, which was why I'd framed the photo.

"Coolest old person ever," I murmured, my smile disintegrating as a deep yearning for my grandmother tore through me.

My bag thumped to the floor, making a loud bang on the polished wood and helping me cut off the suffocating emotions coursing through me. I slumped onto my bed and fell back against the cover, relishing the familiar smell. Gazing up at the twinkling lights above me, I pulled in another breath. It would take time for me to find peace again, maybe I never would, but if I was going to have a shot, I needed to be in my oasis and not living with the guys the way Jimmy wanted me to.

He was right about one thing; I couldn't spend the rest of my life in bed, but I could at least get some space and figure out how to manage my new reality.

I didn't care what he thought. I'd be just fine on my own.

*****

I let out a frustrated scream and dropped the hair tie onto the floor. My nose wrinkled as I tugged at my hair, tempted to rip it out at the roots. I wanted to tie it back in a ponytail, something that should be so easy, but I couldn't frickin' do it.

I slid my fingers through my long locks, and for the first time ever wished I didn't actually have them. My eyebrow peaked as the idea grew in my mind, and before I could think anything of it, I stormed into the kitchen and started yanking drawers open. The kitchen was pretty well stocked, and I was positive a pair of scissors would be around somewhere. The utensils clattered together as I shuffled the contents around.

"Aha!" I snatched out the black-handled scissors and slapped them onto the counter. The long, silver blades glinted under the kitchen lights and my belly quivered.

"Just do it," I muttered. Gathering up my hair, I twisted it around and pulled it over my left shoulder. My heart was pounding and I could only manage quick breaths through my nose as I reached for the scissors. Placing my stump against my hair, I opened the blades wide and slid the lower edge under my locks. I was about to make the big chop when the front door clicked open.

Jimmy's head appeared and his eyes instantly rounded. "What are you doing?"

"Don't you knock?" I paused, the blades poised to take a huge bite out of my hair.

He ignored my question and leaped down the steps, reaching over the counter and clamping his hand around mine. "Do not cut your hair."

I wriggled free of him, unwilling to admit that I was grateful for his interruption. "I can cut my hair if I want to," I spat.

Jimmy reached for the scissors again, his thumb gently caressing the back of my hand. His soft touch did not help at all with my racing heartbeat. I frowned at him.

"I don't think you want to, though. You seem frustrated and ready to kill something right now, and hacking off these gorgeous locks probably won't make you feel better." The way he said the word *gorgeous* and the expression on his face as he gazed at my hair made me freeze.

A small part of me still wanted to clamp the blades together, just to spite him, but his touch on my hand and the look in his eyes made me fold. With a short huff, I dropped the scissors. They clattered onto the counter, and Jimmy's head drooped with a relieved sigh.

I stepped out of his reach and crossed my arms, backing up until I hit the refrigerator behind me.

He studied me with a quiet grin, probably trying to work me out or something. I glanced away from his blue gaze and stared down at my bare feet instead.

"So, ah, why the sudden need to chop your hair?" he asked.

I shrugged. "It's hard to tie up."

"I can tie it for you."

My head jerked up, and I gave him a confused scowl. A smile spread across his lips, the charming one that turned my insides to putty. No wonder girls fell all over themselves to get to him.

My shoulders tensed.

"C'mere, at least let me try." He coaxed me over

to him with a flick of his hand.

I gazed at his long fingers, already knowing what they felt like running through my hair then fisting my locks and giving them a light tug as he pulled my head back and ran his tongue up my neck.

My jaw worked to the side, and I was about to deny his offer of help, but he sauntered around the counter with that sexy swagger of his and stopped right by my feet. I stared down at his scuffed Vans.

His breath was a soft tickle on my forehead as he reached for my left arm and gently pulled off my spare hair tie.

"Turn around," he whispered.

I did as I was told. It was hard enough to breathe, let alone put up a fight. His long, slender fingers slid through my hair, gently pulling the strands. I closed my eyes and tipped my head back, trying not to enjoy his close proximity. One step and I could nestle against his broad chest. His strong arms would wrap around me, and he'd kiss the top of my head, maybe murmur a sweet little something into my ear and make me feel like I could fly.

My eyes snapped open, forcing the fantasy to disappear. That would never happen. No matter how much I wanted it or dreamed about it, Jimmy was not a one-girl man. He wasn't the type to whisper sweet anythings.

I had to stop loving him.

"There." Jimmy stepped back and patted my shoulders. "Does that feel okay?"

I ran my fingers down my ponytail and nodded. "Thanks."

He moved to the counter with a heavy sigh and reached for the scissors. Dropping them into the drawer, he slid it shut and leaned against the countertop. His long fingers splayed over the white surface.

"This is why I want you in the main house. I can help you with this stuff." His shoulders were tense, the muscles bunching beneath his T-shirt. The tattoo on his arm rippled as he clenched his fist and turned to face me. "It's not safe for you to be here on your own."

"I am fine." I flicked up my right hand and moved out of the kitchen. Jimmy stopped me before I could reach the stairs, tugging me back to face him.

"You're not fine. You need help. You can't do this on your own."

I yanked my hand out of his grasp. "Yes, I can. I don't need you!"

His mouth dipped and his forehead wrinkled with an injured frown. "I get that you're still pissed at me, and that's fine, but it's going to take time for you to adjust to this, and whether you like it or not, you need help. Don't be an idiot."

"Oh, *I'm* the idiot!" I pointed at my chest, my hackles rising so fast I couldn't hold back. "You treat me like a piece of dog shit on the bottom of your shoe, and you expect me to let you back into my life. You want to become my little helpmate. Forget it!"

His eyes flashed with anger, and he leaned down so close our noses were nearly touching. "I am *sorry* for what I did! But I can't take it back, and you can't keep running away. If you'd just stuck around in the first place...!" He jerked tall.

"And what, put up with more of your bullshit?" I shoved at his chest, but he didn't even move. I loved and hated how damn strong the guy was. He may have looked small next to his bulky brother, but beneath that shirt was a chiseled work of art. Tight, sinewy muscles wrapped around a perfect frame of unyielding rock.

My nostrils flared and I crossed my arms, breathing like a bull at a rodeo.

Jimmy gazed at me, his face pinching tight before his shoulders slumped and he turned away. Threading his fingers behind his head, he looked up to the ceiling and said softly, "I don't know, Ness. Maybe we could have fought it out and found our way."

"We don't have a *way*, Jimmy. You made sure of that."

He spun back with a sharp frown. "So did you."

I scoffed and threw my arms wide. "How?"

"You ran!" he shouted, his hands flopping down to his sides. "You just split without telling anyone. We had no idea where you were and if you were okay and now, you're..." He pointed at my left arm, his expression crumpling.

Was he fucking blaming me? Saying this was somehow my fault!

I cradled my arm against my stomach, covering

my missing appendage with my right elbow and willing myself not to fall apart in front of him. I sniffed and puffed out a shaky breath, my jaw trembling as I fought for the right response.

"I'm not saying it was your fault," he whispered, raising his hands like two white flags. "I was the asshole. I don't deserve to be forgiven. But I'm determined to make this right, and I just really need you to stay and let me try."

His expression was so full of remorse I couldn't take my eyes off him. Jimmy never apologized— that wasn't his style. But there he stood, calling himself an asshole and looking ready to cry. His lips lifted into a tender smile, his eyes beaming with something I couldn't let myself buy into.

Moving to the stairwell, I gripped the railing and turned to ascend. I pressed my lips together and glanced over my shoulder. His silent torment tugged at my heart, but I steeled myself against any kind of emotion. I was being held together by sticky tape and Band-Aids. I didn't have the courage to risk my heart on Jimmy Baker again.

I had burned his photo and let him go…at least, I'd tried to. I wondered if Josh, the bartender in Payton, had been lucky enough to get over his girl, Rachel. Maybe I should have been calling him for advice.

"Yeah, hey, Josh, tell me. What did you do when the person you love hurt you so bad you didn't ever think you'd recover and now they're trying to win you over?"

I had a sinking feeling the sweet guy would probably tell me I was being a scared fool and I should go for it. I didn't want to call and find out. No, the only way to protect myself was to stick with the belief that the charade Jimmy had in place was simply fueled by guilt over what had happened to me. It wouldn't last. He'd soon be back to his old ways...and I'd be left in the gutter, licking my wounds and cursing myself for falling under his spell once more.

I wasn't being scared—I was being sensible.

Before Jimmy could say anything else to sway me, I dashed up the stairs and disappeared into the safety of my room.

TWELVE

JIMMY

Walking in and seeing Nessa ready to lop off her silken hair nearly gave me a heart attack. Not that she wouldn't look great with short hair, but the idea of her hacking at it in frustration sent me reeling. She didn't need to regret anything in her life. She had enough to deal with.

I let myself back into the main house and headed for my room. Flick had gone out with some chick he'd been eyeing up at the local coffee shop while Ralphie was locked in his room, watching some movie with lots of shouting and gunfire in it. I probably should have knocked and asked to join—I could have used the distraction. Instead, I wandered into my room and paced around aimlessly.

I glanced at my watch and winced. Usually, I'd be out on the town, dancing at a club or with some random chick, getting trashed and having a good time. I sighed in frustration as I scratched my crotch and headed for the shower.

A good time. I scoffed. What the fuck did I know?

I thought I'd had it all. When the presenter for *Shock Wave* called out Chaos in the final, I couldn't believe it. Nessa had squeezed my waist and started jumping up and down, while Ralphie wrapped us all in a bear hug. Flick kept muttering, "Holy shit. Holy shit," until he finally shouted, "We did it!" I started laughing and gazed down at Nessa. She was staring at me and had this dreamy look on her face. Our eyes locked, and we said a million things to each other in that moment. We'd done it. The two of us, who'd started out with this tiny dream, had turned it into something epic and were finally going to make the big time.

I stepped under the hot spray and scrubbed my face.

The sad thing was, we still were heading along the road to becoming full-time musicians—all we'd ever wanted. Except for Nessa. She'd wanted more. She'd wanted me, and I'd done everything in my power to destroy that. I pressed my hand against the white tiles and let the water run down my face, dripping like tears into my mouth.

I thought of her lying alone in the guest house. The only time I'd been up to her room was to check that she really was gone. I hadn't exactly stayed to look around, just seen the strewn clothing and raced back down the stairs, dialing her number. I'd seen her sleeping before, though. She was adorable, the way her dark eyelashes rested on her pale skin. She was like Snow White in the flesh. I'd run the back of my finger down her cheek and for a split second imagined myself doing that every morning for the rest of my life, but then of course, I freaked out and left her…in true Jimmy style.

Dad's advice over the years warned about the danger of getting attached. He'd used him and Mom as the perfect example of how commitment only complicates things.

"Keep yourself free, Jimmy. The only good thing to come from tying myself down to your mother was you and Troy. I could have been a father without the hassle of getting married, and probably been so much happier for it. I could have saved us all a lot of frustration and heartache."

Letting out a low grunt, I snapped off the shower and rubbed the water droplets out of my eyes. I hadn't even sudsed myself down. I didn't care. I was restless, and I needed to figure out how the hell I was going to make it right. My body was aching to hit town and find me a sweet piece of ass, but that wouldn't exactly score me points with Nessa. I couldn't revert back to that anymore. I had to change, like *really* change, and I was afraid I couldn't do it. Sex had been my fail-safe, my natural high. Dad had been right about that—it feels so damn good.

"Nothing makes you more alive, Jimmy."

He'd sold me his lifestyle like it was the only way to live...and I'd bought every fucking word. He must have never loved Mom, because after sleeping with someone I truly cared about, I couldn't think about sex the same way. Screwing those two girls after a night with Nessa had been a weird kind of torture. Their hot tongues and lusty cries couldn't erase Nessa from my mind. I'd worked my guts out striving for a high that never hit. No amount of pleasure made it better, and I'd left that hotel room a haunted man.

Nessa was my best friend, not just some chick who sucked me in with her beauty. Being inside her had been something else entirely. That high took me to a whole new level. I'd felt more than alive. I'd felt like I could fly...and the difference with her was that the feelings had stayed with me, intoxicating me like a bittersweet potion, nearly drowning me when she wasn't there anymore.

Was that love?

Dad would be so disappointed. I'd finally crossed the line he'd always warned me away from. I understand why he did it. Loving someone was a bitch. A constant war raged inside me— sweet memories of our night together were shot down by guilt that was then attacked by frustration and longing. I was a wreck. My mind was consumed with caring for her, protecting her...making up for what I'd done.

Nessa couldn't be on her own. It wasn't safe, and I'd have no chance in Hell of convincing her that she'd changed me if I wasn't around to prove it.

I ran my hand down my face and clenched my jaw. The way I saw it, there was only one solution—if she wouldn't live with me in the main house, then I'd just have to move into the guest house with her.

*****

It was a glorious, sunny morning as I made my way down the path with a bag of clothes in my hand. I squinted up at the blue sky and grinned. After deciding to move in with Nessa, I'd gone to bed and slept like a dead man. A firm direction had finally offered me the sense of peace I'd been longing for. Yeah, I was heading into a hurricane— no doubt about it. But at least I was heading toward Nessa. That thought alone filled me with hope.

I stopped outside the white door and expelled one last breath before knocking and walking inside.

She was sitting at the kitchen counter, nibbling a granola bar and reading something off her iPad. Her slender legs were wrapped up tight in a pair of pale blue skinny jeans with rips in the knees, and her baggy red shirt hung off one shoulder, exposing an edible patch of smooth, white skin.

Da-yum.

She glanced over her shoulder as I walked

in…and then she did a double-take.

"What's in the bag?" She swiveled her stool to face me.

I looked down at the black duffle in my hand and shrugged. "Just my clothes and stuff for my room."

Her button nose crinkled. "Why the hell are you bringing it in here, when your *room* is up at the main house?"

I grinned at her, noticing for the first time that the fly on her jeans was undone. She followed my line of sight and quickly flicked her shirt over her exposed underwear. It suddenly occurred to me how difficult buttoning a fly would be with only one hand. It was just further confirmation of my resolve.

"I'm moving in with you."

"Like hell you are." She jumped down from the stool and planted her stump on her left hip.

"There's still a bed in a spare room." I pointed toward it.

"So?" Her incredulous look was adorable. I loved the way her eyes flashed a dark umber when she got mad.

I headed for the bedroom door, ready to stow my stuff. "So, I'll be sleeping in there."

"No, you will not!" She stomped across to me, her dark hair flying. She yanked the bag out of my hand and with a small grunt, threw it out the front door. It thudded onto the grass and rolled a couple of times.

"Hey!" I spun back with a frown.

"Get out." She pointed through the doorway, her chin held high.

"Oh come on." I flicked up my hand. "I want to be around to help you."

Her eyes rounded. "How many times do I have to tell you that I don't need you!"

The words stung as much as they had the night before, but I puffed out my chest against them and narrowed my eyes, looking first to her jeans and then to the half-nibbled bar on the breakfast counter. "You hate granola bars. You normally have fruit salad, yogurt, and a banana smoothie for breakfast." I leaned down until my nose was practically brushing her cheek. "I can make you those things."

"I need to learn to do it on my own." She shoved me away.

I looked into the kitchen at the perfectly clear countertop. "You haven't even tried to."

"Would you just get out!"

With a slow sigh, I stared down at her and whispered, "Please, let me be there for you."

Her fiery scowl faltered, her eyes filling with wistful longing before snapping shut.

"Out!" She pushed my shoulder, stepping back and putting all of her weight into it until I finally relented and let her drive me outside. She gave me a defiant look before slamming the door in my face. I heard the snap of the lock but couldn't help a grin. I hadn't missed the way her lips trembled as she fought to turn me away.

She wanted me. She just didn't want to let

herself believe it.

I braced my arms against the outside frame and tapped my finger on the wood, chewing on the inside of my lip as I tried to come up with my next move. Nessa always hid herself away when things got tough. Not much could coax her out, except...

A slow smile spread over my lips.

Music.

If anything was going to win her over, it'd be music. With a soft chuckle, I raced up the path. Taking the stairs two at a time, I jumped into my room and grabbed my Fender and the small amp sitting next to it.

Trotting down the path, I set myself up outside the guest house. In the end, I had to head back to the house twice. It took two extension cords to reach the power supply for the amp, but I soon had myself set up. Turning up the volume, I strummed my guitar once to check the tuning, then started playing the opening riff of "Hanging By A Moment" by Lifehouse. I figured if I was going to serenade her, I might as well go all the way.

To be honest, it scared me shitless. I'd never told a girl how I felt about her before, because I'd never felt anything more than lust. But it was different with Nessa, and I needed her to know it.

I closed my eyes and started singing. It wasn't a hard sell; for once, I actually meant the lyrics. I'd spent most of my life denying my need to love someone, but losing Nessa flung a door open inside me, and I never wanted to feel that hollow and desolate again.

Dad's advice could stick it. I smiled and sang a little louder.

I was halfway through the first verse when the guest house door flew open.

"What are you doing?" Nessa stormed into the sunlight, her dark hair catching on the breeze.

"I'm serenading you..." I shrugged. "Until you let me in."

Her mouth dropped open, her thin eyebrows dipping into a sharp V. "Are you kidding me right now? I'm not one of your groupies who's going to swoon at your feet!"

The mocking way she said it wracked my insides. The look of disdain on her face didn't help much, either. "I don't want you to swoon, I want you to let me in the fucking door." I pointed over her shoulder.

She crossed her arms and leaned toward me. "Not going to happen."

I bunched my lips together and drew in a sharp breath. Placing my fingers on the strings, I found the right chord and started strumming again.

"It's not going to work, Jimmy!" she shouted at me. "I can be very stubborn."

"So can I!" I yelled back then started singing.

She let out a frustrated huff and stormed back into the house, slamming the door behind her. A smile toyed with my lips as I accepted her challenge and continued to play.

As the sun rose higher in the sky, I played and sang until my voice was hoarse. I couldn't believe I lasted so long, but every time I entertained the thought of quitting, Nessa's stubborn face would come into my mind and I'd force myself to go one more round, turning up the volume a little louder between each performance.

Flick shot out of the main house after my fifth run-through and yelled at me for waking him. His hair, which I hardly ever saw thanks to his permanent beanie, was sticking out at all angles.

I laughed so hard I had to stop playing for a second.

"Sorry, scarecrow, I'm on a mission."

"You asshat!" He thumped my arm, but I mussed his hair and shoved him away. My guitar twanged in protest. His thunderous scowl told me he was about to tackle my ass to the ground, but Ralphie appeared in the nick of time. In spite of his lumbering walk, the guy was like a stealth ninja, materializing out of thin air whenever needed. With a steaming mug of coffee, he coaxed Flick back into the house, giving me a wink before sliding the glass doors shut behind them.

So I kept playing...and playing...and playing.

The sun was beating down on me, coating my skin with a fine sweat. My cotton shirt was sticking to my back, and I wanted to quit so bad. I figured I'd play the song one more time and then have to give in. Damn her stubborn pride.

With a sigh, I started strumming the first riff yet again. I was about to open my mouth and sing when the door flew open.

Nessa ran onto the grass, her eyes wild with frustration. "You are making me want to kill myself. Can you not play any other songs?"

"I wanted you to hear this one." I smiled at her, making sure it was slow and charming, just the way the girls liked it.

Her gaze darted to my lips, but then she flinched and looked into my eyes. "Well, congratulations, you have officially ruined it for me. I now hate this song."

"Let me in and I'll stop playing."

"Forget it!" Her voice squeaked high.

I snickered and looked back down at the strings. In spite of my callouses, my fingertips were still taking a major hit, but I wouldn't let a little pain stop me. Nessa stalking onto the lawn had given me renewed vigor. I opened my mouth and started singing, "I'm falling even…"

She let out a frustrated growl and stomped back into the guest house. I waited for the door to slam shut behind her, but it didn't. It stood wide open and was the only invitation I was going to get.

With a soft chuckle, I unplugged my guitar and ambled into the guest house.

THIRTEEN

NESSA

I sat up in my room for the rest of the day, listening to Jimmy shuffle around downstairs. I hadn't spoken to him since he walked in the door, except to call down the stairs that this was a temporary situation and he better not unpack his bag.

The band showed up mid-afternoon and practiced for a few hours. I shoved my noise-canceling headphones on and buried myself beneath the covers until the boys quit playing. Then I waited another hour before surfacing.

It was dark out when I cautiously walked down

the stairs. Jimmy's black bag sat on the spare bed, still zipped up tight. At least he'd heard me and respected my request.

I felt like a failure for giving in, but the guy had shown an uncharacteristic determination on the lawn. His guilt must have been worse than I thought. I didn't even want to think about the fact he'd been serenading me with a love song. That was too much to wrap my head around. Part of me didn't want to face him, but hunger and thirst dragged me down the stairs. I glanced into the living area and spotted him on the couch, flicking through a magazine.

"Calypso" by Spiderbait was playing—one of my favorite songs. I couldn't help a smirk. The iPod resting in the sound system was full of all my she-rock favorites, which Jimmy would no doubt be silently suffering through. We liked a lot of the same music, but I *loved* my rock 'n' roll girls with a passion that Jimmy could never quite fathom. In spite of that, I saw his foot tapping to the beat.

He glanced up and smiled at me. "Hey."

I couldn't find my voice, so I gave him a brief smile before moving into the kitchen. I flicked on the lights, illuminating the cleared countertops. Had he done the dishes?

I frowned, feeling like I'd been dropped into an episode of some sci-fi TV show. Aliens had possessed Jimmy Baker and were trying to lull me into a false sense of wonderment before whisking me away to another planet.

"Do you need a hand with anything?" Jimmy

called out to me.

I flinched away from my thoughts and opened the fridge, hiding myself behind the door. "No, I'm good."

"I've ordered some Chinese. I didn't know if you were hungry, but I got you those dumplings you like."

The cool air coming out of the refrigerator was doing nothing to dispel the heat pouring over my cheeks. He'd cleaned the kitchen and ordered food. Who the hell was sitting in the living room of the guest house? Because it sure as shit wasn't Jimmy Baker.

My heart pounded in my ears, and I snatched a bottle of Coke from the top shelf. It was capped, but like hell I was asking the stranger on the couch to help me open it. I closed the door and noticed his blue gaze on me. He put down his magazine and slowly stood. I ducked out of his line of sight, yanking the drawer and pulling out the bottle opener. I pressed it against the cap and tried to hold the bottle still with my stump, but it kept sliding across the counter.

"Can I—?" Jimmy started, but I interrupted him.

"Nope, I'm good." I wrapped my arm around the small bottle, swamping it while still trying to get a good angle to take off the cap, but it wasn't working. Clenching my jaw, I hid my frustration, muttering a soft curse under my breath while digging the opener into the cap. My extra force caused the bottle to skid out from under me, fly off the counter, and come to a crash landing on the floor. The glass smashed, sending shards scattering across the kitchen. The sticky brown liquid coated my jeans and splattered over my bare feet.

"Shit." Humiliation burned my eyes, making it hard to see.

Jimmy raced across the room and quickly surveyed the mess I'd made. "Just stay still. I don't want you stepping on any glass."

His shoes crunched over the mess as he negotiated his way toward me. Coming to my side, he slid his hands under my arms and lifted me onto the counter with ease. He then crouched down to brush a few shards off my clothes and pick one small chunk out of the loose threads on my jeans.

I watched him in stunned silence, my heart melting at the attentive way he gently examined me. Lifting my feet, he brushed his hands over my bare skin to check for any nicks. His touch was warm and soft, sending sharp tingles shooting up my body and straight between my legs. I wanted to wrench my foot free, but couldn't move.

I fought for air until he lowered my foot and gave me a sweet smile. Heading over to the pantry, he pulled out the broom and went about sweeping up my mess. His bizarre behavior was freaking me out. Jimmy Baker didn't clean up messes, he made them. He didn't care about other people; he was only out to please himself.

I gave him a WTF look, which made him pause. "What?"

"What are you doing?"

He looked at me like I was stupid and slowly

replied, "Cleaning up."

"But…"

He shook his head and went back to sweeping, pulling the glass and brown liquid into a pile in the middle of the floor. "We'll need to mop the floor, too. Just to make sure we get everything. I'll grab the cleaning stuff from the main house in a minute."

That was it. I couldn't take it anymore. "Who the hell are you?"

He snickered and crouched down to the tiles, brushing the debris into the dustpan.

"Jimmy, since when do you clean up messes?"

He paused, his shoulders tensing as he glanced up at me. "Since now."

The shards of glass clinked together as they fell into the trash can. Jimmy stowed the dustpan and broom away then turned to face me. His blue eyes were bright, his tender gaze saying more than I'd ever seen before.

It unnerved me. I was the one who usually gazed at Jimmy like that, and he'd always been oblivious. I was used to loving Jimmy in spite of his egotism. It was too weird having him stand there acting like the guy I knew he could be. The one I used to believe existed…until he walked out of the club with his tongue in some chick's ear and his hand on her best friend's ass.

"Don't look at me like that." I dipped my head and kicked my heels against the cupboards. They banged lightly on the wooden framing, creating a steady beat.

"Like what?" He moved toward me.

My head popped up, and I glared at him. "Like you give a shit."

"But I do." He said the words so softly, and with such meaning, a chunk of doubt caught in my throat. It begged me to believe him, but I swallowed it down before I gave in. I wouldn't let myself be fooled again. I'd already decided my heart couldn't take another beating.

I scoffed and shook my head, throwing him a skeptical frown that made his chest deflate.

He closed the space between us and rested his hands on either side of my legs, leaning down so he could look me in the eye. "I know I burned you, but I was trying to protect us—the band, our friendship. I thought I was doing the right thing."

"By ripping out my heart?" I whispered.

Remorse cut into his expression, making his mouth dip. "I figured it'd be like ripping off a Band-Aid. It'd sting, but then things would go back to normal. I'm not a long-term guy."

I leaned away from him, placing my hand on his shoulder and forcing him back. "And that's what you want to be now? You want to play boyfriend? What makes you think you can?"

"Because you left!" His voice pitched, his face bunching with anguish. "You left me, and I went out of my fucking mind." The pads of his fingers skimmed my cheek, running gently down my face before pausing on my jawline. "I finally got a taste of life without you, and I couldn't handle it."

I swallowed, easing myself away from his touch.

Fear was making my throat constrict. I licked my lips and forced my cynicism to remain at the forefront; it was the only thing protecting me.

"That's not a reason to be with me, Jimmy. We've spent every day together for the last five years. Of course you were going to miss me."

"I didn't just miss you, Ness. I *craved* you."

The look on his face could have melted me to the floor. Part of me really wanted to trust him, but he'd severed what we had. And I couldn't pull the shredded threads back together.

He was playboy Jimmy. He couldn't have changed so much in such a short space of time.

I pushed myself to the other side of the counter and dropped down to the tiled floor near the stairs. Jimmy shook his head as I created extra distance between us.

"Don't you get it?" He ran a hand through his hair and blinked rapidly, looking up to the ceiling with a sharp huff. "I need you. I want you. I lov—" He let out a breath then whispered, "I fucking love you." His gaze hit me, giving my heart a swift jolt. I crossed my arms and attempted to hold myself together as he kept talking. "It took you leaving for me to figure that out. I'd never slept with a girl I care about before. Hell, I've never spent a whole night in bed with a girl before, and I woke up beside you and saw you lying there and I just..." He caught his breath, holding it for a long beat before expelling it on a contrite sigh. "I knew I could screw it up, and I had to jump before we crashed."

It still burned, the way he'd gone about it. He'd wanted me to see those girls hanging off him. He'd wanted me to know he'd be going back to some hotel room to screw the living daylights out of them. He did everything in his power to kill what we had.

"I thought I was cutting something off at the pass," he continued softly, "but it was too late. You'd already gotten to me. And I never knew that hurting you would kill me so bad. I didn't think it was possible to miss someone the way I missed you."

Tears restricted the back of my throat while my nose tingled like crazy. I squeezed my left elbow and forced myself to ask, "How am I supposed to believe what you're saying to me?"

His expression hardened, the remorse swiftly replaced with a die-hard determination. "I'm staying here until you do."

I sniggered and gave him a pitiful frown. "Oh great, and then you'll go partying again."

"No." He shook his head, his blue gaze working like superglue to hold me in place. "I'll unpack my bag."

FOURTEEN

JIMMY

I didn't mean to tell Nessa so much, but it'd all come tumbling out, a torrent of confession that I'd kept locked inside for over a month...possibly longer. After Nessa left and I didn't know where she was, I had to wonder if I'd actually loved her all along and never even realized it.

Either way, it was out now. She knew and all I had to do was convince her I wasn't bullshitting.

We hadn't spoken about it again. The rest of the week passed without incident. I spent most of it working out at the gym to get tour fit. The personal trainer was seeing each of us for one hour a day and working us like dogs so we'd be able to play and perform a two-hour concert without keeling over. After lunch, we'd congregate at the guest house for our afternoon practice session. I made sure Nina or one of the guys was always around when I wasn't. It was pissing Nessa off, but I didn't care. She spent most of her time up in her room or puttering around the kitchen, slowly working out what she could do easily and what she'd need to find new techniques for. I'd been cleaning up a lot of spills but thankfully no more broken glass. Watching her look so vulnerable in a sea of shattered glass tore my guts out. I'd wanted to sweep her into my arms and lay her in a bed of pillow fluff.

I tried to encourage her to see the occupational therapist, but she shot me down right away. She was determined to work it out on her own, which only made me more determined to stick around and help her out.

Flicking the damp hair out of my eyes, I walked out of the bathroom and spotted Nessa in the kitchen. She was carefully slicing a banana and popping it into the blender. Her hair was swept over her shoulder, yet to be tied. I kind of hoped she wanted me to do that for her. I loved running my fingers through that silky mass. I could still feel it clenched in my fist as I explored her soft skin with my tongue.

My cock stirred in my jeans, and I turned for the bedroom before it got the better of me. I drew in a couple of deep breaths as the blender started up, composing myself before walking back into the kitchen.

I was supposed to leave Nessa that morning and return to the studio. It was our next recording session with Jace, and if it went as well as the first couple, we'd probably finish up the second song. Torrence wanted to have three tracks down before we released the first one so we could hopefully get back-to-back hits running on the radio. The full album was due for release in December, with the tour due to kick off mid-January. It was an exciting time, and I wanted Nessa along for the ride.

Ambling back into the kitchen, I gave her an easy smile as she poured herself some smoothie.

"Do you want one?" she asked, resting the glass blender on the chopping board before reaching for a second glass.

"Sure." I perched on the stool and let her serve me. The blender was a heavy-duty, glass beast that weighed more than a blender should. It belonged in a restaurant kitchen, and I had no idea where we'd gotten it from. Nessa went to balance the bottom of it with her stump and hissed, dropping the jug. It rocked and swayed on the counter, threatening to topple. I grabbed the lip and steadied it while Nessa cradled her arm against her stomach and sucked in a few deep breaths.

I jumped off the stool, but she held up her right hand. "Sit your ass back down."

"But I can help—"

"I don't want your help! I want you to let me pour you a drink!"

"But your arm—"

"They're just phantom pains, that's all." She inhaled slowly and smoothed back her hair. "SIT!"

I hesitated for only a moment before parking it on the stool again. Nessa shook out her right hand then reached for the blender and poured it one-handed. I saw her arm shaking. She went to steady the jug again, but tucked her stump behind her back before she could.

Damn it. I was buying her a lightweight, plastic, cheap-ass blender.

With her jaw clenched, she poured me a full glass, spilling a little over the side. The thick, milky drink dribbled down the glass and pooled on the counter. I went to get up and grab a cloth, but her glare was so fierce I stayed where I was. Clearing her throat, she slid the glass over to me, and I could tell by the hitch in her lips that she felt a small sense of achievement.

"Thanks." I took the glass and winked at her.

She grinned then caught herself and hid her expression by taking a sip.

I ran my finger up the glass and sucked off the milky drip. It tasted sweet, just like she did.

The idea of leaving her for the day sucked, so I blurted out an invitation. "You should come with us today."

She jerked still then slowly licked the milky foam off her upper lip and gave me a quizzical frown. "To where?"

"The studio."

She started shaking her head before I could say

more.

"Hear me out." I tapped the counter. "Whether you're playing drums or not, you're still part of this band. You're cofounder with me, and you're not allowed to bail on this. You signed a contract."

"Yeah, to play the drums, and I can't do that anymore."

I worked my jaw to the side, resisting the urge to argue. She could totally play the drums again if she'd only let the therapist fit her with a prosthetic and teach her how to use it properly.

Nessa's lips quivered as she bunched them together and fought to hide her distress.

"You need to meet the new guy and be a part of this. You hide in your room every time he comes over. He really wants to meet you. And besides, you're amazing at composition. You could help produce the songs." I stared at her until she caught my eye. I tipped my head, hoping my puppy-dog eyes were in good form.

She rolled her eyes and looked to the floor.

"You have to be part of this. You *are* Chaos, and your name needs to be on this album."

With trembling fingers she tucked a clump of hair behind her ear.

"Come on, you need to get out of this place. The guys miss you. Come hang with us."

Her head was still shaking when she whispered, "Okay, maybe I'll just check it out today and see."

I'd take it.

Clapping my hands together, I grinned at her and chuckled.

She rolled her eyes again and gulped back her smoothie, but I didn't miss the little smile creeping over her face as she rinsed out the glass.

Music made everything better, and Nessa couldn't ignore the tug it had on all of us. It brought us together, and it would be the glue that held us strong.

*****

We piled into Ralphie's bright green SUV cruiser and headed for the studio. I was expecting reporters. They had been camped out there last time, and I'd warned Nessa to prepare herself. She'd given me a stiff nod and then Flick murmured, "They're probably more interested in snapping the new drummer anyway, so don't worry about it."

I shot him a dark glare, which he frowned at until he spotted Nessa's forlorn expression. He winced and went to say something, but I slapped his arm before he could put his foot in it again. He reached back from the front seat and punched me in the leg.

I should have known better than to tussle with Flick.

I was tempted to hit him back but settled for a silent stare-off, until we pulled into the main street and saw the huddle of reporters. Ralphie sped past them and parked in the lot around back. We all jumped out of the car and Ralphie wrapped his big arm around Nessa's shoulders, shielding her from the right. I protected her left side while Flick ambled in front of her, smirking at the cameras as they flashed in our faces. He answered a few questions in his vague, aloof way, offered a few sexy grins and did everything he could to shield Nessa. I was grateful to him.

Questions were shouted specifically at our hottest news, but I didn't let her answer any of them. We hustled her through the crowd and into the secure building. The guard ushered us through and stopped any follow-on traffic behind us.

We jumped into the elevator and all sucked in some much-needed air.

"Still not used to it." Ralphie shook his head.

"It'll die down eventually," Flick murmured.

"Not if we hit number one." I raised my eyebrows at them. It was something we all desperately wanted, but it would come at a cost. I glanced at Nessa's pale complexion and wondered if she could handle it.

She caught my worried gaze and gave me a tight smile. The elevator dinged three floors below the studios. The doors slid open to reveal a sexy blonde wearing a dark-red fitted suit. My eyes naturally trailed down her luscious curves, noting the sway of her hips as she stepped into the elevator with us and filled the cramped space with her rosy scent. She caught my eye and gave me a sultry smile. There was something about her that seemed familiar, and it wasn't until she purred, "Hey, Jimmy. How's it going?" that I remembered we'd slept together. She'd been one of the organizers for *Shock Wave*, and we'd screwed in her office a couple of times during filming breaks. She was like twenty years older than me, but with a body that firm, I hadn't been complaining.

I felt Nessa's acidic glare from the other side of the elevator and cleared my throat, giving the woman (whose name I was struggling to remember) a nod. "Good, thanks."

We rode the next two floors in silence. I held my breath the whole way and wanted to slit my throat when the lady brushed her fingers down my chest. "My office is on this floor now. Feel free to visit me anytime." She winked and sauntered out of the lift.

She turned and tinkled her fingers at me while I tapped the *close door* button as fast as I could. The doors finally slid shut and Flick snickered, holding his nose to hide the sound and dipping his head when Nessa swiveled around to glare at him. I opened my mouth to say something that would ease the molten look of her face, but nothing came out.

As soon as the doors dinged open, she shot through them and smashed straight into Marcus.

"Whoa." He chuckled, catching her against his side before she could fall to the floor.

She brushed her hand down her red cheeks and smiled. "Hey, Marcus."

"How's my favorite Chaos girl?"

She grinned like she always did whenever he made that joke. He wrapped his arm around her shoulder and gave her a quick kiss on the forehead before letting her go and shaking our hands. We'd been hanging out enough not to have to shake each time we got together, but it was just Marcus's way. He was all about eye contact and making people feel important. He asked us how we were each doing and led us through to the main studio.

"Jace is already here."

Nessa stiffened beside me. I went to put my hand on her back and give it a reassuring rub, but she side-stepped me before I could. I had to bite my tongue and clench my fist at my side to hide my frustration. I just wanted her to let me in.

Jace was sitting at the kit, playing "Carpe Diem" by Green Day. He was oblivious to our stares as he played a song with a great beat. The goofy smile on his face was pretty funny. It was cool that Garret, the sound guy, let Jace have a good time while he waited for us.

Damn, he was good. His sticks hit the skins with confidence, jumping from one drum to another as he kept in perfect time to the music. I had to smile, but it quickly faded as I glanced down and saw Nessa's face. Her skin was ashen, her chest heaving as she gazed through the glass at the sticks dancing under Jace's command.

I leaned down and whispered into her ear. "You can do that again, you know."

My soft voice startled her, and she flinched away from me. She forced a smile and nodded, but I could tell she didn't believe me. She was probably still pissed about the elevator ride, too, which so wasn't helping my cause. Why had I checked that woman out? I'd done it without even thinking.

Nessa had no doubt watched me out of the corner of her eye, knowing I couldn't resist. Damn, it wasn't like I was going to act on it!

The song cut off and Jace stopped playing. He spotted us through the glass, and a broad smile stretched across his mouth. Jumping up from the kit, he loped to the door and busted through, stopping short when he spotted Nessa next to me.

He was a giant compared to her, but he acted like he was meeting royalty as he held out his hand and blushed.

"Dude, it is such an honor to meet you." He grinned.

Nessa hesitated for a second before reaching forward and grasping his hand. She said a short thank you then let go of him. A long, awkward silence dropped into the room, and I flicked Marcus a silent plea to get on with it.

He snapped his fingers and clapped his hands together. "All right, let's get to work."

I brushed my hand down Nessa's arm as I shuffled past her, but she didn't return my smile. Her body was rigid. I cleared my throat before walking through the door and pointed at Garrett.

"You cool if Nessa watches over your shoulder? I thought she could help produce some of the songs."

"Yeah, totally, man." Garrett spun in his seat and grinned at Nessa, ushering her over with a flick of his fingers.

She hesitantly stepped up behind him and gazed down at the soundboard. He started explaining the mixes to her, most of which she already knew, but she listened politely anyway.

Relieved that Nessa wasn't standing there like a lost stray, I picked up my guitar and gave it a quick tune. Flick was on keyboards for the number we were recording, so we stood together and made sure we sounded okay. Ralphie did a few bass notes, making us laugh with a funny riff. Jace then joined in, throwing in a few quirky taps and getting an off-the-fly song happening. We all chuckled and messed around until Garrett spoke into the mic.

"Okay, ready to go, dudes."

I smiled at the glass, hoping to catch Nessa's eye. I couldn't really see her but wanted her to know how much it meant to me that she was there.

Turning around, I gave Jace a quick nod and he tapped us in. The music grew around me, and that familiar swell bloomed inside my chest, a whirlwind of notes and sound...my peace in chaos.

FIFTEEN

NESSA

I stood behind the glass, watching the guys play. I wasn't used to facing them. Sure, they'd spin around and smile at me during performances, but I never had the pleasure of really seeing them play. And it was a pleasure...and a heartache.

The expression on Jimmy's face as he dove into the song made me want to fall in love with him all over again, but I steeled myself against it. I couldn't go down that path, not when I felt completely homeless.

"They sound great, right?" Marcus nudged my shoulder with his arm, playfully rocking against me.

I nodded, unable to speak past the lump in my throat.

His gaze was on me, but I refused to look at him. I caught his pained smile out of the corner of my eye before he sighed and said, "I have to shoot off to a meeting, but let me know what you think when I get back. Maybe you can produce a couple of the songs you and Flick wrote earlier in the year. I think it's important your name is on this album."

I nodded again and was forced to turn and smile at his cute grin.

"I know it must sting having a new drummer, but I swear I worked my ass off trying to find someone who had your style...your sound. He's a good fit for Chaos, and we'll find the perfect place for you, too." He patted my shoulder and slipped from the room, unaware of how replaceable he'd just made me feel.

Gazing back through the glass, I stared at the new guy...the new me. As much as I didn't want to admit it, he was freaking amazing. He was built like a demigod with his long, sexy hair and those pouty lips, dark eyes that practically begged you to start unbuttoning your shirt. The girls would be drooling over him, but more than that...he could play. I mean, he could *really* play.

My stomach twisted into a tight knot as I watched his sticks tackle the beat with ease. He held my boys together, carried them through the song like he'd been destined for Chaos his whole life. I couldn't take my eyes off the way his fingers curved around the wooden sticks, manipulating them with such confidence and drive...just the way I used to.

The song came to a triumphant finish and Garrett whooped. "Freaking legends, boys. Let's do it again."

I quietly stepped away from him, clutching my useless stump against my side and easing out of the room. I couldn't watch anymore. My arms were shaking with an overwhelming urge I couldn't satisfy. I wanted to bust in there and yank those sticks out of Jace's hands. I wanted to adjust the stool to *my* height, fix the kit so it was perfect for *me*. And then I wanted to smack the hell out of those skins until my body was coated in a slick sweat and my heart was racing...until I felt spent and sated—released.

I gripped my left elbow as the elevator descended, praying no one would join me. I didn't need some hot-bodied woman in a red suit walking in and making me feel like an ugly loser. Sniffing, I wiped my finger under my nose and headed for the exit. Brushing past the guard, I busted outside and totally forgot about the barrage of reporters who'd be waiting for me.

"Nessa!" They surged forward, like a tsunami set on drowning me.

I lurched back from them, hiding my shorter arm beneath my whole one and squinting as a flash went off in my face.

"How are you feeling?" one of them shouted at me.

I put my head down and tried to keep walking. They squished in around me, making it hard to move.

"Is the arm healing nicely? Are you suffering any pain?" another one called.

"Do you think you'll ever play again?" A photographer yelled the question as he snapped my picture.

My chest restricted, the air in my lungs struggling to break free as I panted through the fray.

"Do you feel you still have a place in Chaos?"

The questions stung, like poisonous arrows sinking into my exposed flesh. It was making me dizzy and nauseated. Shunting to the side, I held out my arm and silently begged for some space.

The move gave them free access to my damaged limb. There was a short collective pause before the cameras started snapping in a frenzy. The world started to spin, and a full-blown panic rose up within me.

"Leave me alone!" I screamed, forcing a nearby cameraman out of the way and making a break for it.

I pushed and shoved until I had enough room to start sprinting. My hair flew over my shoulders as I pumped my arms and aimed for the first corner. Persistent photographers clattered behind me, goaded on by my dramatic resistance.

They were freaking sharks, and they'd smelled my fear. They wanted to taste more, get the juice that would soon be spread over the Internet like chocolate sauce on a sundae.

I was such an idiot. I should have kept my head down—stayed silent and calm. This was basic stuff we'd been taught when first entering *Shock Wave*. I remembered the 'press lessons' so clearly, yet couldn't execute any of it.

Stopping to catch my breath, I leaned against the mailbox and scanned the street. I kind of knew where I was, but home was too far to walk, and I hadn't gotten my head around the LA bus system. Taxis were nowhere in sight.

I was officially screwed.

My eyes started to well with tears as desperation rendered me useless. I blinked and tried to focus, deep down knowing my only real option was to head back to the studio. But the idea of standing there watching the guys play without me was freaking depressing. I had to get away. To get out. I couldn't let them see. I'd been hiding in my room during practices for that very reason. But Jimmy's sweet smile as he drank my smoothie made me weak, and I'd said yes without thinking it through.

Playing had always been my form of escape. It helped me sell the lie that I had everything under control—that I was worthy of playing with them. But now I had no kit to hide behind, and my veneer was cracking. Everything I'd been trying so hard to forget was bubbling to the surface. I didn't want them to learn the truth. I didn't want them to see who I really was.

"Nessa!" A reporter down the street spotted me and my heart hitched.

I sucked in a breath and turned on my heel, bolting down the street and weaving through the human traffic—business people on cellphones, a skateboarder obviously ditching school, and two women power-walking while talking a hundred miles an hour. I swiveled and jumped around each of them, glancing over my shoulder as I went. The reporter now had a buddy, and they were hurtling after me like I was tomorrow's headline.

Cars buzzed past on my right, and I looked for a quick dash across the road but couldn't see one. I'd have to make it to the lights.

My tired body was weakening quickly. Having spent most of my last month lying around in bed, I was well out of shape and my banana smoothie breakfast wasn't cutting it.

I glanced across the street and noticed a tall guy with messy brown hair ambling out of Starbucks. He had a coffee in his hands, and in spite of his large wrap-around shades, I recognized him immediately.

Thank God, an escape.

"Troy!" I screeched, raising my hand and dashing onto the street without thinking.

A car horn blasted and a high-pitched squeal of brakes sounded to my left. The smell of burning rubber hit my nose and froze me to the spot.

I turned, my eyes bulging so wide I thought they might pop out of my head. My heart shuddered to a stop, and I waited for that all-too-familiar impact.

SIXTEEN

NESSA

"Nessa!" Troy's voice boomed across the street, but I barely registered it.

All I could see was a bright red Corvette screaming to a stop at my feet. The bumper was less than an inch from taking out my knees. Breaths shuddered inside my chest, making me crumple forward as my mind flashed with my accident again.

I was flying through the air, and then came the hard crunch. I gripped my stump, reliving the excruciating pain of having my fingers mangled by a burning hot engine.

"Are you crazy?" the driver shouted, but I was still back in Arkansas on a black road in the early morning sun.

"Nessa." Troy's voice tried to break through my fog, but it wasn't until his hand slid gently down my back that I jolted upright and looked at him.

My eyes must have been wild; I could tell by the way his mouth dipped. "It's okay, Ness. You're safe now. I'll take you home."

I fell against his solid chest, burying my face in his brown leather jacket. Cameras clicked behind me and people continued to shout questions. The driver mumbled something but let us walk past before revving his engine and squealing away. I flinched at the sound, and Troy held me tighter, his large arm engulfing me.

Cars stopped for us as Troy raised his hand and ushered me through the traffic. I kept my head down. My body wouldn't stop shaking. Each time I shivered, his arm would wrap around me that much tighter. He was a big guy and I felt like a little kid next to him, but in that moment, I didn't mind. I needed his safety, his protection.

He didn't say anything as he walked me to his car. I remained huddled against his chest, sniffing quietly as my stomach quaked. He pulled out his keys, and the alarm did a double beep before he opened the door and guided me into my seat. I couldn't see his eyes behind the shades, but his expression was grim as he buckled me in then closed the door.

A photographer ran up to the car and snapped a

few shots.

"Back off!" Troy got in his face. "Show some respect."

He didn't touch the guy, but his tone and towering demeanor had the cameraman shuffling back a few paces. He was ballsy enough to take one more photo as Troy slammed into the car and started the engine. He pulled away from the sidewalk and tore down the street, putting as much distance between me and the relentless paparazzi as possible.

"Are you okay?" His voice was soft, like he was talking to a scared kid or something. That was how I felt.

I nodded.

"Where's Jimmy?"

"Chaos is at the studio," I murmured, looking out the window. A group of joggers bounced past the car, followed by a couple holding hands. Their fingers were linked and she rested her head on his shoulder. There was a blissful, relaxed smile on her face. In her other hand was a shopping bag, which swung idly at her side. I looked down at my left stump, my forehead wrinkling. I'd never be able to do that...walk along holding a guy's hand while swinging a shopping bag in the other. It was so pathetically insignificant, but at the same time, it felt huge and devastating.

What guy would ever want me anyway? I was a mutated freak.

I pressed my lips together, the urge to disappear coursing through me. I wanted a cave in the middle of nowhere, a wide-open field with no humans for miles…a black vortex in space.

Troy turned onto the main road then took the freeway. It was the quickest route to my house, and I was grateful for it. I wanted to get out of his car and be on my own for a while.

He kept glancing at me, trying to silently ask if I was okay. I scratched the side of my head, hiding my face from him. I was sick of people looking at me.

"You want to talk about it?" he finally asked.

"I'm not one of your patients, Troy."

"I know, you're way too old." He smirked then trained his eyes back on the road. "Look, I may be used to listening to kids, but the basics of counseling apply across all ages. So, if you want to talk, I'm here to listen, free of charge." Dimples appeared in his chiseled cheeks. He had the same sweet charm as Jimmy, although he wore it with an honesty that was endearing.

I wouldn't let that break me, though. I didn't want to delve into the inner workings of Vanessa Charlotte Sloan. I knew what I'd find…and I didn't want anyone else to see that. Nearly six years ago, I put on a new coat—my Nessa coat—and I was petrified of people seeing underneath it.

I shook my head and sniffed. "I'm fine."

"You're not fine." His long finger tapped the wheel as he checked the four-way stop before pulling through.

I stiffened at his quiet comment. "What the hell are people expecting me to say when they ask if I want to talk about it?"

Troy sighed, flicking on his indicator and turning into my street. "I don't know. Something. Anything. It's better out than in, you know."

His words jolted me. I could hear another voice saying them and my heart spasmed. The pieces of sticky tape I'd been using to seal up the cracks in my soul started to break away. I swallowed and lurched in my seat as Troy stopped outside the gate.

I unfastened my belt and reached for the handle. "Thanks for the ride."

"I can drive you around to the guest house."

"No, I'm good." I shouldered the door open and stumbled out of the car.

Troy leaned across the seat. "Are you okay?"

"Yes," I clipped, straightening up. I sucked in a breath and tried to smile, but all I could manage was an unconvincing flash of movement. "Bye, Troy."

I walked to the code box and punched in the number. The gate lumbered open while Troy's car idled in the driveway. As soon as I could squeeze through, I headed away from Jimmy's brother. I could feel his eyes on me the whole way and ducked my head, wrapping my arms around myself and trying to hold it all in.

But I couldn't.

My mind flashed with the memories I'd been keeping at bay...a mixture of good and bad. The sweet, redeeming ones, which should have brought me so much comfort and pleasure, instead made me feel like I was about to shatter.

I sat by the window, drawing invisible pictures on the glass with my finger. The room was quiet — the suffocating kind that made me want to digest my own head. I hadn't been allowed music since my big fight with Mama. She ripped the stereo out of the socket and marched from the room. The door slammed shut with a finality that warned me I was entering into the longest, and most painful, summer of my life.

I could hear the strains of laughter downstairs. My five-year-old sister, Violet, was giggling. She always giggled. I didn't know how or why. I found it impossible to laugh in that house. Victor, my twin brother, was no doubt doing something adorable — being the perfect child.

I sniffed and resumed my drawings, but my index finger paused on the glass when I noticed a dry cloud of dust at the end of our driveway. A cherry-red Cadillac convertible that belonged in the sixties came barreling up our long drive. I squinted to see the driver. My family didn't know anyone with such an ostentatious car. We drove sensible family wagons in our neighborhood.

The Caddy swerved to a stop in the flat patch of grass parallel to our front porch. I studied the older woman in the driver's seat. She pulled off her large shades and threw them on the dashboard before looking up at the house with a pensive smile. Her long fingers gripped the wheel, and her thin lips twitched as she sucked in a breath through her straight nose before getting out of the car.

She was dressed in black skinny jeans with knee-high

boots. Her well-worn leather jacket and the way her wild, straw-like hair was braided over her shoulder made me wonder how a woman with so many wrinkles could pass as a rocker-chick and make it look so damn cool. I was waiting for her to make the rock 'n' roll sign and poke out her tongue. I smiled. That would have been funny.

The screen door squeaked open then smacked shut. I rose to my knees, pressing my face against the glass while straining to hear what my sharp-tongued mother had to say. Her tone was chilly. The guest was obviously not welcome in our home.

She raised her ringed fingers as two white flags. "I happened to be down here for something else, and I thought I'd swing by and meet my grandbabies."

"I didn't invite you, Mama."

My stomach twisted. Mama? The one who was never spoken of?

I strained to hear more, but they shifted out of sight and earshot. I scrambled to my bedroom door and leaned against the wood. The voices downstairs were still muffled, but it wasn't hard to sense the awkward tension. I heard a few barked sentences and then some murmurs. It was impossible to hear anything good, and all I could hope was that Vincent or my other sister, Veronica, would break the rules later and let me in on what went down.

A quick thumping sounded on the wooden steps, and I eased back from the door. The feet were traveling in my direction. Fear spiked inside me as I listened to the metal key slip into the lock of my bedroom door. It swung wide and my mother stood there puffing.

"See, five altogether," Mama snapped. "Say your hello then get going. I have dinner to prepare."

The taller woman stepped around my mother. Her hazel eyes studied me, narrowing slightly before lighting with a soft smile. "Hello, Vanessa. I'm your grandmother, Rosie."

"Hello." I swallowed and slid my hands into the back pockets of the ripped jeans Mama hated. She'd tried to throw them out twice, but I'd snuck down and rescued them from the trash each time. Her eyes narrowed as she noticed them on me. I glanced away from her glare and locked eyes with my estranged grandmother.

Her smile grew a little wider as she peered around my room. It was a mess—clothes scattered across the floor, half-read comic books open on my dresser, the end of my bed and my desk, music CDs shoved into any spare space I could find. I used to have posters up, too, but the second my parents saw them, they were taken down. So the band members were bare-chested— honestly, it was like living in a convent.

"Why was your door locked?" My grandmother's voice was kind of deep and husky for a woman, but it was soft and gentle, too. I liked it.

Mama stiffened, her bony fingers gripping the doorknob. "She's a bad girl and until she can learn to do as she's told, she'll be staying in here."

My grandmother snickered. "Martha, she's only fourteen. What could she have possibly done that was bad enough to warrant being treated like a convict?"

I glanced at my mother then back to her mother. I couldn't believe they were related. Mama only ever spoke of her beloved father, and we weren't allowed to ask *about the crazy lady who abandoned ship the day after his funeral.*

Mama's lips bunched tight as she whipped around to look up at the woman. "Unlike you, I know how to discipline my children, and they will not run wild and embarrass this family." She pointed her knobby finger at me. "That girl needs to learn respect and she needs to do as she's told, whether she wants to or not. She may look sweet, but she's a devil-child when she wants to be."

Grandmother's eyebrows rose and she nodded, her hazel gaze still locked on my face. I flinched at Mama's words and looked to the floor, digging my toe into the worn carpet.

"Maybe I should take her off your hands then." My grandmother's quiet suggestion was said with a smile and met with a hostile glare.

"Like I would turn her over to the likes of you," Mama snapped.

The tall rocker-chick ignored the derisive tone and hitched her shoulder. "Martha, sweetheart, you have four other children to care for and a big house to run. I'm simply offering to lighten the load. Let me have Vanessa for the summer."

"I will not be giving you my eldest daughter." Mama's hands landed on her hips, her chest puffing out defiantly.

"This is no way for a young teen to spend her summer days. I will not allow my granddaughter to be treated like a prisoner."

"I am the mother in this situation. You don't even know the girl!"

"Then let me get to know her. I'll take her to Chicago

with me. I have a guest room in my apartment. I'd love to have her stay." Her eyes were gentle and kind as she grinned at me. My heart hammered away in my chest, erratic and out of time. I didn't know what to think. I couldn't imagine driving away from the only home I'd ever known to spend a summer with a lady I'd said one word to…but I liked her smile and the sound of her voice.

"You don't know what you're sayin'. She's nothing but trouble."

My grandmother's eyes narrowed in on me, her high cheekbones looking sharp as she scrutinized me up and down. "I'll straighten her out for you."

Mama rolled her eyes. "You wouldn't know the first thing about raising a child right."

"Hey, I raised you and your brother, didn't I?"

"Barely!" Mama scoffed.

Grandmother's nostrils flared slightly as she stood to her full height and looked down at her daughter. "I'm not leaving without her."

My mother lifted her chin and met the challenge head-on. Her fiery gaze, which was capable of making me feel like an ant, had no impact on my grandmother.

The thick bangles on Rosie's wrists clinked together as she crossed her arms and smirked. "I'm sure child services would be very interested to find out about a young woman being locked in her room. How long's she been in here?"

Mama's face blanched. "I am not abusing my child. I'm teaching her a lesson."

"I'm sure when I call them to ask for their advice, they'll let me know."

A cold current passed between them, and I held my breath. Finally, Mama laughed—a cool, brittle sound that made my spine quiver. "You know what, go ahead. Take her. You're right, I have four other children who want to be raised by me. They respect their parents, and I could do without the irritation." She spun to me, flicking her head at my closet. "Pack a bag, Vanessa. You're spending the summer up north."

My expression wrinkled with doubt, and my mother's lips twitched with a small smile before turning back to her mother. "Good luck. I expect you'll return her soon enough. Not even God himself could tame that one."

Grandmother looked over my mother's head, her eyes lighting with glee as she caught my stare. I didn't know if she was thinking 'challenge accepted' or what was going through her mind at that point, but it only ignited the uncertainty within me.

Thirty minutes later, I stumbled down the front steps with an overstuffed suitcase in my hand. All I'd had time to grab was my essentials and a few comic books. I wanted to ask for my iPod back, but I doubted Mama would give it to me. She stood on the porch, her body rigid as I hugged my siblings goodbye. Dad glided his arm around me and gave my shoulder an awkward pat.

"It's for the best." He nodded with a weak smile.

I couldn't smile back.

Mother then stepped up to me and placed her hand lightly on my cheek. I flinched away from her touch. "This is what comes when you don't do as you're told. You get sent away."

My throat grew thick with a caustic acid that burned.

I had no reply for her, so I just stood there like a statue as she kissed my cheek and led me down to the car.

As the cherry red vehicle loomed closer, my legs stiffened and I spun to face my mother. "Why are you doing this? You don't even like this woman."

Mama's nose twitched, her chin trembling slightly as she blinked and refused to look at me. "I'm at my wits' end with you, and I can't go another round. So unless you're willing to tell me that you will do everything I ask, then you are getting in that car and you are giving me a summer off."

My shoulders slumped, my spirits deflating. I wasn't willing to beg; hell, I wasn't even willing to apologize for what I'd done. She couldn't make me into something I wasn't. Besides, it was only one summer, and surely my mother wasn't enough of a psycho to send me off with a serial killer. It sure as hell beat sitting in a room for five more weeks.

Holding my breath, I swiveled toward the car and shuffled through the dirt. It took a massive leap of faith, but I forced my butt into that passenger seat and fastened my seatbelt with quivering fingers.

The engine roared to life as my grandmother turned the key. I gazed down at the messy interior, noting the empty Coke bottles between the seats and the shiny black sound system that was way too new for a car that old. She picked up her phone and handed it to me.

I nervously held it in the palm of my hand as she reversed out of the spot. My family was still on the porch watching us. Violet was sniffing against Veronica's leg, her bottom lip wobbling while Vincent and Victor watched me with stoic expressions. Dad had his arm around Mama's shoulders, but they weren't crying. They didn't even look that sad. Why should they be? The black sheep was finally leaving.

"Just press play, honey." Grandmother put the vehicle in gear and winked at me.

I tapped the screen and hit play like she told me to. A loud bass riff boomed out of the speaker and she reached for the volume, pumping it up until the air was filled with Pink singing "Trouble." Throwing back her head with a merry laugh, she pressed the gas. Dust flew out from the back tires as she peeled away from the house.

I sat in the front seat with my mouth agape, and it wasn't until we reached the end of the drive that I found it in me to smile. As we pulled onto the main road, she started singing at the top of her lungs. A surprised laugh burst from my lips.

"Come on, honey, sing along with me. Here comes trouble!" she shouted with a laugh, shaking her head and letting the wind pick up the thick strands around her face.

As the song came to an end, I sat back with an awestruck smile. "You're like the coolest old person ever."

"Hey." She scowled at me. "Cool it on the old talk, kid. And don't be thinking about calling me Grandma, either. Let's stick with Rosie."

"You—you want me to call you Rosie?" My voice squeaked.

"I sure do, honey." She reached across and patted my knee before sliding her shades on. "And I think I'm going to call you Nessa. Does that sound okay?"

I'd never been called anything but Vanessa, and I

loved the idea of having a new identity for the summer, so I bobbed my head and grinned.

Rosie chuckled. "Good. Now, we have about a twelve-hour drive ahead, and I have fourteen years of news to catch up on, so why don't you start talkin'."

So I did. I talked using more words than I had ever spoken in my life. From my first memory of growing up in the shadow of my perfect twin brother to my passion for music that wasn't composed three hundred years ago. It was the first time anyone had actually been interested in listening. She probed me with questions that would start a whole new flood of information, and we chatted the entire trip. I learned all about her getting pregnant and falling into a marriage that she'd never really wanted. She told me how hard she'd tried to be the best mother she could be, but she felt so misunderstood along the way. Her strict husband never really got her, and so the day after his funeral, she'd finally left and started living the life she wanted. Her kids were grown by then.

"Martha was about to graduate college. She didn't need me anymore, and Scotty had been gone for years, so I high-tailed it to a town that had always fascinated me and became a tattoo artist."

My mouth dropped open yet again. "You're a tattoo artist?"

"I sure am. I own my own shop and everything."

"Wow."

"Your mother would flip a switch if she found out." Rosie laughed. "One day, I'll tell her, and I can't wait to see her expression when I do."

I was still too stunned to really say anything, so I just sat there gaping at her and shaking my head.

"There's nothing wrong with wearing art on your body, kid. It's a way of keeping precious things with you all the time, and telling the world who you really are." The magical glint in her eye won me over, and I decided then and there that by the end of the summer, I was getting me a tattoo.

By the time she pulled up outside her three-bedroom apartment in Chicago, I felt like I knew her better than all the people I'd grown up with. She was a kindred spirit and made me realize that my genes must have come from her.

It was two o'clock in the morning when we piled in the door. She took my bag and lugged it to the spare room, throwing it inside before snatching my hand and dragging me away.

"I know you're tired, but I just have to show you something first."

My insides bubbled with excitement. I'd never been allowed to stay up past eleven o'clock before. It was past two!

She pulled me down the short hallway and opened a door, revealing a music room stuffed full of instruments. There was a keyboard and an electric guitar sitting nearby. A drum kit sat in the back corner, two sticks resting on the snare.

"Wow," I whispered, stepping past her and running my fingers along the strings of the guitar before being drawn to the kit in the corner. I flicked the cymbal and grinned as it wobbled on the stand.

"Guitar and piano are my strong suit, really. I just keep the drums there in case I'm having a bad day and I need to beat the shit out of something." Rosie snorted

and began to quietly chuckle.

I spun to look at her then glanced back at the drums, my fingers tingling with a desire I didn't really understand.

Rosie stepped over to me, her arm gliding up my back. "It works, you know. Better out than in."

My forehead wrinkled, and I looked back at her with my silent question.

She gave me a smile—an old, knowing one that was filled with wisdom. Her arm rested on my shoulder and she pulled me close. "All the hurt you've got bottled up inside there. One of the best ways to get it out is to play." The passion in her voice was inspiring.

"Mama wouldn't let me play," I whispered.

Rosie shifted away so she could look down at me. Her hand was soft as she ran her knuckles down my cheek. "Well, your mama's not here, and I say you can play as loud and as badly as you want if it helps."

I giggled, moving out of her grasp and sitting down at the kit. I picked up the sticks and tested out the weight. Gripping them in my hands, I gave the snare a couple of sharp taps, my insides jolting with pleasure. I grinned and tested out the cymbals then smashed the sticks down on the toms. They sounded good, so I hit them again.

Rosie laughed.

I wrinkled my nose and blushed. "I'm not very good."

"Well, that's what practicing is for." She winked at me then stretched her arms wide. "C'mere, baby."

I hesitated for a second but then rose from my spot and walked toward her. We hadn't really hugged yet, and I didn't know what to expect. My parents' hugs were short and simple, but when Rosie's hands slid around my back and she pulled me close, I felt enveloped. She squeezed me tight and I rested my chin on her shoulder, my fingers digging into her back as I finally let myself be held. I'd never felt anything like it.

"I want you to know," Rosie murmured into my hair, "that I'll always have a hug at the ready. No matter what you're feeling or what you may have done, you can always run to me." She pulled away, holding my shoulders and smiling down at my tear-filled eyes. "We don't know each other that well yet, but I can already tell I'm going to fall madly in love with you...my precious granddaughter."

A tear slipped from the corner of my eye and trickled down my cheek. She chuckled and wiped it away with her thumb, a low hum coming out of her mouth. I didn't recognize the tune at first, but by the time she got to the chorus, she'd thrown in the words.

"Run" by Pink. (One of her favorite artists, I'd discovered along the way.)

She gazed into my face, singing me that song and promising me that I'd always have a home with her. No matter who I became or what I did, she'd be there with open arms to hold me tight.

If only I'd known what a liar she was.

I walked up the stairs and stopped in the doorway of my bedroom, staring at the picture-covered walls and the carefully hung fairy lights. When I'd lain in that hospital bed in Arkansas, I'd wanted to go home, to run into a safe haven that would keep me warm, but it wasn't working. I didn't have a safe place anymore. Rosie was gone, my hand was gone…and I had nothing left.

SEVENTEEN

JIMMY

"Okay, let's take a break, guys." Garrett's voice filled the sound booth, and we lowered our instruments with relieved sighs. We'd been playing hard core for an hour, laying down the track in slightly different ways, mixing it up and trying new things. Nessa had stayed damn quiet throughout the process, but I didn't want to push for her opinion. She usually wasn't shy about giving it. She was just in a weird place and didn't like drawing attention to herself. Once I stepped out of the sound booth, I'd take her to the side and ask her.

Sweat dripped from my forehead. I felt alive as I set my guitar in its stand and walked for the door.

I pulled out my phone as I went and noticed I'd missed a couple of calls from Troy. I had no idea what he wanted, but the guy would no doubt hound me until we'd spoken. My brother was persistent, if nothing else.

Following Flick through the door, I punched in my code and went to dial my brother back when I noticed a serious lack of female behind Garrett.

"Where's Ness?" I shoved the phone back in my pocket.

Garrett looked over his shoulder and shrugged. "I don't know, man. She split about forty minutes ago."

"And you didn't think to tell me?" I snapped.

"Sorry, dude. I didn't notice her go, and we were recording."

Fear coiled in my belly, a dark dread that I'd experienced once before and never wanted to live through again. "Where'd she go?"

"I don't know." He raised his eyebrows at me. "I told you, I didn't see her leave."

"What the fuck, Garrett." I pounded my fist into the edge of the sound desk.

"Hey!" He shot out of his chair and planted his finger in my chest. "You respect the desk."

"You think I give a shit about the desk." I stumbled back, knocking into Ralphie. He steadied me with his arm before I held out my hand to him. "Give me your keys, man."

"Where are you going?" Garrett yelled at me

while Ralphie placed his car keys into my palm.

"To find her." I gave him an incredulous look. Was the guy a complete dumbass?

"You are not leaving this studio." He pointed at me. "We are so behind schedule, and Marcus will kill me if we don't get this track laid down today."

"I'll be back," I muttered, swinging the door open.

"This isn't just about you and some girl, Jimmy. Torrence is a big company, and they won't be screwed with. Now you stay!"

I bristled at his command, but the thing that really had me seeing red was the way he referred to Nessa as some girl. Some girl?

Spinning on my heel, I gave him the blackest look I could muster. It wasn't hard; my insides were raging. "She's not just some girl. Now, I didn't chase after her last time, and I will not be making that mistake again," I thundered. "I'm going to find her."

"You keep pulling this shit and you will lose this contract." Garrett stormed toward me, and the room fell silent. I stood at the door scowling at him. He met my anger head-on, and I let it fuel the inferno within me.

"I just need to make sure she's safe, and then I'll come back." I glanced at Flick, who obviously had a big problem with my decision. His dark eyes were warning me to stay put.

"Maybe we can all look for her together after the session," Jace murmured.

What the hell did he know? Newbie.

My heart pounded in my chest as I looked over at Ralphie. He gave me a quick nod, and that was all I needed. I bolted out the door and heard Flick shout, "Fuck!"

Garrett followed it up with, "You better be back as fast you can, because I am not covering for you!"

I punched the down button for the elevator and leaped inside as soon as the doors opened. Garrett's words chased me, clamping onto my shoulders and making me worry. I hated that I was putting Chaos at risk by ditching on a recording session, but I had to find Nessa. It was all-consuming, and I wouldn't let up until I knew she was safe.

Why'd she run again?

I closed my eyes and thumped my head against the wall, hoping it wasn't because of that blonde cougar who flirted with me in the elevator. Damn it, why'd she have to be so obvious about it?

I had no idea where to start looking for Nessa. She must have had at least thirty minutes on me. At least she was on foot. I'd start by searching the nearby streets and hoping for the best. It was a shitty-ass plan, but it was all I had.

The phone in my pocket buzzed and started ringing. I yanked it free and answered before even checking the screen.

"Hey, Jimmy boy. It's your ol' man." His jovial voice made me cringe.

"Not now, Dad. I'm kinda busy."

Dad chuckled. "Chasing some chick, huh?"

"Something like that," I muttered and squeezed

the back of my neck.

"I just wanted to let you know that I'm going to be in LA soon. Thought we could hit a few clubs and hang out."

My first reaction was a spurt of excitement. It was a built-in thing. He'd been doing this to me for years—calling a few weeks out, planting a seed of excitement then turning up to suck me into a whirlwind of fun. We'd laugh, get drunk, have a blast…then he'd be gone. It always happened so fast I was left a dizzy wreck, piecing together memories and clinging to the fact my father had lavished his undivided attention on me.

For the first time ever, my mind jumped forward to the aftermath. I could feel myself sitting on the end of my bed, a cold loneliness creeping into my soul as I tried to wrap my head around mundane life again. I'd bury myself in music, playing the guitar until my fingers bled and hanging out with Chaos, but it'd still eat away at me. When I couldn't take it anymore, I'd hit the town. More often than not, I'd end up in bed with a girl or drunk off my ass, desperate to relive that high.

But Nessa had taught me how to fly and then she'd left…and I'd experienced the worst low of my life. Dad leaving me was peanuts compared to the despair of living without her.

I needed her. I needed to find her.

A heightened urgency drove me to cut the call short. "I'm kind of busy at the moment, but just, uh, call me when you're in town."

Denying his invitation would only create questions I didn't have time for.

"All right, son. Looking forward to it."

"Yep." I hung up without saying goodbye. The doors pinged open, and I hadn't even stepped out when my phone started buzzing again. I nearly ignored it, thinking it was Dad, but the phone was already in my hand and I spotted the screen.

Troy.

With a heavy sigh, I raised it to my ear. "Not now, man. Can I call you back?"

"It's about Ness."

I skidded to a stop. "Do you know where she is?"

"Yeah, at home...I think."

My mind stuttered, making it hard to see straight. "What do you mean, you think?"

Troy sighed, sending my erratic heart spiraling into my stomach.

"You better start fucking talking, man."

He let out another sigh that made my forearms flex as I gripped the phone to my ear.

"She was running down the street, away from those damn paparazzi and she—she nearly got hit by a car trying to get away from them."

My lips bunched and I closed my eyes, picturing her fear, feeling it in my very core. I ran a hand through my hair and mumbled a string of soft curses.

"She was a quivering mess, so I took her home. I offered to drop her at the guest house, but she didn't want me to, so I sat at the gate until she'd walked past the main house and I couldn't see her anymore."

"You didn't go in with her?" I pulled on the door and lurched back as a slew of photographers rushed me. I retreated into the safety of the building, ducking behind the security guard so I could finish the call.

"She didn't want me to," Troy repeated slowly. "I'm parked outside the house and I haven't seen her leave. I just thought you should know. When she said goodbye to me, she looked lost. I can't help worrying that she's a flight risk."

"Stay where you are and do not let her leave." I closed my eyes, whispering the last few words like a desperate plea.

"I'll stay until you get here."

I hung up, bracing myself for the onslaught that awaited me outside the door. I pictured Nessa trying to muscle her way through them.

Shit. She'd been so desperate to get away from them, she'd run into oncoming traffic. Those fucking leeches. My fists bunched, and I had to remind myself to breathe. The temptation to lash out and punch whoever chased her was damn overwhelming, but we couldn't afford the bad press.

Sniffing in as much calm as I could, I swung the door back and stormed outside. I kept my head down and powered through the swarm. Cameras flashed, the continual sound of digital clicks chasing me as I clipped to the car. I shut my ears off to any questions and revved the engine when a reporter came right up to my window. With a tight smile, I carefully reversed out of the lot, waiting until I pulled onto the road before gunning it for home.

"Please still be there, Ness. Please, baby. Please stay." I murmured the words over and over, gripping the wheel and weaving through traffic in the most important drive of my life.

Dad's call taunted the back of my mind, teasing me and trying to lure me with a devil's finger. It would be so much easier to pretend I didn't care, but I couldn't go back to that soul-destroying loneliness again. I was finally starting to understand that highs were always followed by lows, and I was getting damn sick of trying to pull myself out of them.

EIGHTEEN

NESSA

I turned my back on my room and shot down the stairs. My boots clunked on the tiles, sounding loud and out of place. Music was always playing around me. I hated silence, and I wasn't used to hearing my footsteps. Unnerved, I snatched the remote off the kitchen counter and pointed it at the sound system. "Going Under" by Evanescence started to play. The beat was good, strong, and thrummed through me.

I gazed into the living room, memories from the past year flashing before my mind's eye. Sitting around with the guys, drinking Coke and eating pizza between practices. Me sitting at the drum kit and whacking the skins with a smile on my face. Me sitting on Jimmy, gripping his bare shoulders as I sank onto his long, hard shaft. I blinked against the memory and sniffed sharply before gazing down at my stump.

It couldn't grip anything anymore—not Jimmy's shoulders, not my drumsticks. I pointed the remote at the controls and pumped the music louder until it was blasting through the house at a deafening volume. I dropped the remote and staggered against the counter like some drunk who couldn't handle her liquor.

My chin trembled, my lips shaking as I sucked in a ragged breath.

Digging my nails into the middle of my chest, I leaned over. "How do I get it out now?" I scraped my skin, leaving behind stinging red marks. "How do I let it go?"

Tears blurred my vision as I stumbled to my drum kit—the one thing that had gotten me through so much. The beloved instrument I'd hit the shit out of every time the world was too hard to handle.

It was positioned all wrong thanks to Jace, but I smashed the seat down and placed my foot on the bass pedal. Snatching the sticks off the snare, I held them both in my right hand and started bashing the skins. At first I tried to keep in time with the beat, but my confused body couldn't work out what I was doing. My left arm sat limp in my lap, twitching to play. I couldn't satisfy that need.

"Please," I begged. "Please, just let me play. I can get through this if you just let me play." I lifted my left stump, staring at the rounded end with the straight scar cutting through my skin. "Grow back," I whispered and sniffed. Tears were streaming down my face, blending with the snot leaking out of my nose. "Just...just grow back, please. Grow back." I shuddered, slamming the sticks against the tom drums and shouting, "Grow back!"

The beat rose and swelled around me, pulling at my insides, tugging on me until I let out a scream. I threw the sticks up and caught one with my right hand, plunging it into the snare with a feral growl. It punctured the skin and something snapped inside me...an angry, savage emotion that had been lying in wait.

"Run!" I yelled. "Where? You're not there anymore!" I shoved the crash cymbal and it flew back, knocking into Flick's guitar stand. They toppled over with a loud clang. I heaved in another breath then swung out with my left arm, taking out the ride cymbal. It hurt like crazy, which only enraged me more. I sent the floor tom flying with a swift kick before ramming my boot into the bass drum and upending the whole kit. It crashed and fell around me, the music unable to drown out the commotion.

Dropping to my knees, I punched my fist into the toms on the floor, hammering over and over like a piston on overdrive.

"You said you'd always be there to run to, but

you're not! I'm nobody without you!" I screamed at my dead grandmother. "And I can't play it out! I can't play!" My fist tore through the high tom, leaving a gaping wound. I pulled my hand free, and my chest began to heave with sobs, my face crumpling into an ugly grimace as I slumped to the floor.

I lay on my tousled mop of hair, digging my fingers into the carpet and sobbing like I'd never done before. I felt like the Coke bottle I'd dropped in the kitchen. My insides had shattered into a thousand tiny shards that scattered across the floor. The damage was too great, and there was no way to put me back together again.

I was lost. Homeless.

Rosie wasn't there to hold me, and I couldn't hide behind my music anymore.

I was exposed...an open target with nowhere to run.

NINETEEN

JIMMY

I screamed onto our street, taking the corner way too fast. Slamming on the brakes, I skidded to a stop outside the gate and spotted Troy across the road. I punched in the code while my brother started up his car then followed me up the drive.

I swerved around the house and jerked to a stop, noticing the guest house door was wide open. Shoving the car in park, I leaped out of that SUV, not even bothering to cut the engine. I heard Troy's quick footsteps rushing to Ralphie's car to deal with it as I shot across the lawn.

"Nessa!" I shouted, bolting into the entranceway

and freezing to a stop.

Music was blaring from the stereo, the volume so loud it hurt my ears, but I couldn't move at first. I couldn't take my eyes from Nessa curled in the middle of the floor, a chewed-up drum kit scattered around her.

Her chest was heaving, her eyes squeezed shut as she sobbed into the carpet.

The sight tore my heart out. Nessa wasn't a crier. She kept it locked up tight, hidden away behind her cute little smile. If things got bad, she played.

My jaw hurt as I clenched my teeth together and slowly crept into the room. I turned the music down until it was a mere whisper in the background, but she didn't even flinch. She was too caught up in her own misery, still sobbing and hiccupping. Her hair was a tangled mess beneath her, wet with a combo of tears and saliva.

"You're not here," she whimpered. "Why'd you leave me?"

I could only just make out her murmuring until I got near enough to really hear it. I didn't know who she was talking to or how I was supposed to make it better. Uncertainty flickered through me as I knelt beside her and gently rubbed my hand down her back.

"Ness, it's Jimmy."

She sniffed. "I want Rosie." Sobs cut her grandmother's name short.

It broke my heart. I knew how close they'd been. I remembered when Rosie died and the shell-shocked way Nessa conducted herself. She went quiet for weeks, a husk of the sparkling girl she was. The only time we really saw her come alive was when she played. And oh man, did she play. It'd saved her, brought her back to us. It got her through graduation and then the summer. She'd played through it all, and she'd never once cried.

"I'm here," I whispered, leaning over her and gently kissing her tear-streaked skin.

"She said I could run to her," Nessa murmured. Her eyes remained closed, her expression crushed by despair.

I ran my fingers down her hair, tucking it behind her ear before letting out a quivering breath and saying, "You can run to me. You can always run to me."

Footsteps sounded in the entranceway, and I glanced over my shoulder. Troy stood at the door, taking in the damage and the broken girl at my feet. His face crumpled with compassion before he gave me a look that asked if I wanted him to stay.

I shook my head.

Stepping back, he gently closed the door behind him, but I knew he'd call me later. He always checked in to make sure I had everything I needed. He was my first line of defense, the one I'd call when things turned to shit. He'd carried me through so much, and I'd never even thought about it.

I gazed down at Nessa, knowing what I needed to be for her, but scared shitless I couldn't do it. I wasn't the come-to-the-rescue type. I didn't wear shiny armor, and I sure as shit didn't know how to clean up after myself, let alone look after another human being. But in that moment, watching her so fragile on the floor, my protective instincts came alive.

I wanted to encase her in a titanium shell so no pain could touch her. I wanted to make it all go away.

Scooping her into my arms, I lifted her small body against my chest and clambered over the broken drum kit. I held her against me as I smoothly walked up the stairs. She rested her head on my shoulder, her right hand snaking up and clinging to my neck. Her quiet sniffing continued to punch at my guts, but holding her was easing my torment.

Her bedroom door was open. My breath caught as I eased toward it. The boys had never been allowed in, and we'd always respected that. I'd rushed in and out once, but I hadn't even bothered to turn on the lights. I'd already known as I scanned her disarray that she was gone.

Using my elbow, I flicked the switch, my lips parting as the magic of her fairy lights took me in.

I walked toward her unmade bed, loving that she didn't care about that shit. Clothes were strewn over the floor, her boots a mixed chaos in the bottom of her open closet. My eyes scanned the walls and cluttered shelves, taking in the pictures and trinkets. There was a large photo of me and her on the wall with love hearts and arrows that she'd scribbled around it.

My chest restricted as I laid her down. Her dark hair splayed across the pillow, and I brushed it back from her face. She turned to her side and tucked her stump beneath her chin.

"You okay?" I whispered then stroked my lips across her forehead.

She reached forward and snatched my wrist, squeezing it as she finally opened her eyes and stared at me. Her brown gaze was glistening, warning me there were still more tears to come. She opened her mouth to say something, but nothing came out. Instead, her expression crumpled and she closed her eyes again, fresh tears breaking free.

Her quivering fingers held tight to my wrist, like if I let go she'd disappear into a black chasm.

To hell with heading back to the studio. I wasn't going anywhere.

Climbing over her body, I nestled down on the bed behind her then pulled her against me. She wrapped her arms around mine, holding it like a teddy bear while she trembled. I tucked my knees in the crook of hers, skimming my lips across the back of her head and starting to hum the chorus to "Run" by Pink. I have no idea what possessed me to whisper-sing that song to her, but as I did, her body started to relax. The tears faded away, her quiet sniffles going silent, and eventually her chest began to rise and fall in the even pattern of sleep.

I held her close, gazing up at the fairy lights and wondering if I could really do this. Seeing her fall apart freaked me out. Nessa had always been so solid and in control. She was the one who could make *me* smile on the days I was down. She put up with *my* shit. I'd never had to be anything more than my asshole-self. Hanging out with her had always been so easy, but now it was freaking hard. She needed an anchor, and I was offering to be that for her. Me—the most unstable guy on the planet.

Dad's call still beckoned me, reminding me of the good times and how they were worth the crashing lows. Temptation nibbled at me. The urge to run for my life and slip back into the comfort of my old ways was damn compelling. But then I turned my head and my nose brushed against Nessa's dark hair. Her citrus scent wafted up my nostrils, filling me with a sense of unfamiliar comfort.

The only thing I'd ever stuck at was Chaos. Nessa was Chaos, too, but *us* was something different. She needed a man who could love and protect her with an unwavering passion.

A familiar fear, fueled by self-doubt, coiled inside me as Nessa's grip loosened on my arm and I had the chance to quietly slip away.

TWENTY

NESSA

I woke up alone.

I guess I should have known. Falling asleep with Jimmy was never a good idea.

My eyes hurt from crying, my left arm ached, and my throat felt swollen and sore. I had to get up. I didn't want to, but my bladder wouldn't let me lie there a minute longer.

I wasn't wearing boots anymore. Jimmy must have taken them off before he left me...alone...again. Trudging down the stairs, I took a left into the bathroom and quickly relieved myself, not even bothering to re-zip my fly when I was done. I just wanted to head back to bed anyway. I washed my hand then flicked the light off, nearly jumping out of my skin when a flash of movement caught my eye.

I spun around with a gasp and spotted Flick standing by the keyboard, his beanie perched on the back of his head and a pencil clenched between his teeth. He spotted me and pulled the pencil from his mouth, giving me a broad grin.

"Hey, destructo-girl." He waggled his eyebrows. Glancing over his shoulder, he indicated the kit behind him. "That must have felt so frickin' good."

I gazed past him at the destroyed kit and let out a breathy laugh. I winced and ran my fingers through my hair, grabbing a fistful at the base of my neck. How could he stand there *not* judging me? I'd done hundreds of dollars' worth of damage. I'd gone psycho.

"Don't sweat it." Flick brushed the air with his fingers. "It's the perfect excuse to buy a new one."

I scoffed and squeezed my left elbow. "Why bother?"

Flick drilled me with a hard look. "Because you're going to need something to practice on."

His eyes grazed over my stump before landing back on the music in front of him.

"Cut the bullshit, Flick," I muttered. "You've got a great drummer now."

He grunted and gave me a warning look not to go there. I shook my head and stepped into the kitchen, my jeans slipping down my hips.

"You don't believe in zipping your fly

anymore?" he asked with a smirk.

I snatched my jeans and yanked them back up, throwing him a hot glare. "I couldn't be bothered."

He snickered. "It's the little things that are the biggest bitches, huh?"

I softly cursed and looked to the ceiling, wrestling to zip up the fly. I inched it up bit by bit, begging the teeth to catch quickly. I should have just converted to sweat pants, but I was used to living in my ripped-up jeans. I finally won over the fly but didn't bother with the button, instead rolling the waistband over to hold the jeans in place. It showed off my musical dandelion tattoo that blew across my right hip, and although it made me a little sad, I also liked that it was on display. Rosie designed it for me. She designed tats for every member of Chaos, and we wore them with pride.

I glanced at Flick, gazing at the quarter notes that danced over the sides of his neck. They stemmed all the way down his back, covering both his shoulders, and were a symphony of music right down to his hipbones, divided by a curving set of piano keys that were etched up his spine. It was a freaking work of art and took months for Rosie to complete.

He had a few other little ones scattered throughout—a four-leaf clover above his thumb, a Chinese character on his wrist. Ralphie swears Flick has a little love heart on his ass, too, but I can't quite bring myself to believe it…and I sure as hell am not about to check for myself. All I could pray was that Rosie hadn't put it there, although she probably would have taken great delight in doing so. She'd always thought Flick was the cutest one among us.

"Come over here." Flick tipped his head. I usually hated it when people ordered me around like that, but I was feeling lost hovering on the edge of the kitchen. I shuffled over to the keyboard.

I ran my finger along the beveled edge. "What are you doing?"

"Jimmy asked me to come and hang out here while he smoothed things over with Marcus, so I thought maybe we could write a song together."

"Wait. What?" I jerked back. "Smooth things over? What happened?"

"Well." Flick braced his arms against the keyboard and blew out a breath. "You left and no one knew where you went, so Jimmy freaked out and took off to find you."

A pleasant tingling I didn't want to recognize sizzled in my belly. He freaked out? He took off to find me? My insides bubbled with warmth.

Scowling, I rubbed my stomach. "What does that have to do with Marcus?"

"Um." Flick licked his lower lip. "Well, you know things kind of had to be put on hold for a little while, and Torrence is starting to get pissed that we're not getting through things on their timetable. So, we're kind of under the gun, and Jimmy can't keep skipping out." Flick nodded then glanced down to the keys, saying nothing and everything all at the same time.

A sharp breath punched out of me, guilt coiling around my spine as I tried to mentally justify why I'd abandoned them. Shit, if they lost the deal because of me, no excuse in the world would be good enough.

"You're not going to lose the contract, are you?"

"No." Flick shook his head then cringed and shrugged. "But we're running out of chances."

I huffed, anger masking my guilt. "Jimmy shouldn't have done that. We've all worked too hard and long to lose it now."

"I agree, so next time, just leave a note or tell someone before you sneak out the door." His emphatic, raised eyebrows made me shrink in on myself.

"Maybe I shouldn't come to any more sessions," I mumbled.

"Hey, hey, hey." Flick waved his hand in the air. "Now, don't go getting all drama queen and sulky about it. I'm not saying that. We want you there. We just want to know when you leave, as well."

I rolled my eyes and chewed the inside of my cheek, feeling slightly reprimanded. Part of me wanted to stomp to my room in a huff, but I'd rather eat my own arm than have Flick call me a drama queen again. As if I'd ever be that girly.

To prove my point, I gave his arm a thump and grunted. "What are you working on?"

"A new song. I figured since you're struggling to play right now, maybe you should write instead."

He tucked the pencil behind his ear and played

a few quick chords, his fingers tinkling over the keys. I listened to the notes, liking the sound and rhythm. It had a nice feel, a soft ballad-type piece that could turn into something more rock 'n' roll. It could start out soft with the keys and bass then build nicely over the first verse. There was a depth to the music that lent itself to something from the heart.

"What have you got for the chorus?" I leaned over the keys to check out his scribbled chords on the page.

"No words yet, but I was thinking some kind of tune like..." He played it for me—chords on the bass line while his right hand owned the melody. I nodded as I listened, creating a soft beat with my tongue and lips.

"Yeah, yeah." Flick looked at me, his eyes bright. "I was thinking we could drop out the melody in the bridge and let drums and bass carry us through. It'd be a really good effect before we came crashing back in for the final chorus."

"I like that." My lips were fighting a smile. It wanted to set itself free, but the thought that I wouldn't be the one carrying the song with my beat stopped it from forming.

Flick distracted me by pulling out his pencil and scribbling on his sheet of paper. He popped the pencil in his mouth and played the intro again. My head started bobbing, the melody rising within me.

"Shadows falling. I'm surrounded. Darkness taking over me," I sang. "Shadows rising. I am lost now. No light will help me see." The lines came to me without thought, and I closed my eyes and got carried away. "There's no more road, there's no one waiting. No more arms to set me free. I want to run, I want to scream, I want to let myself break free, but I'm trapped in a dark and sinking dungeon. I want to rise, I want to breathe, don't let this vortex swallow me. Help me out, from this dark and sinking dungeon. Hold me. Hold me."

The music petered off and I opened my eyes. Flick was staring at me. A sad smile slowly formed on his lips.

I sniffed and hid my burning cheeks by looking at the floor. "You know what they say, better out than in, right?"

Flick snickered. "You remember anything you just sang?"

"A little." I wrinkled my nose.

"Good." Flick nodded. "It was kinda dark and depressing, but there's some potential there."

I scoffed and tucked a lock of hair behind my ear. "Those whiny lyrics? I hardly think so. You better not write any of them down."

"Why not? It'd make a great song?"

Fear sparked inside me. "Flick, I mean it. You have to swear."

"I don't want to. I think you should share that part of yourself with the world."

"I'm not sharing that shit," I practically yelled. "I don't want people seeing me that way. I don't want…" I let out a short sigh and pressed my lips together before I said too much. Like Jimmy, Flick saw me as this quiet, tenacious fighter—a girl with spunk. I didn't want him seeing under my Nessa coat and figuring out the truth.

Flick sucked in a breath then paused and leaned toward me. "The world can't stay dark forever, Nessa. The sun always rises in the morning. We could make this a really inspiring song. Fans would love it. You're not the only person who feels like they're sinking."

The sentiment was touching, especially from a guy who prided himself on being dark and mysterious, but if we pursued this song, I wouldn't be attaching my name to it.

Flick brushed his hand down my arm. "You probably don't want to hear this right now, but you *will* find your way."

"How do you know?"

He ran his thumb over his lower lip. "Because you asked someone to hold you, which tells me that buried underneath all that rubble in there," he pointed at my chest, "is someone who wants help. That, to me, is hopeful."

His wise old gaze and gently spoken words made my skin prickle. I wrapped my arms across my waist and stepped back from him. "Shit, Flick, I think some old guy is possessing you right now." I snickered. "Can you please just swear a couple of times and make some crass joke, you're freaking me out."

He whooped with laughter and threw his head back. "Unnerved by the feels. Got you good, Nessy girl."

"Shut up," I muttered, relieved by his loud

outburst.

Placing his pencil onto the stand, he gave me a cheeky grin and waggled his eyebrows. "So, what do you want to do then—get rip-roaring drunk and beat the shit out of something? I think Ralphie still has those padded sumo suits if you want to go a few rounds. I'd be happy to kick your scrawny little butt to the curb."

I giggled. "You're such an ass."

He wrapped his arm around my neck, pulling me into his chest and giving me a noogie. "I love you, too, Nessy."

I slapped at his arms and laughed, enjoying the fleeting moment of normalcy. For a second, I could pretend that everything was right in the world and I wouldn't wake up to a new day feeling untethered.

TWENTY-ONE

JIMMY

Marcus was pretty good about me bailing on the session, especially after I told him what I saw when I ran into the guest house. He understood my reason for having to find Nessa and even bought me a coffee so we could sit down and really chat. I wasn't much of a coffee drinker, but I sipped it down and let him lecture me for a good half hour. I figured holding back my rebuttal would get it over and done with faster.

Look at me, getting all mature and shit.

In the end, he sighed, slumped back in the black metal chair and looked out across the street. We were sitting at an outside table at a little cafe I'd never heard of—Quirky Corner Cafe. Marcus was obviously a regular, though, because they greeted him by name and he actually said, "My usual," and they knew what he was talking about.

His finger tapped on the metal table, making it wobble on its uneven legs. "I get it, man. You're falling in love and it does things to a guy."

I chortled, heat rushing up my cheeks. "I don't—I'm not used to this feeling. I've never..." I blew out a breath. "It's intense and—and terrifying."

"Yeah." Marcus grinned, his hazel gaze going distant. "I remember this one girl in high school who captured me. There was something about her that turned my brain to mush." He chuckled. "I would have walked across a bed of nails to make her smile."

I laughed at the rapturous look on his face. "Did you ever hook up?"

"No way." His eyes rounded. "She was completely unimpressed by all my attempts. I was this dorky senior and she was an eleventh-grade goddess who bewitched the entire student body." He shook his head and snatched his coffee cup, a wry smile creeping over his lips. "She was a troublemaker, but I was gone for that girl." His expression turned dreamy and then he took a sip of coffee, which seemed to snap him out of his reverie.

I sighed. "I never saw Ness. Never saw how amazing she was...until she wasn't there anymore and there was this gaping hole in my life."

"Distance makes the heart grow fonder." Marcus shrugged.

I scoffed. "Disappearance rips the heart from your chest." I pursed my lips then started chewing on my fingernail.

Marcus stared at me, his silent scrutiny unnerving.

I shuffled in my seat, and I have no clue what came over me, but I started talking. "Thing is, I want to be the guy she deserves, but I don't know if I can. I wasn't exactly raised in a home where you commit, you know. My dad started cheating before I was even born. I can't help wondering if Mom knew the whole time, but she was scared of being left alone. When they finally did split, Mom disappeared into work. She just worked, that's all she did. She started up a housecleaning company, and it became the most important thing in her life." I shook my head, not even hearing my bitter tone. "She never cleaned at home, of course. She was never fucking there. But Dad, you know, he would come home for weekends and holidays. He'd take us out and we'd have fun together. He'd take us to Millennium Park and Navy Pier, or Lincoln Park Zoo. We'd spend shitloads of money on candy and rides...and just have fun the whole time. I thought he was the coolest, most generous human being on the planet."

"When did you figure out he wasn't?" Marcus's coffee cup clinked as he placed it back down on the saucer.

My snicker was contrite and disintegrated quickly. "Maybe I'm just figuring it out now," I croaked. "You know, when we got accepted into *Shock Wave*, my dad was so proud. He told me that being a rock star is the ultimate life. I'd be able to party as much as I wanted and I'd get all the girls. I remember thinking, *yeah, I'm going to be just like my dad*. He's the happiest man I know, so what's better than that?"

Marcus's quiet gaze was kind of unnerving. I shuffled in my seat, wishing I hadn't opened this shitty-ass can of worms. "Why do you think you wanted to be like your dad?"

I groaned and looked up to the sky. "Now you sound like my brother."

"I take it he doesn't see your father the way you do."

I barked out a harsh laugh. "Troy hasn't spoken to Dad in years, and Dad doesn't even try anymore. I think he prefers hanging out with me because I don't make him feel guilty for his lifestyle." My eyes grew distant. "It probably eats him alive some days, which is why he works so hard and parties every second he can." I nibbled the edge of my lip. "I used to think I was the lucky one because I got all his attention, but I have this sinking feeling that I won't get it anymore if I commit to Ness. He's going to see that as weakness. If I don't go out and party with him, he's not going to make time for me anymore."

I swallowed, running my finger around the lip of my saucer.

Marcus didn't say anything, just sat there and twirled his empty coffee mug. I stared at a drop of coffee that trailed down the side of his cup—a lone brown tear. For some weird reason, I felt like crying.

"I want Ness more than I need his approval," my voice quivered, "but how am I supposed to be what she needs when no one has ever shown me how?"

A group of people strolled by our table. One of the girls was a tall, willowy thing wearing skinny jeans that hugged her tight, smackable ass. She glanced at me and smiled. Her eyes started to glint like she knew my face. I pushed the shades higher up my nose before tugging down my beanie. I didn't want to be Jimmy Baker of Chaos that afternoon. I just wanted to be a guy shooting the breeze with his boss, trying to figure out how to take care of his girl. Marcus ignored the group, who moved to the crossing. They whispered and pointed at me. Thankfully, the light turned green and they walked across the street, still looking over their shoulders and giggling as they went.

"I can't tell you much, man." Marcus caught my attention as he scratched his stubble. "I've only had one relationship in college that I thought would get serious, but it didn't pan out. However, I was lucky enough to be raised by two people who adore each other...even after thirty-five years of marriage. From what I can tell, it's just about being there. My dad always says that it's really not that complicated. You hold her when she cries, you listen to her when she's ranting, and at the end of every day, you kiss her and tell her you love her...no matter what's gone down." A smile lit Marcus's face. "And at the start of each day, you make it your goal to get at least one thousand-watt smile out of her, even if you have to be a total idiot to do it." He chuckled. "Dad's really good at that."

The look on Marcus's face made me wish for his childhood. Growing up in a house full of laughter and smiles didn't sound all bad to me. I couldn't picture it, though. How the hell was I supposed to make Nessa smile? After what I'd seen in the guest house, I wasn't sure she'd ever smile again.

My heart cracked a little more, and I was once again back to feeling as useful as a blunt knife.

Marcus noted my dark expression and leaned toward me, resting his forearms on the table. "You can't solve this or take it away from her. No matter what, she will never get her hand back, and that's got to hurt. She's having to adapt to so much, and all you can do is stand by her." Marcus blew out a soft breath. "I've never met your old man, and I've only been working with you for a little while, but I can tell you're not a quitter. You are passionate about Chaos. That's why they look to you as their leader. And after today, I can see that you're passionate about Nessa, too. I don't think you need to be afraid that you can't do this."

His words worked like a magic antidote. It helped that he looked completely genuine when he said them. My chest expanded, and I sat forward with a small grin.

Marcus returned it. "Do me a really big favor, though, and don't split on a recording session again, okay?"

I gave him a sardonic smile. "Tell me how to keep her put and I won't."

Pursing his lips, Marcus gazed out across the street and murmured, "We just need to find a place for her."

My stomach twisted into a tight knot as I took in his worried frown. I knew how he felt. Chaos was sounding freaking good without her. Jace was the perfect replacement, so what would we do with Nessa?

TWENTY-TWO

NESSA

I couldn't stop watching people's hands. As Jimmy and the band set up for practice in the living area of the guest house, I sat on the black leather couch and watched Ralphie's fingers turn the tuning heads of his bass guitar before flicking the strings. A low, reverberating bop-bop-bop came out of his amp. He reached to adjust the setting on the speaker, and I watched his long fingers turn the knobs before my gaze traveled over to Jimmy. His fingers were curved around the neck of his guitar, making a G-chord. He strummed with his pick, and an electronic twang filled the room as he checked his tuning. Jace thumped the middle toms, and my eyes shot to his fingers wrapped around the drumsticks. He'd set the new kit up the day before—quietly walked in and puttered about while I pretended to read a magazine on the couch. I cringed and winced as he pieced it all together, setting it up to fit his large frame. The bass pedal thumped, and then he did a quick roll on the snare, a half-smile creeping over his lips before blooming full as he tested each drum with a quick solo.

My insides were charcoal by the time he was done. I could feel chunks of it breaking away and landing in my stomach acid—sizzling and burning until I felt sick.

Jimmy spun around to face Flick. "Should we start with the song you and Nessa wrote while we were filming *Shock Wave*? Jace doesn't really know it yet."

"Good idea." Flick nodded then beckoned me over with a wave of his hand.

"What?" I ran my finger inside the edge of my knee hole and frowned.

"Come sing it with me."

"I don't need to sing it. You sing it."

Flick rolled his eyes. "You wrote it, you douche. Now get up here and sing it with me."

I pressed my lips together, looking away from his pointed stare. He growled in his throat, and I threw my head back and slapped the couch. "Fine! But I'm not taking lead." I stormed over to the keyboard. "I'll just do the harmony."

Flick grunted, but I gave him my *you're not*

budging me look, and he gave in pretty quickly after that. His fingers danced over the keys before he nodded at Jimmy and Ralphie. They came in on cue while Jace sat there listening. He closed his eyes, his head bobbing as he absorbed the tune. I watched his finger tap on his knee as he found the rhythm easily.

Flick's voice came out loud and clear, singing the words we'd spent hours debating over and perfecting. The song was good, and I remembered actually squealing like a freaking prom queen when we were allowed to perform it on *Shock Wave*. Marcus had promised us we'd get it onto our debut album, and I'd been giddy. A song I had written was going to be on a professional album! It was un-freaking-real.

I swallowed, struggling to find my joy, and nearly missed my cue. Flick gave me a sharp look, and I jumped in only two beats late, picking up the well-rehearsed harmony. We sounded good together, although my usual gusto was missing. I wasn't used to singing without a drum kit around me and two sticks in my hands. I didn't know what to do with my body so instead just crossed my arms and mumbled out the words.

Flick cut the song short, obviously annoyed by my serious lack of enthusiasm. He glanced over his shoulder at Jace. "You get the idea?"

"Yeah." Jace grinned. "So, the keys start the song, and then do you want a slow rumble around the third or fourth bar to lead into the chorus?"

"Something like that." Flick nodded. He turned

back, his eyes sparkling before he winked at me. It wasn't hard to see how much he liked the new drummer. The guy was fitting into the group with an ease that made me taste bile.

Jimmy's eyes were on me, so I stepped back from the keys and retreated to my spot on the couch. I didn't want to look at him. Since my total meltdown moment, he'd been super sensitive around me. It was kind of sweet, but I was still too scared to fall for it. The way he'd felt as he held me close and sang "Run" turned my heart into a soft, pliable mess. If I didn't watch myself, I'd be putty in his hands again, and there was no way I'd let myself be that vulnerable around him. He could undo me, take whatever he wanted from me and then hang me out to dry. I couldn't let that happen. I wouldn't survive it.

The song began, and I plonked my butt onto the couch. The music swelled around us, the energy from the beat and melody bringing a smile to everyone's face. Even I felt it, and my lips twitched before I could stop them. A full smile was nearly in bloom, but it faltered. Jace did something wrong. I wouldn't play it that way.

I shot off the couch with a scowl and the music twanged to a stop. Jimmy was staring at me with wide eyes. "What's the matter?"

"It's—it's…" I pointed at the drummer. "You're playing it wrong." I walked toward him. "It's not supposed to be syncopated in that part, and you're bringing the roll in too early after that. It gives the song a totally different feel."

"Okay." Jace nodded, his big lips curved into an accepting smile. "So, how do you want to do it?"

"I'll show you." Without thinking, I reached for the sticks. He hesitated before placing them in my right hand. I went to grab the second stick with my left but stopped. My cheeks flamed red and I stood there like a total idiot, fighting the urge to cry. With a short huff, I threw the sticks back at Jace. He caught one, and the other pinged off his chest then clattered to the floor.

An awkward silence landed in the room, like a heavy, suffocating gas.

Jace calmly collected the stick and smiled at me again. "Do you mean, more like this?"

He played it again. It was closer to what I had meant but not exactly the same. I shrugged.

"Or I could go like this." He played again, almost nailing it. I could hear the song in my brain, having spent so long composing it with Flick, but I couldn't figure out how to relay what I was hearing inside my head. It was hella frustrating.

I licked my lower lip. I had to say something or I'd look like a total, clueless meatball to everyone. In the end, I cleared my throat and lamely choked out, "Make sure the emphasis is on the first beat, not the second, and fix that roll into the chorus."

"Will do." Jace's voice sounded light and chipper, although I could see a silent resistance in his dark eyes. He was being nice to me because of my condition, and that only pissed me off.

At the time, I didn't think about how annoying it must have been for him to have some chick telling him how to do a job he was more than capable of doing.

Jace twirled the stick in his right hand and hit the drums again, killing the beat just right then adding in a little flair of his own before rolling into the chorus. It sounded freaking good, but Jimmy huffed and shouted, "Did you hear anything she just said? Do it right, man!"

He was only standing up for me, which was kind of sweet, but as I glanced at Flick's face, I knew I was in the wrong. Jace sighed, glanced at me, then prepared to do it my way.

"Leave it," I mumbled before he could hit the skins. "Your way sounds better."

A small smile tipped his lips, and Flick gave me a nod of approval. Jimmy's face crested with a glum smile, but I turned my back on it.

"I'm just gonna go." I stepped off the carpeted area and onto the cool tiles. They felt nice on my bare feet.

"Wait," Jimmy called. "You can't. You wrote this song."

"Yeah, Nester, you have to be a part of it." Ralphie rested his forearm on the body of his bass guitar and gave me that goofy smile of his.

For the first time ever, it brought me no comfort. If anything, it made me snap.

"How?" I held up my stump. "You don't get it! I can't be a part of this song anymore. I can't play. And none of you understand how much this is killing me because you all have two fucking hands!" My voice rose to a screaming pitch, making the silence that followed stifling. I huffed out a breath. "You have Jace now, and he's freaking good. You don't need me anymore."

"We *do* need you," Flick argued. "You are part of this band."

"Not anymore." I shook my head. "I'm not good enough. I'll never be good enough." Words that had been haunting me my entire life came out of nowhere—an unguarded confession that I'd never meant to say. I slapped my hand over my mouth and stumbled for the stairwell.

"Ness," Jimmy called after me, but I ignored him, taking the stairs two at a time and locking myself in my room. Pushing my back against the door, I slid down to the floor and wrapped my arms around my knees.

I felt like I'd just flashed the room, like I'd spread my coat and let them see inside. I wanted to take it back so bad, but I couldn't.

The truth was out now. I'd been putting on a show this whole time.

The only thing I'd ever done well was play the drums. I'd hidden behind that ever since I moved to Chicago, but I didn't have that anymore. And now, everybody would be able to see that my mother had been right all along.

I wasn't good enough...and I'd never amount to anything.

TWENTY-THREE

JIMMY

Nessa's door slammed shut and Jace flinched. He gripped the sticks, tapping them on his knee and shaking his head.

"I'm sorry, you guys," he finally murmured.

"It's not your fault." I brushed the air with my hand. "She's dealing at the moment. It's...it's tough."

"Yeah, I get it." His eyes, in spite of their dark color, had a warm understanding that put me at ease. His silent forgiveness of Nessa's outburst didn't quell my raging insides, though. My heart was thundering so loud I could feel the vibrations in my ears. The look in her eyes before she slapped her hand over her mouth and ran...holy shit!

Not good enough?

Was she fucking kidding?

She was everything. She'd won me over. And I *never* thought I'd fall for anyone. She was the heart and soul of this band. We all adored her.

I wanted to help her so bad, but I didn't know what to say to fix it. Maybe if she learned to play again things would get better. Unfortunately, she was resisting any forms of moving forward, and I didn't want to push her away.

"What was all that shit about her not being good enough?" Flick scratched his beanie. "Where the hell did that come from?"

"I have no idea," I croaked and ran a shaky hand through my hair.

"I think I do," Ralphie mumbled.

We all spun to face him.

My eyes narrowed to thin slits. "What are you talking about, man?"

Ralphie swallowed and slowly lifted the guitar strap over his head. He placed his bass in the stand with a heavy sigh then crossed his arms over his chest. A muscle in his jaw worked as he took his sweet time. I was about to tell him to hurry the fuck up when he blurted, "Remember when she moved in with my family senior year?"

"Yeah. After Rosie died. Your parents were Nessa's guardians, weren't they?"

Ralphie winced. "Not exactly. She was eighteen when it happened, so she didn't actually need guardians anymore. We just told you guys that, because…"

I frowned at him. I could feel an impending secret about to be exposed, and I wasn't sure I was ready for it. My shoulders tensed and a low growl rumbled in my throat. What the hell had they been hiding from me?

"She made me swear not to tell." Ralphie's face bunched with uncertainty before he licked his lips and blurted, "But she actually has parents and four siblings."

"What?" Flick whispered. "I thought her parents were dead. That's why she was living with Rosie in the first place."

"Dude, I sometimes wish her parents were dead."

Coming from Ralphie, that was huge. In spite of his fascination with blood-and-guts action movies, the guy was pro-human all the way. He blew out a sigh and slumped onto the stool behind him. He perched his feet on the metal stand and leaned his elbows on his knees.

"I wasn't supposed to know either, but the day before Rosie died, I found Nessa bawling her eyes out in the music suite. I finally managed to figure out what was wrong with her, and when she told me Rosie was in the hospital after a heart attack, I took her straight up there to visit. She kept going on about how she shouldn't skip school. She was fidgety and pale. I just assumed it was worry for Rosie, so I told her this was way more important than school."

I crossed my arms and glared at him, hating that I was hearing about this for the first time...nearly two years after the fact.

"When we got there, this *woman* was in the room with Rosie. She was mean-looking and... you know, a total bitch. She saw me and dressed me down like I was pond scum, and then she started going off at Ness." Ralphie made a disgusted face then put on a voice, "Vanessa, I told you to go to school. Playing hooky is unacceptable. Who is this boy?" Ralphie looked ready to murder something as he spat out the words. "She had this irritating, scathing voice that made you feel like a useless loser." He pointed to the tattoo on his arm. "She spotted this and nearly had a conniption, going on about marking the skin and saying Ness better not have one of those. She started talking about this kid called Victor and how perfect he was and how he'd never do anything so foolish." Ralphie shook his head, a wave of sadness washing over him. "The whole time she was going off, Ness just seemed to shrink in on herself until she was nothing but a bug standing across the bed and looking lost."

"Who the fuck was this woman?" I growled.

Ralphie gave me an intense stare, and I knew the answer before he said it. "Her mother."

"Okay, so the woman's a bitch. Is that why Nessa was living with Rosie?" Flick asked.

"Yeah." Ralphie nodded. "I mean, I think so. At one point, she started yammering at Rosie, saying she never should have agreed to her stupid plan, and the one summer never should have turned into all of high school. Rosie argued back that it had worked in everyone's favor, and the woman finally conceded, saying life had been easier without the nuisance of a rebel child." Ralphie's snigger was dark and fleeting. "But now, her daughter was 'hanging out with hooligans and getting up to who knows what', which of course was completely unacceptable." He blinked, a muscle in his jaw working. "When she said Rosie was going to die and she'd have to take Vanessa back and fix all the damage that had been done, I thought Ness was going to pass out. She looked so scared." Ralphie ended in a broken whisper. "I wanted to rip that woman's throat out, so I snapped and told her to go find the anal ward so they could remove the stick from her ass."

Jace softly chuckled then pressed his lips together with a mumbled apology. "It was a good line, though."

Ralphie flashed a brief grin. "I thought so, but it didn't go down too well. She stormed off to find security, and I was dragged out of there a few minutes later. I didn't see Ness again until—"

"How could you never tell us this?" I snapped. I was pissed. She and Ralphie had kept it under wraps for so long. It felt like some kind of betrayal.

"I wasn't even out of the hospital parking lot when she called. She begged me not to say anything."

"Why would she do that?" I retorted.

"I don't know! Shame, maybe? If my mother was like that, I wouldn't be telling the world! Come on, man, give her a break. She was petrified, and I don't think she could face the idea of saying goodbye." His eyes bored into mine, sending me a silent message that said the idea of leaving me nearly broke her.

I pictured Nessa, petite enough as it is, standing in that hospital room while her beloved grandmother slipped away and her bitch of a mother threatened to pull her out of a world she'd thrived in. I felt like someone had punched me in the chest. Gripping the neck of my guitar, I sucked in a few quick breaths, trying to rein in my fury before I busted something.

"Dude, I wonder what her life was like before Chicago," Flick mumbled.

"Sounds like Rosie saved her." Jace twirled the drumstick with his fingers. "She must have been an amazing woman."

"She was." Ralphie nodded, his lips curving into a broad smile. I flashed a grin, too. Rosie had been the bomb. I remembered spending hours in her tattoo parlor, drinking Cokes and singing while she inked us all. It was the summer before our senior year, and we'd had a total blast.

Ralphie's voice drew my attention away from the memory. "I'll never forget when Bitch Face left to go find security. Rosie grabbed Nessa's hand and said as loudly as she could manage, 'You listen me to me, kid. I don't care what that woman says. You, sweet girl, are fucking perfect, and don't let anyone tell you different.'" Ralphie's eyes glassed with tears and he sniffed. "I thought she'd believed her, but maybe she didn't."

His quiet words were followed by an eerie silence. I didn't know how to fill it; my throat was thick with emotion. A cocktail of anger and grief held my voice at bay. A deep sadness hung in the room as we all mourned for Nessa's loss and tried to figure out a way to bring her back to us.

We'd done it once in the past. Surely we could do it again.

It was depressing to think that back in our senior year, it was playing that had gotten her through. What the hell was going to get her through now?

"Pretty, pretty please..." Ralphie sang the start of the chorus for "F**kin' Perfect" by Pink.

Flick's eyes rounded, a brief smile tugging at his mouth. He turned for his mic. Wrapping his fingers around it, he pulled it to his lips and sang the entire chorus.

The words echoed throughout the house, and we all gazed at the stairs, waiting to see Nessa's skinny legs appear.

Nothing.

Pressing my lips together, I placed my fingers on the strings and stepped up to my mic. I sang the first line of the song, starting at the top and strumming my guitar. Jace and Ralphie came in as the song picked up before the chorus, and it didn't take long before we were all hollering into our microphones, beckoning Nessa down to us with a song that was nothing but the truth.

Rosie knew our girl better than anyone, and

she'd been right. Nessa was fucking perfect, and I was going to do everything in my power to make her believe it.

TWENTY-FOUR

NESSA

The song reverberated throughout the guest house, loud and clear. I pressed my head against the wood and listened. They were singing for me, just like Ralphie had two years ago. He must have told them about Mama. Traitor.

I sniffed and rubbed a finger under my nose.

The song should have made me happy. I should have thrown that door open and raced down the stairs to listen, but I couldn't, because as much as that song meant to me, it also reminded me of losing the most perfect woman I'd ever known and then becoming an orphan.

"Welcome To My Life" blasted through the stereo in the music room. I tapped my sticks against the drums, losing myself in the music. I loved the beat for that song, and the words totally encapsulated how I was feeling as I played in Rosie's music room for the last time.

The funeral had been conducted the day before. There was a smattering of people—all of which Mother disapproved of. She wouldn't let me invite Chaos, so it was mainly Rosie's employees and her music buddies. My mother sat in the pew, straight-backed and stoic. I refused to cry in front of her and held it all in. I even let her snatch my wrist and drag me through the day. I was numb and actually relished that feeling. I didn't want to experience the true pain I was holding in.

Rosie was gone.

The woman who had come into my life, out of the blue, and rescued me was no more. She'd fought to keep me. She'd let me be myself and loved me for it. I'd blossomed in her sunlight. But the day she fell out of the kitchen chair clutching her chest, a bleak darkness descended, and I was sucked back into a life of disapproving oppression.

The drums dropped out of the song. I clutched the sticks to my chest and listened to the words, feeling them in my cracking core. The beat kicked in again, and I smacked the drums, throwing my all into the final chorus until my mother walked into the room and shut off the sound.

My sticks froze midair and I gave her a cold look that she simply raised her nose at.

"Let's go, Vanessa." She eyed the instruments with

disgust then sighed when she noted my broken expression. "If you really want to keep playing, I'll arrange for you to have piano lessons with Ms. Richmond."

That evil spinster?

All I could picture was being forced to sit on a rock-hard piano stool playing classical music while she held a wooden ruler over my knuckles and bashed them every time my fingers weren't curved enough.

"No, thank you," I mumbled, reluctantly rising from my stool and clambering around the drum kit. The crash cymbal wobbled as I brushed past it. I turned and ran my finger lovingly over the edge before tapping it with my nail. It pinged softly, and my nose started to tingle with tears.

"Come, Vanessa. Let's go."

I shuffled after her, picking up my suitcase and lugging it down the stairs. The sky was overcast, the white clouds turning gray and bleak. It'd be raining by the afternoon—how appropriate. The front door creaked as Mama swung it wide, and I caught a whiff of moisture in the cold air.

I shivered and dragged my suitcase down the concrete steps. The case started tipping, threatening to tumble down the stairs, when a strong hand stopped it.

"Let me get that for ya." Ralphie smiled down at me. His nose was red, and his teeth were lightly chattering. How long had he been standing outside my door?

My lips parted. "What are you doing here?"

I stepped onto the sidewalk and shoved my hands into my coat pockets.

Ralphie's eyes flicked to my mother's back before

*landing on me. "I didn't want to miss saying goodbye."
His voice sounded kind of dry and hollow. The sadness
in his gaze tore at my heart.*

*I sniffed and nodded, looking down at my black boots.
"What are you going to tell the guys?"*

"I still haven't thought of anything yet."

*The boulder in my throat was so huge I didn't know
how I was ever going to swallow again. My nose tingled
as I pictured Jimmy and Flick hearing the news. They'd
be furious, but it would only be to hide their pain. Poor
Ralphie. I shouldn't have put him in that position, but I
didn't have it in me to say goodbye.*

*Ralphie's arm snaked around my shoulders, and he
pulled me close and kissed the top of my head. "You
could stay. Mom would let you move in with us, for
sure."*

*I glanced up at Ralphie's face and knew he meant it.
His mother was a gem, cut from the same cloth as Rosie.*

*"She can't stay," my mother interjected. "She has a
home in Mississippi, and her brothers and sisters are
waiting for her. Now, come on, say your goodbyes."*

*I'd barely seen my family in three and a half years.
I'd been sent down for two Thanksgivings and one
Christmas, but it'd been painful. No one had ever come
up to visit me, and if I was one hundred percent honest,
I hadn't really missed any of them. I was the black sheep,
the girl who never quite fit. Even as a baby, I never
bonded with my parents thanks to my twin brother
taking sick and using up all their time and attention.*

*I pulled away from Ralphie. Tears burned the back of
my throat, but I wouldn't let them fall as I walked
toward the car. Dread seeped through me, making my*

legs heavy. My muscles had turned to iron, and I had to drag myself to that wretched vehicle. Mama stood by the passenger door, holding it open for me and giving me an impatient look.

"Would you hurry it up? We've a long drive ahead."

A familiar pine smell hit my nostrils as I approached the open door, and I could see into my future. We'd drive away from that curb and spend the next twelve hours in a silent, stuffy car. There'd be no music, no easy chatter. I'd endure my time staring out the window, feeling my heartstrings stretch and snap as I drove away from the place I belonged. I'd arrive in Mississippi an empty, soulless shell.

I swallowed and stepped back from the car. "I can't do it," I murmured.

"Excuse me?" My mother reached for my arm, digging her fingers into my muscles and yanking me back. "Get into this car."

"No." I shook my head.

"Vanessa." My mother closed her eyes and sighed. "Don't do this to me now."

"I can't go back. I don't belong there."

"You are my daughter!" she shouted. "Now, I didn't ask for you, but you are my responsibility, and you will do as I say."

Desperation made her voice pitchy, but I couldn't give in without at least a small fight. I didn't want to be someone's obligation...not after Rosie had shown me what it was like to feel significant.

"I've never done what you've said," I countered. "That's why you didn't want me back. Life is easier without me, so just let me go. I release you from your *fucking* responsibility."

Mother's nostrils flared, her face pinching tight. She hated bad language, but more than that...she hated losing. She always had, and I'd never made it easy for her. Her chin bunched into a little knot and her lips trembled as she spoke in a low, guttural voice. "How a child like you came out of me is something I will never understand." Her southern drawl grew thick as she leaned toward me, her spittle landing on my cheek. "You are an impossible child, and you break my heart, Vanessa. If you'd only tried to be good like your brother." Her voice cracked before she sniffed in a breath and steeled herself. "You are just so damn stubborn. You wretched child, don't make me drag you into this car!"

Her words sliced like a sharp blade, covering me in little nicks and scratches. They deflated me, like they always did, making me believe that my time with Rosie had been a fool's illusion. I shuffled back to the open car door. I'd let her win if she'd just stop making me feel so small and worthless.

I steadied myself against the door and was about to lift my foot inside when Ralphie's voice stopped me.

"Pretty, pretty please..." he started singing, his low voice picking up the chorus of "F**king Perfect" and turning it into the most beautiful song I'd ever heard.

I froze, absorbing the sound and feeling my insides tingle as he grew louder. Soon, he was bellowing the words, screaming out that I was fucking perfect and sending my mother into a near state of cardiac arrest.

"Stop it!" she screamed at him. "You stop cussing, you filthy boy!"

It made me laugh, watching her face get all mottled

like that. *Every time she shouted, he'd just sing that much louder, and soon I was laughing so hard my stomach hurt. She heard me and her face morphed with a look of shock and despair. Her eyes welled with tears and she stared at me, shaking her head, before finally whispering, "I can't do it, either."*

Moving to the trunk, she yanked out my case and dumped it on the curb. Her expression remained crumpled and wounded as she slammed the passenger door shut and moved to the driver's side. She stopped before getting in and gave me one final look. "I wash my hands of you, Vanessa. You are on your own."

She sniffed and slipped into the car, starting the engine and peeling away from the curb without looking back. There was something so definitive about the way she did that I froze for a second.

My mother had just disowned me. I had no one.

The air in my lungs grew thick and chilly until an arm landed on my shoulder.

"Jimmy would have killed me if I'd let that woman take off with our drummer." Ralphie patted his chest, looking relieved. He sucked in a breath and brushed his gloved finger down my nose. "Should we go tell Mom I've adopted a sister?"

The tight grip on my chest loosened a little, and I grinned up at him. "I love you, Ralphie."

"Not as much as I love you." He wrapped his big bear arms around me and hoisted me off the ground. I squawked then started laughing as he jiggled me in the air. "Let me go." I chuckled.

"No way, drummer girl. We are never letting you go." Ralphie threw back his head and whooped before

yelling at the sky. "Nothing can separate Chaos! We are indestructible!"

If only he'd been right.

I closed my eyes as their serenade came to a finish. A thick silence followed, only broken by the sound of footsteps coming up the stairwell. I tensed, my back going stiff against the wood.

"Ness?" Jimmy lightly tapped on the door.

I'd been expecting Ralphie's voice, and maybe if it had been my big bro, I would have opened the door, but I couldn't face Jimmy. I didn't know how much Ralphie had said, but I didn't want to see the pity on Jimmy's face.

I gripped my stump and pressed my lips into my knees.

"Can I come in?"

I shook my head.

The handle above me wiggled, and I braced my legs, pushing back against the door even though I'd locked it. He didn't put up much of a fight, sensing my resistance and knowing I wouldn't budge in a hurry.

"Ness, please. Let me in."

"Go away, Jimmy," I croaked. "Just leave me alone."

I held my breath, waiting for another fight, but he soon sighed and shuffled away from the door. I slumped over, laying my head on the carpet and listening to the soft movement downstairs. To my surprise, they gave up the practice and left. I had no idea if Jimmy stayed because I closed my eyes and welcomed the oblivion of sleep.

I drifted toward my only escape as a deep sadness rattled inside of me. The four of us were supposed to be indestructible, but we weren't.

I never in a million years thought I'd be the one to break us.

TWENTY-FIVE

JIMMY

It had been quiet since I tromped down the stairs and shrugged at the guys. We all looked to Ralphie, silently appealing for more, and he filled us in on every detail he remembered. I couldn't believe her mother had spoken to her that way. Shit! If Ralphie hadn't been there, asking her to stay, we could have lost her for good.

We all grew restless and agitated as we listened to the story.

By the time Ralphie got to the part about her mother squealing away from the curb, Flick lost it. Lightly kicking the keyboard stand, he barked,

"That fucking bitch," and huffed out of the room.

Jace took his cue and sauntered out. "I'll catch you guys tomorrow."

I nodded but didn't say anything. Sliding my hands into my pockets, I gazed at Ralphie with a long, intense stare that eventually had him squirming.

"I can't believe you never told me, man."

He looked to the ceiling and sighed. "She made me promise."

"I thought I was her best friend," I muttered like an immature prick. "I thought I was the one she told everything to."

Ralphie gave me a droll frown. "You've always been more than that. She probably finds it easier to talk to me because she doesn't want to jump my bones."

I flashed him a warning glare, my cheeks burning red.

He chuckled. "I can't believe you never noticed her goo-goo eyes." His light-gray gaze stripped me bare and he murmured, "Or maybe you just didn't want to see it."

I closed my eyes with a heavy, guilt-ridden sigh.

"Look, man, I know this sucks, but we can't force our Nester out of hiding. We just have to be patient. The girl she became when she lived with Rosie is still in there somewhere. She just can't see it right now, but she will...eventually." His pause and the way he whispered *eventually* revealed his doubts and worry.

My forehead crinkled. He mirrored my sad

frown for a second before he cleared his throat and hitched up his jeans. He gave me a light slap on the shoulder as he loped past. I stayed where I was, gazing at the lonely instruments in the practice area and wondering what the hell to do with myself. I ended up pacing around the bottom floor of the guest house until I thought I'd lose my mind. Finally, I headed up to the main house to do a workout in the downstairs gym. I pushed weights until sweat was dripping into my eyes and my muscles felt like Play-Doh. After a shower, I stuck around to drink beer and play *Mortal Kombat X* with the guys.

We tried to forget that Nessa wasn't with us, but it was a lingering dark cloud and no amount of distraction could dull the pain of her retreat. The sky was a deep midnight blue when I wandered back down to the guest house. I wanted to check that Nessa was okay. She'd no doubt be hungry, and I hoped she'd found the leftover pizza in the fridge.

I eased into the quiet house. It was dark and tranquil, and for a second, I flashed with panic that she'd left. I crept up the stairs and listened against the wood, holding my breath until I was sure I could hear her breathing. From what I could tell, she was still lying against the door. I pressed the light on my watch. Shit. She'd been there a long time.

With a heavy sigh, I descended the stairs and turned on the lights, illuminating the practice area and kitchen. I yanked the fridge open and grabbed a bottle of water, pleased to see the pizza was no longer in there. She must have gotten up for a mid-nap snack…at least that was something. I shut the fridge and spun on my heel, feeling restless. It was too early to go to bed, but I didn't know what the hell else to do with my time.

Snatching the remote off the counter, I pressed 'play' and rolled my eyes as Avril Lavigne came through the speakers. Nessa and her she-rock music. I shook my head but found myself grinning. I actually adored that she was a rocker-chick and aspired to be like those sexy women who weren't afraid to speak their minds and give the world the finger when they needed to.

I wanted that Nessa back—the spunky one who told me where to stick it when I was being an asshole, the feisty one who told me I'd been drinking too much or that I needed to practice the guitar more. The one Rosie had unveiled and coaxed out of hiding. That Nessa had never been afraid to tell me anything…except that her parents were alive and kicking. Oh yeah, and that she was in love with me.

"Since the ninth grade," I murmured with a sigh, flopping onto the sofa.

I glanced at my laptop, still sitting there from the night before, and pulled it over. Opening the lid, I went to YouTube—my go-to site—and typed in Chaos. Clips our band had been making over the past three years popped up and I scrolled through them, re-watching us play and talk to the camera. We were so passionate about the music and being a band. I ran my finger down the screen, tracing Nessa's smile and grinning when she laughed. I watched her ringed fingers dance in the air as she introduced the song we were going to perform. She flicked her long braid over her shoulder and bounced around to the kit.

She'd never be able to braid her hair like that again...not on her own anyway.

My eyebrows creased. I opened up a new screen and typed in a different search, leaning toward the screen and concentrating as I watched the clip.

I was so absorbed in my research that I didn't even hear Nessa walk in. I caught a movement over the edge of my laptop and glanced up as she came around the corner and noticed me on the couch. Her lips rose with a soft smile before she looked to the floor. The dark locks of shiny hair fell over her face, creating a curtain. I longed to sweep it over her shoulder but bunched my fingers into a fist and remained where I was.

If I tried to approach her, she might flee back up the stairs again.

Music wafted around us and I looked up at her, staring into her beautiful brown eyes and not saying anything. She gazed back at me, searching my expression until she started to move forward. My heart hitched, an unfamiliar feeling I'd never experienced with any girl except her. The first time I'd felt it was when she kissed me, her sweet tongue brushing inside my mouth. I hadn't meant to start it, but we'd freaking won *Shock Wave* and we were high on the sheer thrill of that. She'd been standing at my feet smiling at me, and I just grabbed her face and kissed her. She'd sighed into my mouth and responded, making my heart hitch. I should have backed off then, but she'd felt so damn good that I'd ignored the unfamiliar twinge and lifted her into my arms. As soon as her legs had wrapped around my waist, it was a done deal. I couldn't have stopped if I'd wanted to.

My eyes traveled the length of Nessa's tight body. Her cute little butt perched on the couch beside me, and she tucked her hair behind her ear.

"What are you watching?" Her nose wrinkled as she looked at the computer screen.

"Um..." I licked my bottom lip and shifted the laptop away.

She started to snicker. "Are you watching a clip on how to braid hair?" Her eyebrows rose, along with the color in my cheeks.

"I..." I scratched the back of my beanie before yanking it off and patting down my tousled hair. I threw the beanie onto my keyboard and hitched my shoulders. "I wanted to learn, you know...in case you ever wanted me to...do it for you."

She swallowed—a loud, audible one—and the shocked look on her face told me she'd never expected such a sweet gesture from the likes of me. I reached for her dark tendrils of hair, running my fingers through the long strands.

Her pale skin started to bloom red, and she blinked a couple of times before nervously tittering. "Seriously, who is possessing you right now?"

I chuckled and shifted to face her properly. "Just

shut up and let me try."

Her smile was dubious, but she didn't fight me when I gently pulled the hair over her shoulder and attempted to braid it. It was damn tricky. Her silky strands had a mind of their own and kept slipping out of my fingers. I held my tongue between my teeth and twisted the hair like the video showed me. Nessa sat on the couch, fighting a smirk.

Eventually, I managed to wind the hair into a sort of braid. It had a big bulge about halfway up on the right side, but for a first attempt, it wasn't too bad. I held it up, unable to mask my pride.

She looked down and cringed before clearing her throat. "Not bad."

I dropped the braid and rolled my eyes. "Shut up."

"No, really." She reached for my arm. "It's good. Thank you." The way she said the words and the look in her eye told me she meant it.

Damn, I wanted to kiss her so bad. Her lips were full and pink, and I wanted to taste them again, to skim my tongue over their sweet softness. To make matters a million times harder, she wet them with her tongue, so they glistened.

My hand twitched to clamp around the back of her neck and pull her into me, and I was so close to giving in when she whispered, "I'm sorry."

I leaned back, confused. "For what?"

Her nose twitched and her lips pulled into a frown. "For not telling you about my mother." She shrugged, looking ready to cry. "For not coming down when you sang to me. I just…" She sighed. " I don't know what's wrong with me at the moment."

Her eyes glinted in the soft light from the lamp behind me, turning them to a light nutmeg. I reached for her face, cupping her left cheek and brushing my thumb along her jawline.

"It's okay," I whispered. "No one's judging."

She blinked a couple of times, giving me a brief, watery smile before dipping her chin. Avril Lavigne started singing "Fall To Pieces." I couldn't decide if it was the perfect song or not. It said everything…maybe too much. It seemed to suck the air out of the room as Nessa sat there, trying not to look at me.

Finally, at the end of the first chorus, she glanced up. I caught her gaze, holding it steady…unwilling to let her go.

Screw it. I had to kiss her.

I leaned forward before she had time to pull away and gently pressed my lips to hers. She didn't stiffen and back off like I expected her to. Instead, she released that little sigh I remembered and melted against me. I inwardly smiled, relishing her taste and dipping my tongue in for some more. Her mouth opened up to me, and I shifted my hand to the back of her head, shuffling closer before deepening the kiss. Our tongues touched and teased each other. A hot fire, sparked from vivid memories, ignited in my belly and shot straight down to my cock. It grew quickly, straining against my jeans as I skimmed my hand down Nessa's arm and found a perch on her hip. My thumb snaked beneath her shirt, lightly caressing the soft skin above her jeans.

Nessa curled her fingers into my tee, sucking on my bottom lip before diving into a deep kiss that made me heady. Our breaths mingled together, a steamy sonnet of moans and gasps. My hand splayed over her bare back. Her skin was so tight and silky. I traced her ribs, weaving a pattern around to her spine. She wasn't wearing a bra. A giddy glee flashed through me, and my fingers drifted around the side of her body, my thumb brushing that smooth curve of her pert breast.

She jerked and pulled away from me with a gasp. "We can't—we—what are we doing?" She wriggled away from me, pushing my arm out from under her shirt and shifting so far back she nearly toppled off the couch. She caught herself just in time, steadying her back against the arm of the couch and running her fingers into her hair.

My braid came undone easily, having no tie to hold it in place, and the strands of hair split apart, fanning over her shoulder. I swallowed and looked down at my hands.

"We were kissing," I finally said.

"No, we…" She shook her head. "We can't."

She jumped off the couch and straightened her shirt then paced over to the drum kit. Her finger skimmed the rim of the high tom and she stood there, not looking at me.

"I don't want to hurt you." I slowly stood, shoving my hands into my pockets when she whipped around to stare at me. I gave her a soft smile. "I just want you to let me in. Are you ever going to forgive me?"

Her mouth opened and shut a few times before she grimaced and huffed out a quick breath. "It's not—It's about trust, Jimmy. You don't do long-term and I can't...I shouldn't." She squeezed her eyes shut and ran her fingers down her arm, lightly feeling the scar on the end of her stump. "I'm not strong enough to deal with this, as well. I've got no outlet right now, and I'm struggling."

"No drums." I made a sad face and nodded.

"No drums," she whispered, her eyes filling with a despair I couldn't handle.

"You don't need them. You can survive this. You're amazing and strong and..."

"Shut up, Jimmy," she whispered, softening her command with a weak smile. "I'm not."

I opened my mouth to argue, but she cut me off with a shake of her head. Her expression told me not to try. It was an effort to press my lips together. I wanted to launch into a speech about how perfect she was and that her mother was full of shit, but she probably wouldn't believe me.

I had to break the tension somehow, so I decided to go for humor—some very risky humor.

"We need to find you another outlet then." Tipping back on my heels, I looked at her with a charming smile and winked. "Maybe sex would work."

She scowled back. "Is that all you think about?"

"Only with you."

"Yeah, right." She rolled her eyes. "You infuriate me."

"But I'm kind of irresistible, though." I waggled my eyebrows, and she laughed before she could stop herself. It didn't last long. Her lips were soon back in a tight line, but I held on to the triumph of that fleeting sound.

She tried to give me a glare but couldn't hold it, her lips soon flashing me another smile. She shook her head and retreated toward the stairwell.

"Goodnight, Nessa."

She stopped and looked over her shoulder. "Goodnight, Jimmy."

Her smile was brief but genuine, so I took it, holding it tightly inside my chest. I carried it to bed with me and let it linger in my dreams, hoping it would see me through until I could get another one out of her.

TWENTY-SIX

NESSA

Jimmy's kiss stayed with me all night. His tongue taunted me, sending rocket fire straight through my body. I squirmed in my bed, tossing and turning as I relived the night we slept together—the feel of him inside me, the heat of his passion making me euphoric. He took me to another plane and I had relished every second of it, until I'd woken up alone and realized with a sinking sense of dread that maybe I'd made love while Jimmy had simply had sex.

My nightmare had become a reality, yet I still couldn't resist him. I'd given in so easily to his kiss the night before. It wasn't until his magic hand had skimmed my breast that I'd jerked back to reality. My body hated me for it, but my mind was relieved. I'd remembered, in the nick of time, who Jimmy Baker really was and that his words and sweet ways (the hair braiding!) were simply a balm for his own guilt.

I'd known ever since I met him that Jimmy cared about people. He was a sweet guy with a good soul, but he never let himself love anybody...not all the way. And after everything I'd gone through, I couldn't settle for anything less than all the way. I was smart enough to know that I needed stability and a constant love that could never be questioned.

My resolve, however steely, was starting to bend, though, and it scared me. I didn't want to fall under his spell again, yet another part of me was desperate for it.

I shook my head and flung the guest house door open. Jimmy wasn't around and I worried he'd be up at the main house, but I had a few more apologies to make, and unless I wanted guilt to eat me alive by the end of the day, I had to get them over with.

Ralphie was on the couch in the main house, his feet buried in a beanbag and his eyes glued to the TV screen as I walked in from the back lawn.

"Hey, Nester."

Grunts and huffs came out of the TV, and I glanced up to see two cartoon characters battling it out in an arena. *Mortal Kombat X*. Seriously, the guys were addicted. I would have rolled my eyes if I hadn't noticed Ralphie was fighting Erron Black—my favorite character to beat. So far, I'd been the only one in the house able to kick his ass.

"No way," I murmured. "Are you seriously beating him right now?"

He gave me a sheepish grin, tipping the controls to one side while his tongue poked out the edge of his mouth. It reminded me of Jimmy braiding my hair, and I scowled at Ralphie, leaning forward and knocking his elbow.

"Watch it," he growled, but I knew he wasn't mad. The guy didn't know how to display that emotion.

I flopped onto the couch, sinking into the soft cushions and punching my boot into the beanbag before muttering, "I need to talk to you."

He paused the game and flicked off the TV, shuffling around to face me. The move surprised me, but I guess a lot of weird shit had been going down since I lost my hand. Ralphie never paused a fight, and he never turned off the TV to give someone his full attention. I was becoming more and more convinced that the guys had been possessed by sensitive love fairies. It was freaking me out, but maybe I liked it a little.

The music coming through the speakers could be heard now that the TV was off. I listened for a moment before smiling up at my friend—the brother I'd lived with for eighteen months when I refused to return to Mississippi. The one who'd always been so good to me.

"Are you mad?" He winced, his nose crinkling into a funny shape.

"For telling them about Mama?"

"I prefer to call her Bitch Face, but yeah."

I snickered at his deadpan expression then nudged him with my elbow. "That's okay. I probably should have told them when it happened. I just wanted to put it behind me."

"That's why I agreed. But when you lost it yesterday, I couldn't hold back anymore. They wanted to understand where you were coming from." He slumped back into the couch and gazed at me. "You don't really believe that trash your mom said to you, do ya?"

My smile faltered and I cleared my throat. "Anyway, I came here to say I'm sorry for being a bitch at practice, and yelling at you. I was...frustrated."

His lips tipped into a half-smile, his bright gray eyes soft and forgiving. Nerves skittered through me as I wondered if he'd launch into some big spiel about how perfect I was, but he showed a little mercy and softly said, "I know we don't get what you're going through, but that doesn't mean we don't love you and want to help you. You can't quit on Chaos, you're not allowed."

I scoffed and leaned my head back, gazing up at the ceiling. It was a high stud and made the living space feel expansive and airy. My eyes tracked along the white beams and stopped at the big skylight. I stared up at the cloudless sky above us and watched a bird fly overhead. Freedom. It reminded me of those days I'd sat alone in my Mississippi bedroom, wishing for the power of flight so I could take off and never return.

"Nothing's the same anymore," I mumbled. "I don't know how to make this work."

Ralphie made a pensive sound in his throat before nudging me with his elbow. "You and Jimmy slept together, didn't you?"

I jerked and turned to face him, my eyes so wide they actually hurt. "He told you that?"

"No." Ralphie shook his head. "But something went down between you two, and it's my most logical guess."

I sighed and rested my head against his shoulder.

"Best sex of your life?" he asked.

A slow smile spread over my lips, and I couldn't help a small whine.

"Really? He outclassed Simon McPinhead?" His mock surprise made me giggle.

My cheeks flared pink, and I thumped him in the arm. "I can't believe I told you that."

"Sweetie, you didn't have to tell me that. I walked in on that...and I'm still having nightmares, by the way."

I chuckled then groaned and covered my face with my hand. "Simon McMurphy. What was I thinking?"

"I have no idea, but that was one awkward summer."

I grunted. It was always destined to be awkward. It was my first summer without Rosie, and I was not in a great place. Simon was sweet. Neither of us had done it before, and we fumbled our way through a few times. It went from clumsy to enjoyable, and although it didn't make my limbs sizzle, it was a weird kind of comfort. I felt obliged to date the guy for the entire summer break and it was tres bizarro. Jimmy had been sullen and moody, Flick didn't like the guy much either, and Ralphie's cheeks burned red every time he saw us together. I was silently begging for college to start so Simon would give me his final kiss goodbye then move three states away.

"Jimmy loves you, you know?" Ralphie said it so simply, like it was the most uncomplicated thing in the world.

My scoffing laugh was short and hard. "Jimmy loves a lot of girls."

Ralphie tugged at the chain dangling from his baggy jeans, running his fingers across the silver, linked metal. "You're different. I haven't seen him like this before."

I went quiet, knowing exactly what Ralphie meant. Jimmy *was* acting weird. I wanted to like it...to love it even, but I was finding it so unnerving. I couldn't push past my own wariness long enough to see it for what it was.

It was just so much easier to think of Jimmy as an asshole and blame him for everything, but he was making it really difficult.

I chewed on my lip, not wanting to admit any of that to Ralphie. I had to change the subject and change it fast. Thankfully, music came to my rescue and "Teenage Dirtbag" by Wheatus started playing. I sat up with a smile and looked at Ralphie. He grinned at me and started mouthing the words.

I giggled. The song meant everything to us. It was the one Chaos had played to win the school talent show back in our sophomore year. We'd killed it, and the entire student body had fallen instantly in love with us.

The chorus started, and I mouthed the words with him, throwing my inhibitions to the wind while dancing on the couch like an idiot. Ralphie had always been my goofball pal. It was easy to let myself go with him. The bridge started, and he went for dramatic, singing with exaggerated facial expressions, running his fingers down my cheek and staring at me with his big, puppy-dog eyes. My stomach quivered with giggles. I licked my lips then kicked in with the girl's part, batting my eyelashes and twirling my hair around my finger. Ralphie chuckled, then we both started banging our heads as the music grew with intensity. At the same time, we threw our heads back and sang, "Oh, yeah! Dirtbag!"

I started playing air drums while Ralphie played air guitar as the song came to an epic finish. It felt good to play again, even though I wasn't touching anything. A fresh, light feeling rose in my chest, and I giggled as the song faded out.

A slow applause sounded behind us, and we spun around to see Jace watching us with a big grin. My cheeks turned red, so I slumped back onto the sofa, ducking down so he couldn't see me. He just laughed some more and wandered around until he was standing in front of us.

He tugged the beanbag away from Ralphie and sat in it, giving me a sweet smile.

"Nice playing."

"Thank you," I replied with a dry smirk.

He let me have it, tucking his hair behind his ear and reminding me of a sexy surfer.

"Hey, listen, I'm sorry about yesterday." I didn't know what compelled me to apologize to the guy who'd replaced me, but it felt kinda good, like a small weight lifting off my shoulders.

"No, that's cool. I get it." He nodded, looking as though he actually did.

I tipped my head in question, and he gave me a closed-mouth smile before admitting, "My dad lost both his legs in a fire about six years ago. One of his crew got trapped in the building, and he went in after him."

My lips parted, my throat swelling so tight I wasn't sure I could breathe.

"I'm sure he'd be happy to chat with you, if you ever want to blow off some steam or ask him anything. It took him a while, but he's in a really good place now." Jace smiled, his relief obvious to see. "Hand me your phone, I'll program my number in. No pressure or anything, just if you want an ally, you know? Someone who really understands."

I passed him my phone and couldn't speak as I watched Jace's fingers fly over the screen. He stood from the beanbag and gave the phone back to me with another sweet grin.

"Thanks," I whispered; it was the loudest I could manage.

"Well, I'm out. Mom's cookin' meatloaf tonight, and I know it sounds weird, but hers freaking kicks ass and I'm not missing it."

He ambled out of the living area, and I turned to Ralphie. "He still lives with his parents?"

"Yeah. We invited him to move into your old room, but he doesn't want to. I think he likes being around to help out the family."

"Good guy," I murmured, my heart still racing as I imagined the horror of having my body so badly burned I lost my legs. Both legs. How the hell did he cope?

I drew in a shuddering breath.

"I'll come with you, if you want." Ralphie nudged me with his elbow.

"To where?" I glanced up.

"To see Jace's dad."

"Oh." I nodded, still not sure if I was ready. It was so much easier to be angry and pretend everything was fine. I didn't want to admit that I'd lost my hand and I'd have to learn how to live without it. I hated the idea of wearing a hook—oh yeah, I'd Googled them. I'd seen pictures of metal and hard-plastic hooks that had a special attachment to hold a drumstick at the right angle. It looked freaking alien. According to the insurance policy Rosie had left me, I could afford a simple design that would suit my needs, but... I didn't want anything to change. I didn't want to accept the fact they had.

My throat swelled with emotion.

I wanted to go back to the night before we won *Shock Wave*. It killed me that I couldn't.

I had no control, and I hated that feeling.

Ralphie leaned forward and turned on the TV. His game came back up, and I went to rise off the couch to go and find Flick—my final apology before I retreated to my room again.

"Where you going?" Ralphie grabbed my arm and pulled me back down, passing me the remote.

"Ralphie," I snapped. "I can't."

"I know, but *we* can." He wiggled the remote, encouraging me to hold the right side with my right hand. He leaned against my arm and held the left side with his left. "Unpause it," he softly commanded.

I gave him a wilting look that he ignored.

"Unpause it, woman. Let's play."

With a soft grunt, I did as I was told, and we tried to play together. Two bodies, one controller, and a whole lot of laughs.

TWENTY-SEVEN

JIMMY

The first thing I heard when I opened the front door was Nessa's laughter. It was a sweet, contagious sound that I initially didn't recognize. In fact, I didn't fully believe it until I heard Ralphie shouting, "Go, Nester, kick his ass!"

With a curious frown, I peeked into the living area and watched Ralphie and Nessa arm to arm on the couch trying to control a *Mortal Kombat X* fighter with a shared controller.

Nessa's smile was at least a thousand watts. I leaned against the wall, my gaze transfixed to her beautiful face. I didn't realize it was possible for someone to take my breath away, but she did. I couldn't believe it took me so long to notice how pretty she was, how effervescent she could be. I was so caught up on living the lie that partying and one-night stands was the only way to feel free that I completely blanked on the fact that security could mean freedom, too.

Ralphie was right—I hadn't wanted to see it, but my eyes were wide open now, and it was one fine view.

"Yes!" Nessa bobbed on the couch, breaking into a deep chuckle that was plain adorable. Ralphie pointed at her and laughed some more, which only set her off again. I hadn't seen her that free and happy since the night we won *Shock Wave*.

The only problem was, it was Ralphie who was making her smile, and I wanted it to be me. It still bugged me that she'd opened up to him about all this shit and I'd remained an oblivious idiot. Those two had history together that I'd never be a part of. He was her confidante...and I wanted to claim that role. Hell, I wanted to claim all of them—best friend, lover, soulmate.

I slid my hands into my pockets, unable to take my eyes off the duo as they kept playing. They were so absorbed in the game, they hadn't even noticed me, and I was cool with that, because I needed time to think.

I needed to figure out a way to show Nessa how much her disappearance had changed me. I needed her to trust me again, to let go and let me in. I wasn't chasing her out of guilt. Yeah, it was a heavy burden, but that wasn't what was driving me. I wanted Nessa to be my girl.

Nibbling on my fingernail, I stared until my vision turned fuzzy and a thick resolve stirred in my chest. It was time I upped the ante. I had to do something I'd never done before.

It was time to take a girl out on my first date.

TWENTY-EIGHT

NESSA

I'd felt lighter over the past few days. Apologizing to the guys and having them all forgive me was a soothing balm. I sat in on their next practice and even complimented Jace when he switched up the drumming again. He really was a great fit for the band. I didn't want to think about what that meant for me in the future. I couldn't do 'future.' I was simply living from day to day, and that had to be enough.

The occupational therapist had called again, and I'd said I was busy. She kind of put the hurt on me.

"You may pick up bad habits that will make things

more difficult for you in the long run. Please, let me help you."

I muttered something about giving her a call in a week or two, but we both knew I'd just told a big fat one. Yes, I was stubborn and probably an idiot.

I kicked my right leg over my left and bounced it up and down in the air. The guest house was quiet, and the main house was empty. Ralphie was out with Flick and Jace playing paintball, and I had no idea where Jimmy was. He'd been a little scarce the last few days. It was a nice reprieve, but again, I found it unnerving. Everything he did put me off-balance. One minute, he was braiding my hair and the next, he was giving me tender smiles and enough space that I felt like an ocean had formed between us.

Yanking a comic book off the side table, I slapped it onto the couch and started flicking through it. I'd read it already, so I just skimmed the awesome graphics. I wished I could draw like that. The artwork was freaking amazing.

The guest house door clicked open and I immediately tensed, listening carefully to the clip of feet as someone walked over the hard tiles and came to a stop on the edge of the carpet. I looked up and my lips parted (damn traitors) as I took in a very sexy version of Jimmy Baker.

He hadn't necessarily done anything different, per se. He was wearing his favorite pair of beat-up jeans with a black fitted T-shirt and his faded leather jacket. His lucky pick was around his neck, and his tousled hair was mussed to the side. His eyes looked a little bluer than usual as he stood there smiling at me.

"Let's go." He tipped his head toward the door.

I pressed my lips into a straight line and raised my eyebrows. "Where are we going?"

His smile flickered with a touch of out-of-character apprehension before he nodded and said, "I'm taking you on a date."

My face bunched with confusion. "Since when have you ever taken a girl on a date?"

He let me have my snarky reply, even nodding as if he was agreeing with me. His contrition was kind of endearing. "This will be my first time."

Oh man, that face! How the hell was I supposed to say no?

I slowly stood from the couch, pulling my tank top straight and eyeing him skeptically. "Why do you want to do this? Really?"

He huffed out a sharp breath and threw his hands wide. "To prove to you that I'm not full of shit. I want to show you how much you mean to me."

Like I could say no after that. My heart squeezed to putty, thumping in my chest and urging me to run into his arms, yelling, "I believe!"

Thankfully, my stubbornness kicked in before I made a complete fool of myself. I scrutinized his expression.

He raised his eyebrows then pulled a funny face, which made me giggle. I bit my lips together and lifted my chin.

"Okay, maybe, um…let me go change."

"Thank you." His smile radiated relief and triumph.

I ignored the giddy butterflies dancing in my stomach and raced upstairs to find a long-sleeved top that would hide my stump. I went for a black, scooped neck T-shirt then threw on a few long silver necklaces with various things dangling off them. The intention was to draw people's eyes away from my arm. I grabbed my jacket and pulled it on as I walked down the stairs. Jimmy smiled up at me then stepped forward and gently tugged my hair over the collar, arranging it around my shoulders.

His touch was so sweet and endearing. He was making it impossible to stand strong against his charm. This date was the worst idea ever.

I nearly opened my mouth to back out, but then Jimmy leaned forward and asked, "You need help with your boots or anything?" His warm breath kissed my skin, sending prickles of desire bubbling up my arms.

I sniffed and shook my head. "No, I'm good." I walked to the door and slid into an old pair of slip-ons I'd bought a few years back but never worn. They weren't really my style, but they were lace-less and easy to wear, so style could stick it.

Jimmy opened his car door for me and buckled me in before walking around to the driver's side.

"Too weird," I murmured, yet found myself loving the gesture.

Gentleman Jimmy was a dreamboat.

I cringed, mortified that I'd thought something

so incredibly girly and pathetic. I wasn't used to this role. I wasn't the swooning type. Sure, I'd been pining after Jimmy for years, slowly growing to love him with each passing day, but he'd always been enough of an asshole to stop me from becoming a lovesick sap.

The new Jimmy, he could do even more damage than the old one. I had to be careful. I had to guard whatever pieces of my heart I had left.

We drove up the coast, stopping at a fancy restaurant that didn't really suit either of us. It was on the edge of a cliff, looking out across the Pacific Ocean. One wall was completely glass and lined with tables for two. Candles flickered in the middle of each table and the lights overhead were dim, creating a warm, luxurious ambiance. Cutlery clinked elegantly on plates, creating a syncopated rhythm to the classical piano music drifting over the room.

We got a few weird glances from the rich, stuck-up patrons around us. I was tempted to smirk and give them all the finger, but Jimmy was trying so damn hard I didn't want to get us kicked out. They were dressed in expensive suits and tailor-made dresses. The jewelry was subtle and sparkly while various perfume scents floated up my nostrils as we walked to our table. I felt like a goldfish swimming in a tank of piranhas.

The waiter pulled out my chair, and I slid into it then jerked back when he tried to lay a thick, white napkin over my knee. I shot him a tight smile and mouthed an apology, gently taking the cloth from him and doing it myself.

Jimmy leaned forward with a snicker as the waiter walked away. "I had to pull a few strings to get us in here. Marcus was a really big help. He knows people who know people, you know?"

I smirked at Jimmy's nervous chatter. It was kind of adorable.

A new waitress came over and introduced herself. She was a bubbly blonde with bright blue eyes and a toothy smile. Her black slacks and fitted white blouse hugged her curves, giving her a classy sensuality. As she walked away to fill our drink orders, I noticed Jimmy's eyes skim her body.

My gut plummeted. Damn it, I was so close to letting him in, to believing gentleman Jimmy was a real person. But he was just Jimmy in disguise. And yeah, I'd loved that guy, too, but I'd been burned by him, and my wounds were still pretty open and raw.

I held in my angst, scanning the menu and looking for the most expensive items I could find. Bitterness chipped away at my innards, killing off the butterflies and reopening the seals I'd placed over my wounds.

I couldn't believe I'd let him braid my hair, zip my fly, and tie my boots all those times. I couldn't believe I'd let him kiss me again. I was such a weakling when it came to him. One look at his sexy face and I was done for. Why the hell was he torturing me this way when he obviously wanted to be out on the town again?

Guilt. That was all I could think.

Once he'd gotten me into bed and I'd proven that all was forgiven, his guilt would be vanquished, and he could go back to being free-spirited Jimmy again.

The waitress returned with two Cokes—couldn't get away with trying to drink alcohol in the high-class establishment. Jimmy thanked her with that charming smile of his, and she blushed.

"Are you ready to order?" She kept her eyes on him while I remained an insignificant nobody on the other side of the table.

Jimmy looked across at me, raising his eyebrows in question.

I pasted on a cheesy smile and said, "Can we just have a couple more minutes."

"Sure thing." She directed her grin back to Jimmy before leaving us. I watched his gaze flicker over her ass then he turned back to the menu like nothing was out of the ordinary.

"Maybe you should ask her out," I muttered.

"Excuse me?" Jimmy slapped his menu closed and gaped at me.

"You know, since you've opened yourself up to the idea of dating, you could ask her out...or maybe you want to wait until she's finished her shift and you can just bang her behind the restaurant before she goes home."

Jimmy's face blanched, his eyes taking on a stormy quality that actually made me feel bad for my bitchy tone.

I pursed my lips, my gaze dropping back to the menu. "You can't hide it, Jimmy. I saw you checking out her ass."

Placing the menu down with a forced calmness—I could tell by the way his fingers were trembling—Jimmy clenched his jaw and looked at me. "So she's got a nice ass. It doesn't mean I want it."

I stared at him deadpan, my eyes drilling into him until he leaned forward and harshly whispered, "What? Why are staring at me like you want to shove your fork through my eyeball?"

"You were totally checking her out," I quietly barked back.

"So? She has a nice ass. It was hard not to look." His eyes bulged. "And for your information, it does nothing for me compared to yours."

His words touched my soft spot, and my defenses rose in swift retaliation. "Oh, please. You can't help yourself. When was the last time you went two days without having sex?"

His skin mottled slightly, his fine features taking on a hard quality as he gritted out, "I haven't had sex since you took off on your little road trip. Actually, before that. I haven't had sex since we argued in the kitchen, the morning after..." He dipped his head. "You know."

My eyebrows shot up and I shook my head. "Bullshit."

He gave me a pointed look that said otherwise. My heart lurched.

No freaking way. Jimmy hadn't had sex in two months? How was that possible? The guy had been sleeping around since he was in the tenth grade.

We won the talent show, and he suddenly became the sexy rock star at school. Girls fell all over themselves to get to him, parting their legs and doing whatever he pleased. Sleeping with Jimmy Baker became a status symbol, and he rode the wave with a goofy smile on his face.

Every time we played at a bar or club, he always left with someone. I'd watched him walk out the door with a different girl on his arm so many times I'd lost count.

"Stop gaping at me like that." He shook his head. "I'm telling the truth."

I could tell by his pained expression that he really was. "But—but why?" I stuttered.

"Seriously?" he practically yelled.

I guess he had a right to be frustrated with me. He'd been telling me he loved me, and working his ass off trying to prove it, but I just couldn't make myself believe him.

I chewed on my lip and sighed, placing my menu down on the starched white tablecloth. "You were screwing *two* other girls the night after we did it."

"Something I will eternally regret, believe me."

"I can't, Jimmy. I can't believe you. I mean, part of me wants to, but the thought terrifies me. I don't think you realize how much you wounded me. I thought I'd finally won you over and you..." I shook my head, unable to finish. He'd flicked me off, just the way my mother had. I was too much work, too much effort to stick around for.

He reached across the table, but I pulled my

hand away before he could get a hold of my fingers. His lips bunched into a tight frown and his nostrils flared. "I can't take that back. No matter what I try, I can't do it. And I am sorry that I hurt you, but there's only so many times I can say it. You need to get over yourself and open your eyes. Because I am sitting right here, working my ass off to win you back. I don't know what else you want me to do! How the fuck do I get you to trust me?"

His voice rose, echoing across the restaurant. A few soft gasps followed in the wake of his little outburst, and we were soon being stared down by an army of disapproving glares.

I dipped my chin, tucking my left arm against my stomach and covering it with my right.

"Just take me home," I whispered.

"Fine," Jimmy muttered, dumping his napkin on the table and shoving his chair back. I rose as smoothly as I could, keeping my head down as I walked out of the restaurant. The night breeze ruffled my hair and gave me goosebumps. I turned my back on the flashy restaurant and gazed across the darkened coastal road. I wished there was another way for me to get back to the guest house, but I had no idea where I was, and I didn't want to have to pay some ridiculous taxi fare.

I waited by the car while Jimmy paid for our drinks, steeling myself for what would no doubt be a painful ride home.

TWENTY-NINE

JIMMY

The car was stifling. I was too frickin' peeved to do anything but stare straight ahead and drive Nessa's stubborn ass home. I guess she had a right to be ticked with me. I'd never had a girlfriend before, and even though that waitress had a fine body, I had no intention of screwing her. The thought hadn't even crossed my mind. I was simply looking.

If I tried to sell that line to Nessa, she'd probably roll her eyes and tell me I was full of shit. I gripped the wheel, keeping my gaze on the dark road ahead. It was supposed to be a perfect night—

romantic. But I guess I didn't know how to do that.

I was so angry with myself for screwing it up before it even started, and of course I took it out on Nessa, lashing out at her when she called me on it. It was slightly satisfying seeing her shock when she realized I hadn't had sex in a while. It felt like a frickin' age, and I was restless for release, but the only girl I wanted doing that for me was Nessa. My stubborn little drummer who was refusing to look past her hurt and let me in.

Sure, I'd gratified myself to get me through those moments when memories of our night together consumed me so quick and fast that I'd had to release or combust...but it wasn't the same. I wanted to bury myself inside her, to feel her breath on my skin as she writhed and moaned beneath me. My pants became tight and uncomfortable. I shifted in my seat, trying to ease the growing sensation. If she looked at my lap, she'd no doubt assume it was the waitress setting me off, but it couldn't be further from the truth.

I breathed out a heavy sigh and glanced at her. She was staring out the car window. She hadn't even looked at me since we walked out of the restaurant. I wanted to get inside her brain and figure out what was going on up there.

The way she'd kissed me and melted against my body at the beginning of the week told me she still wanted me. I knew it was buried underneath there, but I couldn't seem to unearth it.

I resisted the urge to reach out and touch her shoulder, to quietly make amends, but I didn't want to start up a fight in the car when I was supposed to be concentrating on getting her home safely.

Thoughts taunted me the entire drive. I was a fucking failure...just like my dad. I'd made my grave, and now I had to lie in it. The idea that maybe my father had been right all along fluttered through my brain, but I cut it off before it could flourish. That was bullshit!

I remembered the night he broke down and admitted that love had destroyed him. He was drunk off his ass and never told me who the woman was, but he'd blubbered on about love burning him and saying the only way to stay safe was to keep the girls at a distance.

"It's a better life, Jimmy. Trust me. I don't want you to get hurt."

I'd bought into his every word, shocked by his tears. My dad never cried, and he broke down all over me. I'd been fifteen years old and horrified by his confession. Thing is, I didn't know if I could believe him anymore.

One night with Nessa had been more satisfying than all the sex I'd ever had. Just being with her, braiding her hair and taking care of her, made me feel like...a man. I'd never felt so whole in my life, and it was killing me that she wouldn't let me go all the way.

I wanted to be her boyfriend, the person she thought of first when she needed help, the person to make her smile and laugh, the one to convince her of how beautiful she was. That was my job. Not

Ralphie's, not Flick's…mine. But she wasn't letting me do it.

Pulling off the freeway, I headed for our street, the silence between us so thick I could barely see through it. I opened my mouth to say something, anything to break through the mist, but I had no words. I'd said all I could say, and it still wasn't good enough.

The gate to the house opened slowly, grinding along the track at a snail's pace and only adding to the heightened tension swirling around us. What would happen when I pulled the car up to the guest house?

I was guessing she'd slam out of it and head for her room. I couldn't let that happen. Going another night pacing the house while she wallowed in her cave would kill me. We had to have it out. If she didn't want me, then so be it, but I wanted to be damn sure that she didn't before I was willing to walk away.

As I predicted, Nessa slammed out of the car and stormed for the guest house. I raced after her, not even bothering to lock up my vehicle. She tried to close the door on me, but I caught it and nudged it open before she could. She gave me a fierce glare, but it was tempered by the glistening sheen in her eyes.

I gave her a soft smile and gently closed the door, but it only made her flinch away from me.

"I'm not going to bite you," I snapped.

She huffed and stalked into the kitchen, yanking open the fridge door so hard and fast the bottles rattled. She steadied them with her arms, giving me a warning look to keep my mouth shut. I didn't say anything. The only sound to fill the place was my shoes tapping over the tiles.

I snatched the remote and got some music going in an attempt to shatter the thick tension between us.

"True Love" by Pink started playing.

Nessa banged the fridge shut and I spun to face her, my arms crossed tight. We glared at each other, both breathing through our noses like irate bulls. The lyrics swirled around us, saying everything we couldn't. Nessa's lips twitched, her hard look starting to break apart.

I exhaled and stood back, resting my hands on my hips. I couldn't take my eyes off her. She was so beautiful and vulnerable...and pissed at me. I'd never wanted her more.

The words of the first verse seemed to be hitting Nessa right in the chest. I was an asshole, but she loved me. I could see it in her eyes. She didn't want to feel that way, but she did...and so I moved toward her.

She let out a shuddering breath then whispered, "I really hate you," in time with the lyrics before closing the gap between us and grabbing a fistful of my shirt. She pulled me against her and crushed her lips to mine as the chorus kicked in.

Her tongue swept inside my mouth, hot and hungry as she wrestled to take off my leather jacket. I gave her a hand, flicking it off my arms while continuing to kiss her. The jacket slapped onto the tiles, and the second I was freed, I reached for her face. Running my thumb across her cheek, I deepened the kiss until she gave me that sweet moan I wanted.

I smiled, sucking her bottom lip and slipping the jacket off her shoulders. She let me remove it. The leather thudded onto the floor, and my hands went roaming.

The scorching heat between us made our movements clumsy and frenetic. I ran my hands over her fine ass, giving it a squeeze before picking her up. She wrapped her legs around my waist while our tongues continued to dance.

"True Love" swirled around us as I walked her to the couch. My knees hit the back and I flopped onto it, bringing her with me. I grunted as our chests smacked together, but her hot tongue swallowed the sound. She was set on devouring me. I was set on letting her.

Yanking on my belt buckle, she wrestled to undo it. I helped her slide the leather open then zip down my fly. My pulsing cock sprang out of my boxers as she jerked them down.

"Hang on," I mumbled into her mouth. "Let me…"

"No, I need you now," she panted into my mouth, grabbing onto me and giving a little squeeze.

My brain went fuzzy, stars scattering my vision. Her hand felt so good wrapped around me, I wasn't about to argue with her. Instead, I tipped onto my side and pulled a condom out of my back pocket.

Yes, I'd been extremely hopeful going into the date and sure, it wasn't happening quite the way I'd planned, but at least it was happening.

Maybe if I'd realized what she'd really been up to, I wouldn't have gotten so carried away, but all my brain was thinking in that moment was that Nessa was letting me have sex with her. Two months of pining was finally coming to an end.

I shimmied the jeans down to my knees while Nessa jumped up and stripped off her lower half. Her deft fingers were getting better at the one-handed deal. My eyes traveled her body as she inched her jeans off, pulling her panties with them. My cock throbbed in anticipation, so I ripped the condom packet open with my teeth and quickly wrapped myself, looking up with a little smile as she sat on top of me. I splayed my hand over the tight, smooth skin on her thighs. Part of me wanted to force her back so I could take my time exploring her, but she wouldn't let me.

She positioned herself above me and slid down, encasing me in a tight hold that killed off all power of thought. I groaned, a deep guttural sound that only grew louder as she rose and fell on my lap. I dug my fingers into her hips, tipping back my head and closing my eyes as the intoxicating sensation took hold of me.

Her breath kissed my skin as she braced her arms on my shoulders and brushed her lips across my cheek. I moaned again, feeling delirious. Nessa increased the tempo, panting into my ear as I filled her.

Having gone so long without it, my urge for release came quick, like a freaking explosion that couldn't be held back. I clutched her ass, holding her onto me and shuddering as I came. It was a struggle to breathe, and my heart hammered hard and fast. My eyes stayed shut until the fog of ecstasy began to lift, and I managed a light chuckle.

"Holy shit," I murmured, creeping my eyes open to smile up at Nessa.

She gazed down at me, her brown eyes drinking me in as she drew a pattern on my cheek with her index finger.

"Feel better?" she asked.

"Oh yeah." I chuckled again, running my fingers down her thighs. I liked her weight on me, the way she fit against me so perfectly.

"So, we're all good then." She made a move to get off me, and something inside me pinged tight— a warning bell. I gripped her legs and held her in place, my eyes narrowing at the corners.

"Jimmy, let me go."

I shook my head.

Her frown was edgy. "Look, we both got what we wanted—a moment of passion that we've been hankering for—but now that's done. We can move on and you can go be yourself again."

I closed my eyes in an attempt to wrap my brain around what she was saying. She wriggled on my lap trying to set herself free, but that only sparked my indignant rage. It came flooding out of my mouth the second my eyes snapped open.

"What the fuck did you just say?"

THIRTY

NESSA

His temper took me by surprise. I thought he'd be on a post-sex high, his mind still muddy, but he was staring at me with eyes as sharp as razor blades.

"Come on, Jimmy, stop lying to yourself. You're not boyfriend material. You don't want to stay, and I'm not some charity case." I fought a little harder, and he finally let me off his knee. I stood and moved away from him, tugging down my shirt and refusing to let myself give in.

We'd had hot sex. It was freaking amazing, and it would allow him to drop the charade and stop messing with me.

But he just sat there, staring at me like I'd punched him in the guts.

I spread my arms wide. "I know you feel bad and partly responsible for what happened to me, but I don't want to be the girl who locks you into some relationship out of guilt! Consider yourself forgiven. I've had my last hurrah with you, and now I can let you go." I pointed to the door. "So just go. Go, Jimmy!"

Reaching for his jeans, he slowly pulled them back up his fine legs. I tried not to watch his taut thighs disappearing behind the fabric, but I couldn't help myself. He did me no favors by leaving the fly open, either. I waited for him to stand from the couch, snatch his jacket and storm from the room.

Instead, he flopped back onto the cushions and shook his head. "What the hell are you on? That's fucking bullshit!" He ran his fingers through his hair. "I'm not staying for any of those reasons."

"Then why are you!" I stepped back toward him, my voice pitching high as I desperately tried to run from the blatant, terrifying truth. "Let me go! Stop torturing me and let me go!"

He snatched my wrist and yanked me back onto his lap. I wriggled and tried to kick him, but he spread my legs over his knees and wrapped his arms around me. Holding the back of my head, he contained my struggles and spoke into my ear. "I am never letting go again, don't you get it! I *can't* let you go!"

My body stilled. His voice was quaking, like he was fighting tears or something. My own started to burn my eyes, and I squeezed them shut while my chin trembled against his shoulder.

"Ness, when I said I love you, I meant it. Do you have any idea how terrifying that was for me to say? But like hell was I going to let you believe anything else." He clasped my head and pulled me back so I was forced to look at him. His eyes were glistening, his desperate expression enough to tear me apart. His fingers dug into my hair as he whispered, "It's the truth. I didn't think I was capable of this emotion, but you...I love you, and I don't ever want to stop."

I sniffed, letting out a shaky sob before catching myself. Tears trickled down my cheeks, and I could barely find the voice to speak. "You could have any girl you wanted." I lifted my stump and tapped it against his chest. "I'm a broken mess. You don't want me."

He let my head go and snatched my stump, pressing it against his lips before murmuring, "I want you. *Only* you."

"But why?" I squeaked.

He rubbed his chin over my scar, his face morphing with a look so intense and pure that it owned me. Dropping my arm, he held my face again, ensuring I couldn't look away. I gazed into his vibrant blue eyes, and I swear I caught a glimpse of his soul as he whispered, "Because you're fucking perfect. You're perfect, Ness."

My lips wobbled into a smile. The tears running

down my cheek tickled the edge of my lips. I ran my fingers along his jawline and brushed my thumb across his mouth. I expected him to open it and give my thumb a little nip, but he didn't.

He just kept looking at me like I was the world's most precious possession. He was waiting…for me. He'd come as far as he could go, and now it was my turn to actually close the gap between us and start something amazing. Something that would change our lives forever.

My insides shook as I stared at him, my lips only parting enough to let out a shuddering sigh. With the back of his knuckles, he brushed my tears away, his touch so soft and intimate. It opened a door inside me. The veil over my eyes lifted and I saw him—the new Jimmy, or maybe just the original version that had been buried so deep for so long that it'd taken me leaving him to unearth it.

"Jimmy," I whispered, a nervous smile creeping over my face. "Make love to me."

"I don't think I've ever done that with a girl before," he croaked.

"Good." I leaned forward, lightly running my tongue across his mouth. "I want to be your first."

"My only," he whispered then cupped the back of my head and claimed my mouth.

THIRTY-ONE

NESSA

He tasted the same, but his kiss was completely different. He owned me, and I owned him. I sighed into his mouth, rocking on his knee as the temperature inside me began to build again.

Jimmy pulled back, rubbing his thumb across my cheek and shaking his head.

"It has to be different," he whispered.

"What do you mean?"

His eyes lit with a smile, his lips twitching as he slowly pulled my shirt off. He threw it over my shoulder before skimming his fingers down my arms. His thumb hooked under my bra strap, gently sliding it free to make way for his lips. They pressed gently into me, followed by his tongue. I closed my eyes as it skated over my skin, traveling the curve of my breast. His hand cupped me lightly before pulling the fabric away so he could suck my nipple.

I let out a shuddering breath. While his tongue worked its magic, he unclasped my bra at the front and slid it off my arms. He rolled my other nipple between his fingers, and I tipped my head back and fisted a handful of his hair. His slow, gentle assault soon had me panting. Heat was pooling between my legs, and it was taking everything in me not to tug him to the floor. I wanted his weight on top of me, to feel him grinding into me until my heart raced and my mind was ready to splinter.

"Jimmy." I breathed his name, dipping my head to rest my cheek against his scruffy hair.

He circled his tongue around my nipple, giving it one last suck before pulling away and mumbling into my skin. "Can we take this upstairs?"

I swallowed and despite my reservations, I whispered, "Yes."

He gripped me against him and stood. I wrapped my legs around his tight torso and kissed his neck as he carried me up the stairs.

My body tensed as he neared the door. Jimmy had only been into my room once, and that was when I'd been too distraught to put up a fight.

"Are you okay with this?" He gazed down at me, and all I could do was nod.

His electrifying smile made it easy to let go...to

let him in, and so I clung tight to his shoulders as he flicked on the fairy lights and walked me to the bed. The room glowed, illuminating our faces with a pale magic that was enchanting.

He placed me down on the bed and I ran my fingers up his back, bringing his shirt with it. His jeans were already undone, so I slipped them off with my feet and soon he lay next to me completely naked. I lounged on my side, resting my head on my elbow and dragging my finger down his chiseled torso. I traced the dips and tight curves, running the back of my knuckles over his rock-like abs. His stomach quivered and he let out a soft chuckle.

"Ticklish?" I asked.

"Maybe," he murmured, turning his head to look at me.

I gave him a wicked grin and brushed my teeth over my lower lip.

He groaned. "You are so damn sexy." He rolled me onto my back, nestling himself between my legs and kissing me solidly. His hot tongue dove in and out of my mouth, teasing, tasting, and sending my nerves into a frenzy.

His hardness poked into my thigh, ready to undo me in one swift movement, but he wouldn't advance. I tipped my hips, digging my fingers into his shoulders, but he pulled back with a soft chuckle.

"I said it had to be different," he whispered again. Gliding down my torso, he started a slow, delicate exploration that spanned my entire body.

It began with the tattoo on my collarbone. He traced the bird with his tongue before navigating my breasts. It was a pleasant torture that I couldn't get enough of, especially when his fingers inched between my thighs, touching my sweet spot. His fingers slipped inside me while his thumb worked some kind of wizardry that soon had an electric current sizzling through my nerves. It built with power, lighting every inch of my body until I thought I might explode. I gasped, fisting his hair and giving it a tug as an orgasm rocketed through me. I arched my back and a strangled moan escaped between my lips.

"Holy crap, that feels good," I panted, slapping my arm onto the bed and gripping a handful of sheets as he kept going, kept twirling until I couldn't take anymore and bucked him off me. "Get inside me right now."

He chuckled and edged to the side of the bed, no doubt looking for a condom.

"Wait." I snatched his arm, nerves racing, but I had to ask. "You're clean, right?"

"Yeah." He gave me a confused look. "I got myself checked after..." His eyebrows rose as deep red shame lit his cheeks.

I ignored it, refusing to let that memory taint the moment. I nibbled my lip then murmured, "I'm on the pill."

His eyes narrowed as he grasped what I was getting at. He shook his head. "Baby, I've never done it unwrapped before."

"Exactly," I said softly. "This time has to be

different, right?"

He gave me his lopsided grin, the first one I fell in love with. "Are you sure?"

"Very." I sat forward, running my arm up to his shoulder. "If I'm your only and you're mine, then there shouldn't be anything between us."

His hooded eyes gave me a dreamy look, and he reached for me with his lips again. I closed my eyes, losing myself in his kiss. His hard chest felt smooth and tight against me as he lowered us back onto the bed. I wrapped my legs around his waist, desperate for him to slide inside me—make me whole again.

But he pulled back.

Bracing his arms against the bed, he gazed down at me and whispered, "Look at me, Ness."

I opened my eyes and stared up at him, my breath catching in my throat as he nestled himself on top of me. His thumb brushed my cheekbone, his intense gaze sucking me in as he pushed into me. We both gasped, our eyes popping wide as he shifted then dove back in.

"Shit, that feels good," he murmured on an awe-filled breath.

"I know," I panted. "It's like so much better, right?" My brain could barely comprehend the hot, slick sensation as he quickly found a heady rhythm that threatened to paralyze me. His eyes stayed trained on mine the whole time.

I'd never done that before, looked someone right in the eye as he moved inside me. It was the most vulnerable, intimate thing I'd ever done, and I knew in my heart that it was a first for Jimmy, too.

I searched his gaze, basking in the wonder of it and giving him a soft smile until his tempo increased and I had to tip my head back with a moan. He chuckled in his throat, a deep rumbling sound, before dipping his head to kiss me. He began to move even faster, creating a sweet friction and turning the fairy lights above us into hazy stars. I bit my lip and dug my fingers into his firm ass, driving him harder until I was moaning a sweet song.

He joined me, groaning into my hair and finally letting out a strangled gasp as he shuddered inside me. I felt it all as he emptied a part of himself into me. His muscles were taut as he rode out the wave. I pressed my heel into his back, brushing my teeth against his shoulder as he finished.

And then we both turned to overstretched elastic, our limbs losing all power. I flopped my arms wide and became a limp starfish on the bed. Jimmy rested his weight on me, his quivering arms doing little to hold himself up. I didn't care; I loved my new blanket and was happy to wrap myself within it for the rest of eternity.

Jimmy's lips pressed against my ear and softly mumbled, "I like loving you."

I snickered. "I like loving you, too."

He rolled off me with a sweet, sleepy smile, pulling me against him and wrapping his arms around me. His knees tucked up behind mine, and he kissed my shoulder while I closed my eyes and drifted away to a place where dreams did come true and happiness wasn't a myth.

THIRTY-TWO

JIMMY

I stirred, my nose twitching as I was pulled out of dreamland. The first thing to register was a citrus fragrance. I buried my face in a head of luscious locks and inhaled deeply, a languid smile forming on my lips. My other senses quickly awakened. I became aware of Nessa's warm, smooth back nestled against my naked torso. Skin-on-skin—the best feeling in the world. I brushed my lips over her shoulder. She didn't even move. I skimmed my fingers up her naked thigh with a playful grin. She let out a little murmur in her sleep, and I was so damn tempted to wake her. My eager cock told me I was up for another round.

Rising onto my elbow, I gazed at her moonlit face. Her dark eyelashes rested on her milky white skin, and she almost looked like she was smiling.

I wanted to brush my knuckles down her face and press my lips into the crook of her neck, but I didn't dare. She looked too peaceful to disturb...and it wasn't like I was going anywhere, right?

My stomach clenched.

I fell back onto the pillow with wide eyes and gazed up at the unlit fairy lights. I was spent after our night together. I'd never made myself that vulnerable with anyone before. It was damn intimidating, and I understood why my father always shied away from it. It was so much easier to screw them with your eyes closed and walk out the door. Vulnerability felt like a weakness, yet it took so much courage and strength to be vulnerable with someone. It was a weird contradiction.

A deep sadness I didn't understand stirred in my chest as I thought about my old man. I wondered how many hotel rooms and women's bedrooms he'd snuck out of over the years. I'd tried to compete with him for so long, to turn into him, and now I lay next to a girl who actually loved me in spite of who I'd been.

It was humbling, and I didn't deserve it.

I was still so capable of fucking up this whole thing.

It scared me that I might not be the man she needed. Whether I liked it or not, I was my father's son. I'd done everything I could to be like him. I'd won his pride and approval—his attention. I'd followed his advice to the letter.

An old, familiar fear curled in my belly, and the urge to hold on to all I'd ever known raced through my limbs. It took me back to the morning after my first night with Nessa. All the doubts and phobias landed on me with a force I hadn't reckoned on.

I held my breath, trying to rein in my galloping heart. A corrosive unease tugged at my body, and I rolled to the edge of the bed, reaching for my jeans and a quick escape.

I had no idea what the hell was wrong with me. Five minutes earlier, I'd been relishing the bliss of sleeping naked beside a woman I loved, but when had fear ever played fair? It gripped me in an iron hold and reminded me of all the things I couldn't be...all the shitstorms I was capable of creating.

I didn't bother with my boxers, just slipped my jeans over my bare ass and crept for the door. I needed some air, a second to breathe and pull myself together. The idea of hurting Nessa again killed me. I promised I wouldn't let her go. I couldn't lose this fight, but how did I win when I felt so incapable?

I burst out into the crisp night air and sucked in two big lungfuls. Bracing my hands against my knees, I gazed down at the thick grass beneath me, cool and damp on my bare toes. Standing tall, I scrubbed a hand over my face and stared up at the night sky. It was crystal clear with a bright moon. I gazed at the round orb, silently looking for a simple way out of my panic attack. I loved Nessa. What the fuck was I so afraid of?

I wanted to be with her. To love her...to be everything I hadn't been before.

Maybe that was it.

I didn't know what I was doing. I didn't know if I had it in me to stay the course.

The phone in my back pocket buzzed. With a frown, I yanked it free and glanced at the screen.

Dad.

That built-in joy at seeing his number skimmed through me until I saw the time—12:36...in the fucking morning.

I touched the screen and lifted it to my ear. The first thing I heard was blaring music in the background. Laughter and static conversation filtered into the phone, and Dad had to shout above it all.

"Hey, Jimmy boy!"

He was already drunk.

I cringed. "Hey, Dad. What's up?"

"Where are you, man? I'm in town. I texted you two hours ago. You have to come join us."

My phone had been on silent all evening. Thank God. I curled my toes into the moist lawn. "Who's 'us'?"

Dad chuckled. "Just some pretty eye-candy I picked up at the airport."

Usually, I'd ask for directions and run for a good time, but all I could think about was the night after I'd first slept with Nessa. I grimaced, remembering how hard I'd fought for a high that never hit me. A spurt of disgusted anger fired through my belly...and then a broad smile grew on my lips. I tipped my head back with relief.

I had absolutely no desire to go out, get trashed, and have sex with a complete stranger. I wasn't a lost cause after all. The thought made me chuckle.

"I can't tonight, Dad. I'm done."

There was a confused pause. "You're done? What does that mean?"

"I can't party with you anymore." My relief was soaked in sadness as I licked my lower lip and said aloud a truth we both knew was inevitable. "I know that means your calls will dry up and we'll drift apart like you and Troy, but I've finally come to realize that he's been right all along. Your life lessons suck."

He didn't reply right away. There were a few mumbled words and then a flurry of movement. The music in the background died down, muffled by what I assumed was a door. Dad huffed out a breath and said, "Where the hell is this coming from?"

I squeezed my eyes shut. "How could you lead me so far astray? Love *is* real, Dad, and it doesn't have to drag you down or destroy you."

"Love is *not* real," Dad barked. "It will only get you burned."

"No, acting like a selfish man-whore gets you burned."

"You don't know what you're saying." Dad swore under his breath. I could sense that he was pacing. "You're a kid! You don't know what it's like to have your heart ripped out of your chest. I am telling you, the lessons I've spent so long trying to teach you will keep you safe and protected."

His venom was thick, reminding me of the time he fell apart—his blubbering-mess moment that scared me down this twisted path in the first place. A path that nearly made me lose Nessa.

I held my breath then let out a slow sigh. "I've found a girl who puts all your theories to shame. She was right in front of me this whole time, building me up, making me a man...and I nearly lost her because of the bullshit you've been feeding me."

Dad scoffed. "It wasn't bullshit, it was pure gold. You know my motto: Live free, die happy. You'll regret tying yourself down. They grow old, they get crabby and demanding. They become people you never thought they could be. Don't give them a reason to expect anything from you. You have your fun and you cut loose. It's the safest bet."

He made it sound so easy. Freedom like no other, but...

"I don't want safe anymore. I want *real*. I don't care if it gets hard. I'm never going back to your way."

"Give it a few years, Jimmy boy, and you'll see what I'm talking about. You'll change your mind."

"No, I won't." I shook my head, my earlier fears evaporating. They flew out of me like bats into the night, and the knot in my stomach came loose. I sucked in a breath and said with a smile, "My mind is set. I may be a fuck-up, but I am *not* ruining this.

I'm never losing her again."

There was a long pause, like Dad couldn't wrap his brain around what I was saying. Finally, he grumbled, "You're not sounding like my son anymore."

"I'll always be your son, but that doesn't mean I have to turn out like you."

I hung up before any more could be said. My hands were shaking, and I nearly dropped the phone as I tried to shove it back into my pocket. I'd never stood up to him before. His word had always been truth. It was weird letting him go, but I also felt like I'd grown my own set of wings.

I didn't need to stand at the end of the driveway looking for his car. I didn't need to hang off his every word, worried that I'd lose him like Troy did.

My father could come or go—I no longer gave a shit. The only person I cared about more than anything was lying upstairs, alone in her bed…but not for long.

With a relaxed smile, I sniffed in the cool night air and ambled back to the guest house. My resolve was set; my fear had finally gone. I was in this all the way. No more running at first sight of the sun.

THIRTY-THREE

NESSA

I breathed in through my nose and let out a pleasant moan. I hadn't opened my eyes, but I could sense the room was filling with early morning light. My muscles were languid after my night with Jimmy. We'd made soft, sleepy love sometime in the early hours, and I felt like I'd been soaking in a hot tub all night. My body was relaxed and limbless. It was so good it almost felt like a dream.

Maybe it was.

My tummy muscles contracted at the thought. Would Jimmy be there when I opened my eyes? I was too afraid to look, too afraid to reach across the bed and see.

I squeezed my eyes tight and strained for noises but couldn't hear anything.

My heart sank. I should have known better than to fall asleep next to Jimmy Baker.

Would I ever learn?

Pulling in a breath, I crept my eyes open and nervously looked to the other pillow...and found a beautiful set of blue orbs smiling back at me.

My heart did a double-take.

He was still there.

His grin was sappy and sweet as he murmured, "Good morning."

He had earplugs in and his phone rested in the palm of his hand. I gave him a tentative smile and reached for the bud in his ear. He shifted closer to me, placing his hand on my hip and giving me a shy grin.

I picked up the tune and knew immediately that he was listening to "Sight of the Sun" by Fun.

My throat swelled, my eyes filling with instant tears. He couldn't mean those lyrics. I wasn't worth them.

His smile grew a little wider as he brushed a finger down my hairline and tucked a long lock behind my ear. He ran his knuckles under my chin and rubbed his thumb over my lips.

I reached for his shoulder, tracing the lines of his tattoo while I listened to the song. I could tell by the look on his face that he meant what he was listening to.

He wasn't running scared anymore...and he didn't want me to, either.

The sentiment was sweet, but did he really understand what he was saying? I wanted to believe it. The idea of us together forever filled me with a ravenous yearning, but how could I tie a guy like Jimmy down? He was a superstar and I was...one-handed Nessa.

My heart hiccupped and spasmed as I gazed at his beautiful face, indecision warring within me. Could we honestly do this?

I wasn't sure.

Rising on my elbow, I pressed my bare chest against his body and slid my tongue over his lips. He palmed my naked back, slowly gliding up to my neck as we deepened the kiss. The song continued to play in our ears as we made out in the early morning sunlight. My eyes remained open as I nestled myself on top of him and brushed the tip of my nose against his. He smiled at me, reaching for my lips and sending sparkles skittering down my spine.

Looking into the future terrified me, so all I could do was take our precious now and make it beautiful.

THIRTY-FOUR

JIMMY

We spent the weekend in bed.

All the Torrence studios were fully booked for recording, so Marcus had told us to take the weekend off. Perfect timing.

That's why I'd planned the date for Friday night.

I'd texted Ralphie and told him to keep the guys away from the guest house. I didn't want anything disturbing our utopia. Thankfully, Ralphie wasn't the questioning type (or maybe he'd just figured it out), so we had the place to ourselves.

Most of the time was used up exploring each

other's bodies and then sleeping, but we did stay up until two one morning watching *The Tonight Show* and some stand-up comedy clips on YouTube. With Nessa tucked under my arm, we ate popcorn and laughed our heads off, the sheets tangled around our legs and the fairy lights twinkling above us. It was the furthest thing from a noisy nightclub you could get...and I'd never felt so contented.

On Monday morning, I forced my ass out of bed and took a quick shower while Nessa slept. Flick and I had stuff to do that morning, and the afternoon was going to be spent at the recording studio. I was looking forward to it, but Nessa wouldn't be there...and that weighed me down. Chaos without her wasn't right, and it gutted me that she was still resisting treatment and refusing to find a place for herself among us.

I poured some milk over the protein powder and gave it a vigorous stir. I wasn't in the mood for breakfast, but I did want to get started on Nessa's smoothie. She'd bitch that she could do it on her own, but I'd simply argue that a guy had a right to make his girl a smoothie. It didn't have anything to do with her hand.

Her hand.

My gut twisted again.

Snatching the remote, I pressed 'play,' not even caring what would come out of the speakers. I was getting used to Nessa's girly rocker shit; in fact, I kind of liked it. Not that I'd ever admit that to her. "Rock N Roll" by Avril Lavigne slammed through the sound system. It was one of Nessa's favorite songs. I did a little spin on my heel then slid to the cupboard.

I set the blender on the counter and was about to reach for a banana when Nessa came skipping down the stairs in nothing but her skintight jeans with the rips in the thighs and a purple bra with lime-green edging. My mouth filled with saliva as I traced the curve of her pert breasts and traveled the planes of her flat stomach. She was one sexy chick.

The tattoo sprinkled across her hip rose just above the waistband of her jeans, and I wanted to run my tongue over it again. It'd become one of my favorite spots on her body.

"Do you know where my Rock T-shirt is?" She made the rock 'n' roll symbol with her hand and I shook my head, still transfixed by the slender curves of her body.

She tipped her head to the side and rested her hand on one hip and her stump on the other. Her eyes narrowed as a cute little smile formed on her lips.

"If you did know where the T-shirt was, would you tell me?"

I shook my head. "No."

She laughed and looked up to the ceiling. Her dark locks fell from her shoulders and her long neck looked too edible to ignore. "You are nothing but trouble." She pointed at me with a playful smirk.

"Some-some-how…" I started singing along with the song and moved around the counter, shuffling across the tiles as I performed for her.

She laughed then took her turn, singing the build-up to the chorus while dancing down the stairs and pointing at me. Her hypnotic hips begged to be captured, but I stopped at the base of the stairs and let her walk down the last two, throwing my head back and singing with her as the chorus kicked in. We shouted out the lyrics, banging our heads in time with the beat and meaning every word coming out of our mouths. Nessa's hair flicked back over her head as she raised her arm and perfect middle finger to the sky.

I laughed, snatching her hips and yanking her into my arms. She wrapped her legs around my waist and we finished off the chorus, our lips drawing ever closer with each beat.

She breathed the word "Hey" into my mouth, and then followed it up with a tongue chaser. She tasted sweet, her soft tongue dancing with mine as the music blared around us. I squeezed her ass then glided my hand up her back. Her skin was smooth beneath my fingertips, sending rocket fire down to my jeans.

I could have taken her right there on the stairs, and I would have, too, if Flick hadn't burst in the front door and shouted, "Oh, you guys are sleeping together now? That's gross!"

I ignored him, thrusting my tongue into Nessa's mouth and deepening the kiss. She moaned against me, sucking my lower lip before pulling away.

"Hello! Earth to gross people! Shit to get done today!" Flick kept yelling at us, but all I could see was Nessa gazing down at me, and all I could hear was the music swirling around us. Her brown eyes sparkled with playfulness while her fingers threaded through my hair. Damn, she loved me so fucking much.

I smiled back at her, drinking in the look in her eyes, deep down knowing I'd never really deserve it. I was one lucky son of a bitch.

"Yeah, shit's still not getting done!" Flick shouted again, his voice ringing clear as the music died away and Avril's voice filled the air. I mouthed the lyrics to Nessa while her smile grew even wider. As the beat kicked in again, she stretched her hand behind her back and from the disgusted snort Flick made, I'm pretty sure she'd raised her middle finger right at him.

I started laughing and murmured, "You are so freaking hot." She swallowed my words with her lips and tongue.

Flick huffed and yelled, "I'll wait in the car!" before slamming out of the house.

Nessa stayed wrapped around me, kissing me with unchecked passion until the song faded to a finish. If I could have put the song on permanent repeat, I would have, but Flick started honking the horn, and I'd never hear the end of it if I didn't go.

I squeezed her very fine ass then lowered her to the floor and kissed the tip of her nose. "See you tonight."

"I'll be here." She smiled big, but it didn't reach her eyes.

I tried to pretend I hadn't seen that slight look of

despair and uncertainty. I didn't want to end a make-out that epic on a downer.

Walking to the door, I threw on my jacket and slid my wallet and phone into the back pockets of my jeans. Nessa was watching me, I could feel it, so I paused at the door, gripping the edge of the wood and looking back at her.

"Why have we never done a cover of that song?"

She crossed her arms and shrugged. "There wasn't a you and me before."

I smiled at her. "There's always been a you and me, baby...and there always will be."

My words threw her—I could tell by the blush in her cheeks and the way she dipped her head and tucked some invisible strands behind her ears. I liked the way I could catch her so easily.

I winked at her and walked out of the house with a soft chuckle. Flick assaulted the horn again, cutting off the sound. I glared at him as I slipped into the car. He just thumped me in the arm and laughed.

"You dog! I knew there was something up between you two." He reversed out of the parking spot and shot down the driveway. "Is that why she took off in the first place?"

I winced. "Shut up, man." I had no idea how long it'd take me to get over the guilt of that. She'd lost her hand because of me. I'd probably always blame myself.

"Well, I'm glad you finally got your shit together." Flick nodded, checking the road before pulling out. The gate rumbled closed behind us. "I like the idea of you two."

"You didn't seem too keen in the guest house."

"Come on, man." Flick made a face. "Ness is like my sister. Seeing her shirtless with your tongue down her throat was disgusting, but that doesn't mean I don't think you guys are a good fit, you know."

"Yeah." I snickered, pressing my fingers into the top of the window frame and gazing at the evenly spaced houses. "I don't know if I deserve her."

Flick glanced at me but didn't say anything.

I let out a sigh and scrubbed a hand over my face. "I've never woken up beside a girl before and stayed. I mean, this weekend has been epic, and I want to stay that way forever. I'm so determined, but…"

"But what?"

"I'm still my father's son. What if I can't do it? What if I screw up again? She's not playing with Chaos anymore, and I don't know if she'll agree to come on the tour. With her not around, I'm worried I'll…" I shook my head, not wanting to admit how much of a man-whore I could be. I'd never had to deny any girl anything. They fell all over me, and I pretty much caught them all. They'd be screaming my name at concerts and trying to dance with me at the after-parties. I'd have my trail of groupies telling me they loved me as they lifted their shirts and asked me to sign their breasts. It was hard to ignore that kind of shit.

Sure, the idea wasn't as appealing as it had been

before, and even though I'd grimaced at my dad's invitation, that didn't mean temptation wouldn't flare up and bite me in the ass again. Without Nessa there to ground me...

"Dude, being someone's son isn't a choice, but how you act is. Make a decision, every day, to be the person you want to be, and if that's a guy who's committed to his girl, then be that guy. She doesn't have to be lying next to you for you to make that decision."

So simple, so easy...not!

"Besides, you're whipped now." Flick snickered. "It's not like it's going to be that hard."

I shot him a sharp frown and grunted.

Flick's eyebrows rose. "Don't tell me you're not. You're watching YouTube clips on how to braid hair."

"How the fuck do you know that?" My eyes bulged.

"I borrowed your laptop the other day." He smirked. "The page was still up." He started laughing at me like I'd tucked my manhood away for the rest of my life.

I punched him in the arm and he just laughed harder.

Shaking my head, I trained my gaze out the windshield, my jaw working to the side as I tried to dodge my embarrassment.

Flick's laughter died away, and when we pulled to a stop at the intersection, he looked over at me.

"It's going to be all right, man."

"Yeah." I sighed. "I just want her there with us."

"Me too," Flick muttered, running his thumb over his lower lip. "But how? I mean, she can't learn to replay in time for the tour, and Jace is fan-fucking-tastic. We can't lose him just so Ness can come back in."

"But she's the original," I snapped. "She's the one who deserves to be there."

"Maybe so, but she's not. She won't even talk to an OT. She's not moving past her injury, and we can't jeopardize our contract with Torrence again. We've worked too hard, man." There was a lick of fear in his eyes. "Don't even think about trying to propose a delay when we meet with Marcus today. The guy's only got so much patience."

I glanced away from him. "But she needs more time," I muttered.

Flick gave me a droll look then pulled through the intersection. "Exactly. She needs time, which means she won't be ready for this tour, but she might for the next."

I ran a hand through my hair—my fingers were shaking. I didn't want to do anything without Nessa. "I hate the idea of leaving her behind."

"Then bring her along as your number one fan." Flick winked at me, but I couldn't crack a smile.

Like Nessa would ever agree to that. It would kill her to travel the country with us, sitting backstage while we went out to perform. I wouldn't ask that of her, which left me with only one choice...I'd have to leave her behind and just hope like hell I could stay the man she needed me to be while I was away.

THIRTY-FIVE

NESSA

Watching Jimmy walk out the door after our weekend of hot sex and serious bonding hurt real bad. He'd unpacked his bag on Sunday afternoon, and I smiled every time I relived him shoving his clothes into the two bottom drawers of my dresser. I wanted to stay wrapped in our bubble of blissful unawareness, but life wouldn't let me. Jimmy and Flick were off to meet with Marcus to discuss tour details.

The big tour.

Ugh!

The guys would be gone for three months,

traveling the country and performing night after night. The tour was starting in LA—three back-to-back concerts. Marketing figured the first night would be a guaranteed sell-out...and I wouldn't be there.

Jace would be in my place, banging them sticks and making the crowd wild with his kick-ass beats. Sure, I'd be invited backstage, but I wanted to be *on* the stage, pumped high with adrenaline as the music swelled around me and took over my senses. I loved performing, hearing a crowd chant or sing along. Having the blood thrum through my veins as cheers and applause followed a song. It was a rush I wasn't ready to live without for the rest of my life.

I gazed down at my stump, brushing my fingers over the scar. I didn't know how to be a drummer again. I didn't know how I was going to move past the safety of the guest house and get on with my life. Before the accident, even in spite of the Jimmy bullshit, I wanted to spend my days playing, writing songs and entertaining people, but that had all been taken away, and I wasn't sure how to pull myself out of that dark and sinking dungeon.

"Hold me," I whispered. At the time I'd sung that song, I'd been thinking about Jimmy's arms around me as he carried me up the stairs while I cried and snotted all over him.

But Flick had said that maybe it meant I wanted help.

I looked at my phone on the kitchen counter. Maybe Jimmy wasn't the only person who could help me. I unlocked my screen and found Jace's number. Part of me didn't want to text him. He was still the guy who had replaced me, and what little pride I had left wanted to thump him one, but...I sighed and started texting.

Can I come over?

Jace replied in less than a minute. I smiled and called Ralphie, asking for a ride.

Less than an hour later, we pulled up to a neat L-shaped home in Claremont. The walls were olive green with a dark-brown tiled roof. Deciduous plants grew in the garden, and spattering the barked area were a few flat stones that created a rickety pathway to the door.

I held my left arm against my stomach as I followed Ralphie. Nerves were wreaking havoc on my insides, burning through my guts and making me ill. I had no idea why. Maybe it was because every time I dared to venture away from the guest house, things turned to total shit. I cringed as memories from my studio debacle and then the epic fail of my dinner date with Jimmy skittered through my mind.

Ralphie rang the doorbell and we waited. There was a quick shuffling of feet and then the door swung open.

"Hey, guys." Jace grinned at us. His broad shoulders filled up most of the doorframe. I looked up at him as he ushered us inside. He just winked at me and led us through an archway and into a living area where a man sat in a wheelchair.

He had dark eyes just like Jace's and those pouty lips, as well. The thing that made him so significantly different from his son was the lack of hair on his head...and his limbless lower half.

"Well, Jace, you didn't tell me she was so pretty." His booming voice and bright smile jolted me. For some reason, I expected the man to be quiet, reserved...slightly sad. He was legless! But he sat there gazing up me like it was the most normal thing in the world.

"Don't be a flirt, Dad. She's young enough to be your daughter." Jace rolled his eyes and walked out of the room.

His dad chuckled. "Nothing wrong with admiring the beauty of God's creation." His wink made my lips twitch with a smile.

"Hi, Mr. Tolson." I stepped forward and extended my hand.

"Cut the mister crap and call me Phil." He chuckled, taking my hand and giving it a firm shake. He shook Ralphie's hand then indicated for us to take a seat on the umber-colored three-seater adjacent to him.

Jace returned with a tray of drinks, placing them on the mahogany coffee table then passing them around. I grabbed my icy lemonade but couldn't take a drink. My eyes kept darting to Phil's legs and the way his gray trousers were tucked beneath his stumps. His legs had been amputated mid-thigh on both sides. I wondered how he managed every morning. All the simple, everyday things like going to the bathroom and getting his own breakfast had to be challenging.

Ralphie spoke over my head, keeping up polite conversation while I stared at the man. Eventually, he cut his answer to Ralphie's question short and brought my gawking to an end.

"You want to ask me something?" His dark eyes studied me, his knowing gaze making me look to my lap.

I sat up straight and placed my glass down, nearly spilling it as I tried to land it on the sandstone coaster. I shook my head with a tight, bashful smile. "No, sorry. I didn't mean to stare."

He shrugged. "You get used to it. People aren't trying to be rude. They're just naturally curious about things they don't understand. It's the way we've been designed."

I swallowed when he reached under one of his stumps and adjusted it in the chair. I ran my gaze up his arms, noting the strength in his biceps and shoulders. I rubbed my stump, then squished it against my belly and covered it with my right arm.

"You don't need to hide. What's happened, although tragic, is the truth, and no matter how much you don't want it to be, that reality is not going to change."

My lips started to tremble.

"It took me a long time to figure that out. I kept going to bed each night and praying I'd wake up with limbs in the morning. A new day would dawn, and I'd throw back the sheet and find two stumps. I'd slump into depression before the day had even begun. All I wanted to do was live in my bedroom and shut out the world."

My heart beat wildly as I gazed up at him. He understood.

Phil smiled at me, resting his elbows on the arms of the chair and leaning toward me. "The thing was, I was trying to fix something I couldn't control when I should have been trying to master the things I had total control over."

"What can you control?" I whispered.

His eyes crinkled at the edges. "My perspective. You see, I was focusing on all the things I couldn't do and all the things I'd lost, forgetting about everything that still awaited me. I'd been a firefighter, saving people's lives and leading a team of men. Then I was turned into this pathetic excuse...half a man." He snickered and shook his head with a pensive smile. "It wasn't until my wife keeled over in the kitchen one day that I snapped out of it." A slow smile grew on his face as he retold the story. "The kids were at school. I was wallowing in my bed. She shouted out my name then promptly fainted. I heard her thump to the floor, and my heart nearly fell out of my chest. I didn't even think, I just acted. Dragged my sorry ass out of bed and hauled myself through the house until I reached her. I'm not saying I saved her life. It didn't need saving—that woman has no stomach for blood. She'd sliced her finger pretty good, though." He shook his head, a fine sheen forming over his eyes. "In that split-second, when I thought I'd lost her, the debilitating fear as I dragged myself to the kitchen, then that overwhelming relief when I knew she was going to be okay... It made me realize I was wasting away and missing everything. After that, I determined to figure a way to start living again."

I blinked at the stinging sensation in my eyes. "But it's not the same."

"No. It will never be the same." He nodded, looking calm and peaceful in spite of that fact. "I just hate to think you'd miss out on something amazing because you thought you couldn't. Don't let the tragedy win. You are bigger and braver than that. I mean, look at you, you're a rock star."

I snorted. "I thought I could be."

He leaned forward, his eyes sparkling as he said, "You *will* be one. Maybe not like what you were before, but you are the only thing that can kill your passion. If you want to keep it alive, then you do it. You fight. You hold on and you don't give in. All I ever wanted was to take care of the people I love, and I don't need legs to do that...just like you don't need two hands to play."

It was a great speech and I guess I found it inspiring, but it wasn't enough to kill the doubt within me. The idea that I'd never be good enough still festered in the back of my mind. Learning to play again would be damn hard, and although I was opening up to the idea of trying, I couldn't imagine ever being good enough to play on a stage.

Meeting with Jace's father helped, though. It made me realize that I couldn't take any of this for granted and I couldn't keep shutting out the world or I'd miss everything. The most important thing I could do was live in the now and enjoy every second of Jimmy's company before he left me to tour the country.

THIRTY-SIX

JIMMY

The first part of the meeting with Marcus and the Torrence execs went well. The tour was all set, and it was predicted that we'd have sell-out crowds in most of the big cities. The marketing team was gearing up and tickets would go on sale within a few weeks. I was happy to go along with it all until they started talking about reshooting Chaos shots without Nessa in them.

I shook my head before they'd even finished talking.

"She's part of it."

"Unless she's going on the tour, she's really

not." The marketing lady with her perfectly styled hair and French-manicured nails gave me a plastic, unyielding smile.

I scowled back at her. "She's part of Chaos. She's written half the songs on the album! You take as many pictures of Jace as you want and you Photoshop him in or do whatever the hell you do, but you are not removing Nessa from this band."

Marcus cleared his throat, looking slightly nervous as he shuffled in his seat and leaned across to me. "If she's not performing with you guys, we can't promote her on the posters," he whispered. "I hate it just as much as you, but—"

"No." I shook my head with a cynical laugh. "I don't actually think you *do* hate it as much as I do, because you weren't there when we started, and you haven't played beside her for the last five years. She has always had my back, and she will always be part of Chaos."

"Which is why she took off and got us all into this situation?" the woman murmured.

I shot out of my seat, my nostrils flaring as I got ready to stalk around the table. "You listen to me, you—"

"Okay." Marcus stood up with a friendly chuckle, slapping me on the back and squeezing my shoulder before I did something stupid. "It's all cool. I'll hook up a photoshoot for these guys in a couple of weeks. They're pretty busy with recording stuff right now, so maybe by the end of the month?"

Miss Marketing tore her icy gaze away from

mine to check her calendar. "We need them before tickets go up for sale. Make sure they're with the graphics department before the end of the month."

"Done." Marcus grinned.

I opened my mouth to protest, but Flick kicked me in the shin before I could. I gave him a death glare, which he ignored, rising from his seat and thanking the executives as we left the room. I stormed into the hallway, my blood pumping. The urge to hit something thrummed through my veins.

"Keep it together, man," Flick sing-songed when he caught up to me.

He knew what I was like. In middle school, I'd managed to break a chair against the wall when a teacher treated me unfairly. The jackass wouldn't hear me out, and I'd lost it. I'd lost it a lot back then...until Troy bought me a guitar. I channeled everything into the instrument, spent my summer before high school mastering it as best I could, and then I met Nessa. At the time, I'd been completely unaware of how she'd made me who I was. It wasn't until she suddenly hadn't been there that it dawned on me.

That was why she had to be a part of it.

Bile gurgled in my stomach as I imagined enduring a photoshoot without her. She couldn't be cut from this band. It wasn't right!

I stormed past reception, ignoring the secretary's quizzical stares. There'd no doubt be some hot gossip flying through the Torrence hallways over the next couple of weeks. I punched the down button on the elevator and winced.

Marcus caught up to us, jumping in just before the doors closed. I couldn't look at him, so I kept my eyes trained on the silver control panel as we descended two flights to the recording studio.

"I know this sucks," Marcus muttered, "but we just have to make the best of it."

"There is no best of it," I retorted. "Without her, the band isn't whole. I don't give a fuck that we have a new drummer who kicks ass. He will never be Nessa!" I shouted as the elevator doors pinged open.

The dark-haired hottie spun at the sound of her name, her eyebrow peaking when she saw me. I stopped short, the thick air in my lungs whooshing out as I glimpsed her sweet smile.

"Hey." She grinned at me then lifted her chin in greeting to Flick and Marcus.

"What are you doing here?" Flick flung his arm over her shoulder before fist-bumping Ralphie and Jace.

"I was hanging out with Ralphie and thought I'd come down and check you guys out." Her eyes landed on me again, and she gave me a sexy wink.

She looked lighter somehow, and it set something loose in my chest. I ambled over to her, running my hand down her back and giving her butt a light tap.

She threw me a warning look, her brown eyes rounding. We'd already talked about keeping our relationship within the original band only. We weren't too keen on anything going public, so I slid past her, pretending her sweet citrus scent didn't have any kind of effect on me.

"It's nice to see you." Marcus kissed her cheek and opened the door for us.

I shot him a *keep your mouth shut* look over the top of her head, and he gave me a quick nod. We all trailed into the studio, even Nessa. She took a seat on a stool in the corner, obviously wanting to hang out while we tuned and got ready. I kept glancing at her, hoping she wouldn't do a runner like last time.

Her relaxed expression told me she wouldn't, so I started to chill, pulling the guitar strap over my head before tuning up. Damn, it was good to have her around. Just her presence in the studio was enough to lighten my mood. I didn't know how I was going to tell her about reshooting the publicity stuff. The execs had been spinning the story that Nessa was still in recovery but would hopefully join the band soon. They had obviously changed their minds and were gearing up to launch Jace onto the world, something I knew would send the chicks wild. It was going to work out great for Torrence, which was why they probably didn't give a shit when I kicked up such a fuss about Nessa being removed. As long as they still got a kick-ass band that could bring them in some big bucks, they were happy.

I strummed my guitar and looked at Ralphie, who did the same. We messed around for a minute, making sure we were in tune, and then Flick came in with his guitar, too.

"I'm ready to go when you are, guys," Garrett

spoke into the room.

I turned with a nod, giving Nessa a tight smile as she rose to leave. My guts sank when she jumped down from the stool and shuffled for the door.

"Just a sec." Marcus held up his finger while reading a text on his phone. "Jimmy, can I have a quick word?" He tipped his head toward the door. "The rest of you just hang tight, this will only take a minute."

Nessa gave me a curious look as I walked for the door. I just shrugged and eased out of the room.

Marcus walked backward until we were hovering by the double doors that led to the elevators. It was a darker space with the overhead lights not reaching that far, but it wasn't dark enough to hide Marcus's reluctant frown.

"What?" I snapped. "Is exec pissed at my little outburst? They're going to fucking make me apologize, aren't they?"

Jace started kicking around on the drums. I looked through the glass and watched Nessa standing nearby. She said something to Flick and he smiled, coming in with a guitar riff that I recognized but couldn't quite place. Nessa then pointed at Ralphie, who brought in the bass line. She spun with a laugh and grabbed the mic off the stand to sing "Come On, Let's Go."

Her hips swayed as she moved her body, lighting up the studio space like a freaking firework.

My lips parted, my eyes transfixed as she threw

her inhibitions to the wind and owned the floor.

"Listen, I just..." Marcus's words trailed off as he noted my expression. His head turned toward the studio and he sucked in his breath.

Nessa had the most adorable smirk on her face as she sang, her body still moving to the beat. She was wearing a white tank that showed off the top of her cute little bra, and when she dipped forward then threw her hair back, I swear my heart forgot how to beat. Her hair spun around her as she danced out Flick's solo. She strutted around him, laughing and getting into the music before skipping over to Ralphie.

"Are you seeing what I'm seeing?" Marcus sounded as mesmerized as I was.

"Holy shit, yeah."

We both chuckled like two goofy idiots. "I think we just found a place for our girl."

I looked down at Marcus, my grin wide and giddy. I couldn't wait to tell Nessa that Chaos had a new lead singer. Damn, it was going to be fucking fantastic!

THIRTY-SEVEN

NESSA

"You want me to what?" I looked at Jimmy's goofy grin then across to Marcus who was bobbing his head like an excited monkey.

I hated to burst their little bubbles, but... "No way."

I crossed my arms, wishing I'd never touched that damn microphone. I'd just heard the music and couldn't resist. It was only me and the guys. It was safe, easy to be front and center because no one was watching me...at least I thought no one was watching me. I was used to hiding behind a drum kit. There was no way in hell I'd go up in front of a massive crowd, especially since my accident.

I pressed my arm against my stomach as Flick said, "Why not? You'd be awesome."

"Agreed." Ralphie raised his hand while Jace bobbed his head—another excited monkey.

The guys were all insane.

"No." I shook my head, not missing the disappointment cresting over Jimmy's expression. "I—I can't, you guys. I'm not a lead singer, I'm a drummer."

"But you *could* be a lead singer." Jimmy grinned at me. "You have an amazing voice, and you've been singing all this time, just not front and center."

"Exactly! *Not* front and center. I'm not like you. I can't woo a crowd."

"You wooed me." Jimmy raised his eyebrows.

I rolled my eyes. "You're different."

"How's he different?" Marcus pointed at him. My cheeks flushed pink. "I was completely enraptured. I couldn't take my eyes off you. You lit the room, sweetie, and you would be a huge asset. I mean, Jimmy brings the girls, but with you up front, we'd have a slew of guys drooling over Chaos."

Jimmy's brow dipped and he threw Marcus a sharp look that could have sliced his head off.

I pressed my lips together to hide my grin. "You don't have to worry," I said to him, "because I'm not doing it."

Marcus gave me a confused frown and glanced over his shoulder at Jimmy, whose expression had once again fallen to a look of searing disappointment. He stepped around our manager and stood in front of me. "Please," he whispered, his puppy-dog gaze trying to do a serious number on me.

I scoffed and stepped back from him, glancing around the room again. Garrett was even standing at the door with a keen grin.

"No! You guys, no! I'm not going on tour with you, and I'm not going up on a stage night after night so people can laugh and point at the one-handed freak show!"

Marcus gave me a sad smile. "That's not how they'll be seeing you."

"How the hell do you know?" I pointed my stump at him. "Look at me! I'm ridiculous!" My voice broke as I heard words I'd tried so hard to forget coming out of my own mouth.

Jace cleared his throat, catching my attention as he shuffled in his seat, looking a little hurt and offended. Guilt punched my chest inward and I closed my eyes, thinking about his dad.

"I'm—I'm sorry." I meant the words for him, but I actually said them to the whole room so all but Jace and Ralphie thought I was simply apologizing for not buying into their master plan.

Yes, not being part of Chaos anymore made it hard to breathe, but the idea of putting myself out there on a stage was too much to comprehend. I couldn't do it. I wouldn't...and so I walked out the door and made a beeline for the bathroom.

No one would get it. I barely understood it

myself...until I snapped the lock behind me on the bathroom door and spun to face the dreaded mirror. It was a massive piece of glass and impossible to hide from. It captured my gaze and held me steady, not letting go for even a second. Puffs of air shuddered out of my chest as I stared at my pale white complexion, and against my will, I was transported back to a different mirror in another time and place.

"Take that makeup off this instant!" Mama shouted at me, thrusting a damp cloth into my hands.

She stood behind me, gazing over my shoulder into the mirror. She seemed like a dragon, her lips pulled into a tight line that made deep wrinkles form around her lips. Her eyes were dark and fiery, her nostrils flaring.

I glared at the cloth in her hand then glanced at my reflection. My eyes were ringed with thick, black eyeliner, and my lashes were coated in mascara that was now running down my cheeks. My lips had been painted a deep grape color, but it had faded and now they just looked bruised.

I raised my chin and glared into the mirror. "No. I like wearing makeup."

Mama rolled her eyes and shook the cloth at me again. "Look at yourself! You're ridiculous! Traipsing around this town looking like some freak show." She snatched the leather collar around my neck and yanked it until it popped off. I winced and rubbed my skin while she threw it in the trash beside my desk. My throat grew thick with tears, but I was never going to let them fall...not in front of her.

"The sheriff found you on the outskirts of town trying to hitch a ride to who knows where. You have humiliated this family, Vanessa. Victor would never do something so stupid."

"That's because Victor doesn't have a life! He listens to Mozart and reads books the size of dictionaries for fun! I don't want to be like that. I want to go and party and dance and sing and have a good time."

"You are fourteen years old. I will not be letting you go out and turn into some party animal. Now take off that makeup."

"No!" I screamed the word right in her face.

Mama drew in a quick breath then grabbed the back of my head, clamping the cloth over my face and wiping away the makeup while I struggled and screamed. She was taller and stronger than me and her fingers were like iron, squeezing into my scalp to reduce my thrashing. Her nails left scratch marks in my skin and it hurt like hell, but I didn't stop fighting. She didn't either, until my face was pale, with faded black lines running down my cheeks.

She finally let me go, and I stood there snorting out my nose. I felt like I'd just been violated. She straightened her blouse and gave me a tight smile.

"That's better. Now, get changed. We're going down to the station so you can apologize to the sheriff for making him take time out of his day to drive you home." Mama walked to my closet and pulled out a dress. It was the pale-pink one with puffed sleeves and a frill around the hem. She'd made it for me to wear on Christmas Day, and I'd sat by the tree watching my siblings unwrap gifts and wanting to slit my wrists. "I want you to look your best now." She laid the dress on the end of my bed.

"No." I shook my head. "I'm not wearing that again, and I'm not apologizing. I didn't ask him to drive me back."

"Vanessa." Mama closed her eyes and drew in a slow breath. "I am your mother and you will do as I say. Now stop shaming this family and get yourself ready."

She clipped past me, flicking the door shut behind her. I crossed my arms and glared down at the pink monstrosity. There was no way in hell I was wearing that thing in public. She couldn't make me do it.

"You better be getting ready!" she called while bustling past my room.

I raised my middle finger at the closed door and stomped over to my stereo, finding the most appropriate song I could think of and blasting it. "One Day" by Simple Plan began to play, and I closed my eyes with a smile. Reaching for the volume, I cranked it up full bore until the music was blaring so loud the windows were vibrating.

It didn't take long for the door to swing open. My mother stood there like a raging bull, her shoulders tight as she stormed into the room and yanked my stereo off the desk. The plug came flying out of the wall and the music cut off, replaced with an ominous silence. Mama loomed over me, hugging the stereo to her side and giving me a warning look that made me want to drop to my knees.

"Is this really what you want to be? Some rebellious loser?"

"I just want to be me. Let me be me!" I shouted.

"If I do that, you'll never amount to anything. You're not good enough, Vanessa. I am trying to train that devil's heart out of you!"

"By making me wear frills," I pointed at the wretched dress, "and live a life that's suffocating me? I'd rather die than grow up to be like you!"

Her hand cracked across my cheek, hard and fast. My fingers shook as I brushed the back of them over the stinging pain. Mama had never hit me before. It hurt like a bitch.

"You do not speak to me that way." Her voice trembled.

I stepped back from her, my lip curling with disgust. Anger surged through me, and I snatched the dress off the end of the bed and started tearing at those damn frills. "I hate this thing! I hate this house! I don't want to be here anymore! You can't make me something I'm not!"

"Vanessa!" Mama screeched. "Stop it! Stop it this instant!"

She dropped my stereo and lunged for the dress, trying to save it before I ruined the whole thing. I'd only intended to rip off the frill, but when she started up the tug-of-war, I fought back like a zealot. A loud rip tore through the room, and we were both left clutching half a dress and puffing like crazed maniacs.

A quaking sob burst out of Mama's mouth as she snatched the other half from my hands and hugged it to her chest. "You make everything so difficult." She sucked in a shaky breath. "I don't know what to do with you anymore, but I'm done fighting." She crouched down and grabbed the stereo, wrapping the torn fabric *around it. "Now, I am going to fix this dress and you will wear it down to the station."*

I opened my mouth to protest, but she raised her finger and kept talking. "And you will stay in this room until you are ready to do as you are told!"

She slammed the door so hard I flinched, but then came the worst sound of all—the sliding of a metal key into the hole and the snapping of a lock.

She'd made me her prisoner.

I clenched my jaw and gently rubbed my tender cheek. I wanted to curl into a ball and cry like a baby, but instead I stood tall and pulled my shoulders back. She was going to try to bend my will. Like hell I was going to let her.

I spent three weeks in my room before Rosie showed up and rescued me. Mama reduced my meals to bread and water. She'd come past my door three times a day to take me to the bathroom and give me fresh food. She had the dress with her every single time and she'd say, "Are you ready?"

And I'd say, "Never."

I ran my fingers down the mirror as a sad frown floated over my expression. I'd never bonded with my mother. Victor was so sick as a baby that he took up all her time, and I was left to be quickly fed, then put back in my crib.

It's not like I needed to be close to her, but it would have been nice to be loved…accepted. As I stood in that bathroom reliving one of my worst memories, I couldn't help picturing my mother standing in a crowd and looking up at the stage.

I'd always felt safe behind my drum kit. Barricaded by metal and skins, I could set myself free, but I couldn't do that on center stage, because all I'd be able to see was her face glaring up at me and telling me I was ridiculous.

THIRTY-EIGHT

JIMMY

Nessa spent forever in that bathroom. It was really hard to play and record, not knowing what was going on, but Marcus promised me he'd stand post and eventually they returned. She looked pale and shaken, but her eyes weren't puffy from crying.

She stood behind Garrett while we finished up the session, and I chose not to say anything more. As soon as we got back to the house, I wrapped my arm around her and walked her up to our little oasis. I made love to her, taking my time and sending her over the edge until she fell into a sated sleep beside me.

I couldn't drift off that easily. Images of Nessa lighting up the stage danced through my brain, affecting my dreams and waking me multiple times throughout the night. How had I never seen it before? She'd always been tucked away behind that kit when her real place should have been standing beside me.

Opening my eyes, I ran my fingers through my hair and glanced at my girl. She was awake, staring at me with a sad smile.

I rolled over to face her, brushing my knuckles down her cheek. "What is it?"

She pursed her lips, gliding her hand over my chest and tracing the bass clef on my right pec. "I'm going to miss you when you leave."

I sighed. "So come with me."

She winced. "I can't."

"Not even to be my groupie?" I smirked at her unimpressed frown.

She shook her head. "I think it'll be too hard following you guys around. Plus, I don't want the press." She held up her stump. "I hate the idea of this being flashed all over the news."

I took her stump and kissed the end. "You're beautiful with or without your hand."

She softly chuckled, wriggling her arm free and tucking it behind her back.

"So, that's it? You're just not going to perform anymore?" I rose up on my elbow so I could look down at her. "Don't forget I know you. We may have only been sleeping together for a little bit, but you've been my best friend for five years. I can see you miss it."

She smiled at me, running her hand up my arm. "Which is why I'm going to meet with the OT this week and start learning how to play again."

My chest buzzed, but not with the same excitement that I thought it would. Now that I'd seen her sing, I didn't want her hiding behind a drum kit again.

"It's going to take time, though, and I'm only learning for myself...not to perform." Her lips dipped into a frown. "You guys have Jace now, and he's amazing."

I ran my finger down her hairline. "Sing up front with me."

She groaned and tried to roll away, but I boxed her in with my arms.

"You didn't see yourself yesterday. You were like a beacon and you belong on the stage with me. This could be so incredibly epic."

"No, Jimmy, it won't. I'm not..." Her face bunched as she cringed and bit the inside of her cheek.

"Not what?"

"I'm not..." She shook her head.

I wanted to probe for more, but her eyes started to glass over, and I didn't want to make her cry. Lifting myself up, I nestled between her legs while my elbows sank into the mattress.

I picked up a lock of her hair and rubbed it. "Well, maybe when you sing that duet with me at Cole and Ella's wedding, you'll get a feel for it.

You'll see how much a crowd adores you."

Her eyebrows flickered and she dug her fingers into my back. "I can't sing at the wedding."

My gaze shot to hers. "What? But the duet was your idea."

"I know, but that's when I thought I'd be singing it behind the kit. I'm not going to stand next to you on a stage."

I rolled off her, flopping onto my back with a frustrated sigh. "Then who the fuck's going to sing it with me?"

Her fingers crept up my stomach then flattened over my chest as she shuffled her naked body next to mine. Her leg came over my thigh, trying to distract me. I gave her a knowing scowl.

She grinned then dipped her head. "I guess we'll just drop that song off the playlist."

"But that was going to be our surprise for them."

"I know, but they don't know it's coming, so they won't be disappointed."

Her light caress tickled. I clamped my hand over her fingers.

My jaw worked to the side as I resisted the urge to mutter, "Well, I will be!"

"Come on, don't be mad at me. Please." Her sweet voice unraveled me, and I looked across at her, running my fingers over her forearm.

"I'm not mad, I just don't get it. You are beautiful and have the most amazing stage presence. I know you're passionate about music and performing, and I don't understand why you're not jumping at this chance."

"I'm not beautiful, Jimmy. I—"

"Excuse me?" She did not just say that.

I spun her over and grabbed both her wrists, pinning her arms above my head. "You're talking about *my* girl right now, and she is one hot specimen."

She grinned, but shook her head, so I kept going.

"She's got these amazing eyes the color of cinnamon and these beautiful pink lips that just make you want to kiss them all day long."

I hovered just above her face, my body going crazy as I resisted the urge to crush my mouth against her. She rose to kiss me, but I pulled back, gazing down at her. "You don't believe me, do you?"

"I don't care what you're saying right now, I just want you to kiss me." She strained her neck to reach me, but I sat back a little farther. With her arms pinned above her, she had no hope and let out a groan before glaring at me.

"You kiss me right now, Jimmy Baker."

I smirked, squashing her beneath me as I reached for my phone on the bedside table. She started to wriggle and squirm, sending my body into overdrive. I nearly plunged myself inside her but pulled back so I could make my point loud and clear.

With a grin, I pressed play and "She Is Beautiful" came through the little speaker. I loved playing that song. I loved the rhythm and the way my fingers felt on the strings. I loved shouting into the mic and banging my head to the beat. But I'd never in my life had so much fun performing that song...and I didn't even have a guitar in my hands.

Nessa giggled beneath me as I sang to her, but the sounds coming from her mouth soon changed as I touched my tongue against her skin, running it over her breasts then up her neck. I sucked her chin, and her sweet moan set my heart racing. As her leg wrapped around my thigh, I could no longer resist and thrust into her. She cried out and moved against me, hungry and eager. I met her beat for beat, the song surging around us as we crushed our lips together and lost ourselves.

I let go of her wrists so she could wrap her arms around me. The smooth skin of her handless arm ran up my back, digging into my muscles as I drove a little harder. She gasped and moaned beneath me, her sweet breath kissing my skin.

I puffed into her ear. "You are beautiful. You're my beautiful. My perfect."

She didn't say anything, just pressed her lips against my shoulder and clung to me. I needed her to believe the truth, but I had a sinking feeling she never would...which meant she'd never have the courage to stand on stage with me.

It was looking more and more likely that I'd have to accept the fact Nessa would not be joining us on the tour. My perfect solution hadn't even had time to blossom. I wanted to fight with every breath to convince her she was wrong, but there was only so far I could push her. I was scared if I fought too hard, I'd drive her away again.

THIRTY-NINE

NESSA

Ella and Cole's wedding was that weekend. Jimmy and I hadn't spoken again of the duet we'd added to the song list months ago. I still remembered coming up with the idea. The guys had all scoffed, saying it wasn't our kind of music, but I'd told them to stick it. It was the perfect song for Ella and Cole, and we were doing it. Jimmy had just smiled and said, "I'll sing it with you, Ness."

I'd been so happy about it back then, so honored that they'd ask us to play at the reception...but now I wasn't even sure if I wanted to go.

Tucking a lock of hair behind my ear, I followed

Jace up the path to his front door.

"Thanks for coming again," he said over his shoulder. "When Mom found out she'd missed you last time, she wouldn't let it go. She's been bugging me every day since to get you back here."

"That's okay." I smiled. "I kind of wanted to thank your dad anyway and tell him I had my first session with the OT."

Jace stopped at the door, turning to look down at me. His smile was sweet as he nodded. "Good girl."

I made a face and brushed off his compliment in an attempt to dispel the heat rising in my cheeks. It had felt good. She was really patient when I met with her to discuss some of the things I wanted to achieve. Playing the drums again was my big one, and she'd said we could work our way toward it. I could either choose to learn one-handed or I could get fitted for a hook. I wasn't sure which idea I preferred more, but she went on to say how beneficial a hook could be for me. She'd showed me pictures of the two I could choose from. They were much the same—a rounded hook on the end of a tubed casing that would fit over my stump. They both had a special circular attachment that a drumstick could slide into. I'd brushed my finger over the picture and imagined myself wearing it. It looked cumbersome and uncomfortable.

"You'd get used to it. Bodies adapt to suit their needs," the OT had said.

"Plus, we'd get to call you Captain Hook." Ralphie had tapped me on the shoulder with a playful grin. The OT and Jimmy gave him equally dirty looks until his smile disintegrated and he shuffled dejectedly over to his beanbag.

I squashed my grin at the memory and flicked my hair over my shoulder as Jace swung his door open and ambled inside with a loud, "Hello, family!"

"In the dining room," a sweet voice called back.

Jace looked over his shoulder and winked at me. "Hope you're hungry."

I wrinkled my nose, about to say no, until I caught a whiff of the most delicious smell. It was cheesy and home-baked, the aroma swirling through the house like a magic finger beckoning me to hurry.

Jace's dad sat at the head of the table and raised his hand in greeting as I walked into the room.

"There she is." Phil smiled. "How's my rock star doing?"

I really hated him calling me that when it was so far from the truth, but I forced a smile and muttered, "Good, thanks."

I took his hand and he pulled me forward to peck my cheek. A round-faced lady with a short pixie cut and nutmeg eyes bustled into the room, and I stood tall to smile at her.

My mouth watered as I eyed the homemade pizza she was carrying.

"Well, hello, welcome." Her smile took over her entire face, making her rosy cheeks rise. She had straight white teeth and broad, glossy lips. Setting the plate in the center of the table, she came around with her arms spread wide. She pulled me into a hug before I could even say anything. "It's so nice to have you in our home. Jace can't stop talking about the band." She rubbed my back and patted it twice before letting me go.

I swallowed, lost for words as I resisted the urge to pull her back against me. Her loving, unhindered touch reminded me of Rosie.

Pulling out a chair, she indicated I take a seat then pushed the chair in for me before organizing everyone. I soon had a huge slice of pizza on my plate with a green, crisp homemade salad sitting next to it. Dressing was shoved at me from one direction while Parmesan cheese was thrust from another. I took both, not wanting to be impolite.

My stomach grumbled as I lifted the pizza to my lips, and it was an effort not to groan with pleasure as I took my first bite.

"This is really good, Mrs. Tolson."

"Oh, please, call me Caroline." She brushed the air with her fingers and winked. "And thank you, sweet girl. Pizza's one of my specialties."

"So." Phil shuffled in his seat. "How's life been treating you?"

"Okay." I brushed the crumbs off my lips. "I met with an OT the other day, and I'm going to start working on drumming again."

"Fantastic." Phil slapped the table with a chuckle.

"Thank you for your encouragement." I grinned and went to take another bite.

"You're most welcome. So, what seems to be

bothering you now?"

The pizza was in my mouth, but I couldn't clamp my teeth around it. I set it down on the plate and shook my head. "Nothing."

His eyes narrowed slightly, and my cheeks heated with color. I didn't want to tell him. I barely knew the family, but something about being at their table and eating delicious food with them made me spill my guts. I didn't mention my mother—I hadn't spoken of that woman since she disowned me. I did, however, admit my hesitation about performing on a stage again.

"What are you so afraid of?" Phil's perceptive gaze was trying to strip me bare.

"I just...don't like the idea that everyone will be staring at me...and my..." I lifted my stump and sighed, my shoulders drooping. "I just don't think I'm rock-star material. I don't know if I ever was. I think I've spent so long playing pretend, and now I have to face the truth."

"What truth?" Caroline tipped her head, looking somewhat mystified.

I shrugged. "I'm not legit. People are going to see that if I put myself out there."

Phil made a *pfft* sound with his lips and waved his hand in the air. "Who cares what anyone else thinks."

"I kind of do. I mean, it would affect the whole band. What if they're only coming to see Chaos so they can check out the one-handed freak? That's not what they want. They deserve real fans." I spun the fork in my hand, accidentally hitting the plate.

It pinged loudly then clattered onto the table.

Phil gave me a kind smile. "Not to burst your bubble, sweetheart, but I don't think people would pay that much just to come to a concert and laugh at you. They'll be there for the music, just like you will be."

I made a face. "I think you're wrong. I think the drama of my situation would take over the music and turn the tour into a gossip-fest rather than a celebration."

"Okay." He nodded and took a sip of his drink. I was expecting things to get really awkward—I'd just contradicted my host. But then he pressed his elbows into the table and threaded his fingers together, leaning toward me with a little smile.

"Being limbless can make you feel like you're roaming the world with a neon sign above your head saying *look at the freak*, but I've found that if you don't make a big deal out of it, no one else will, either. If you're cool with you, then everyone else will be, too."

I wrinkled my nose, thinking of my mother as she scoured makeup off my face. "I haven't found that to be true," I croaked.

"I know it's tough, but accepting who you are is the most freeing thing you can ever do." He pointed his long finger at me. "I dare you to look in the mirror and tell yourself that you're amazing and beautiful just the way you are."

"Fuckin' perfect," Jace murmured beside me.

I let out a breathy laugh and shook my head. "I don't do mirrors. I don't...like them."

It sounded so lame and pathetic. I'd never admitted that to anyone before. All three of them sat there looking at me with sad curiosity, and I felt compelled to explain.

"You can't lie to a mirror. What you see is what you get. There's no hiding."

There was a long pause and I kept my eyes down, heat rushing up the back of my neck as I tried to wipe an invisible stain off the tablecloth.

Phil cleared his throat and I glanced in his direction. "I think, Nessa, you'll find that lying to a mirror is easier than you think." He raised his eyebrows. "Telling the truth is the hard part." His quiet words hit me right between the eyeballs.

My mouth dried up like the salt flats, my tongue feeling thick and useless in my mouth.

Caroline snickered at the other end of the table. We all glanced down at her while she gave her husband a loving, teasing smile. "It's easy for him to talk the talk—it took him months of practice to be able to tell himself he was all right just the way he was. I could barely get this man out of bed in the beginning." She pointed at him and winked before turning to me with a sweet smile. "You'll get there, Nessa. All good things take time."

*****

Phil's and Caroline's words stayed with me for the rest of the day, perched on my shoulder and playing over in repeat.

What if I had been lying to myself? What if I was

worthy?

I hadn't seen myself, but singing "Come On, Let's Go" in the studio had been so much fun. I'd felt free and alive, so pumped with adrenaline that I'd been oblivious to Marcus and Jimmy watching me.

But the thought of doing that in front of an entire crowd froze my insides solid.

Jace drove up to the guest house and left the car idling as I got out.

"Thanks for lunch." I held the door open and smiled at him.

"No problem. Come anytime." His nose wrinkled. "Sorry if my dad's a little intense on the whole self-help thing. It's become his MO since the accident...a way for him to feel useful."

"That's cool." I shrugged. "I don't mind."

I put on a brave smile and kept it in place as I waved goodbye. Jace honked the horn before disappearing, and I spun on my heel and headed back to the guest house, hoping Jimmy would be there to distract me with his luscious lips and magic hands.

But when I walked in the door, Jimmy was busy chatting with a gorgeous blonde. I couldn't see her face. She had her back to me and was leaning into Jimmy as he read over her shoulder.

"Yeah, that's right." Jimmy pointed at the sheet of paper they were looking at together, but all I could focus on was the way her curvy hip was less than an inch from his jean-clad thigh.

I slammed the door shut, and they both spun to

face me.

Two sets of blue eyes hit me, both round with surprise, then in unison crinkled at the corners.

"Hi, Nessa." The woman's smile was bright as she waved her hand in greeting.

Jimmy flicked his thumb at her. "You remember Jody? She's Ella's best friend, and she's agreed to sing the duet with me."

My insides deflated. They shouldn't have but they did, and I couldn't even explain why. I didn't want to sing the duet, so Jimmy found someone new. Smart move.

"Hi." I raised my hand and looked between them.

Jody tucked a large curl behind her ear and looked between me and Jimmy. "I hope you don't mind. I just called Jimmy today to check on the order of things, and when he mentioned you weren't doing the duet anymore, I was so disappointed I offered to sing in your place."

I nodded, forcing a smile.

"Morgan will give her speech, and then we'll kick in with the song. It'll flow beautifully."

"Sounds awesome," I croaked and made for the stairwell.

Jimmy cleared his throat and put his hands in his pockets while Jody gave him an awkward smile. I ignored them both, clutching the railing and dashing up the stairs.

"It's okay that I'm doing this, right?" Jody's voice was soft, but I still heard it.

"Yeah." Jimmy cleared his throat again. "Of

course it is."

"Okay, cool. Well, maybe if we could run through just one more time before I have to go collect my baby girl."

"Sure thing."

I listened to Jimmy pick up his guitar and start strumming. His voice sounded smooth and clean as he came in with the first verse. I leaned against the doorframe as Jody's voice came in for the rest of it. They sounded good together, their harmonies blending nicely.

She was so incredibly beautiful, and next to Jimmy...they'd look amazing together. I gazed down at my stump, my face bunching with disgust.

Phil said not to care, but I wasn't just thinking about me. Chaos...Jimmy...needed to look good up there, and I couldn't help him do that.

FORTY

JIMMY

I adjusted my collar and checked it out in the mirror. Stretching my neck and rolling my shoulders, I tugged on the bottom of the white shirt and smiled. Yep, I looked good.

Nessa had picked our outfits months ago, her enthusiasm carrying us through. We were decked out in black skinny jeans, white shirts, and black leather waistcoats. We also each had a skinny black tie that hung loose around our necks. I'd actually styled my hair for once, taming the wild locks into submission with a little product. Nessa was going to love it.

I pulled the worn scrap of paper from my back pocket and read over the song list again. It was going to be a fun wedding, and I was looking forward to performing. Although Nessa was refusing to get up there with me, at least she'd be with Troy at one of the tables. I'd be able to look over at her and give her a wink. I'd been doing it ever since we'd started playing together. It was like a little energy boost in the middle of my performance, and I didn't know what I'd do without her when I left on tour.

I walked out of the bathroom and found Jace and Ralphie carrying the instruments to the van.

"We'll be good to go in about ten minutes." Flick came into the room and raced across the tiles to grab a couple of mic stands.

"Perfect." I glanced up the stairs and grinned.

Nessa was in her room getting ready. I could hear her humming. I didn't know the tune; she was probably just making it up. She sounded perfect, and it kind of killed me that she wasn't willing to share a little of that goodness at the wedding, but I wouldn't push it.

I gently tried to persuade her after Jody left, but Nessa was a stubborn girl and there'd be no swaying her. I just had to accept the fact she wasn't ready.

It was fucking hard, but I had no other choice.

The guys strolled back in, clearing the last of the stuff off the floor and collecting the last two cables we'd need.

"Garrett's going to meet us there," Flick

murmured and looked at me.

"It's good of him to help us out."

"I think he likes it." Flick grinned then pointed over his shoulder. "Should we get going?"

"Yeah, just waiting for Ness." I ran my hand over my styled hair and grinned, looking forward to seeing her sexy bod walk down the stairs. I had no idea what she was going to wear, but she'd look hot no matter what.

"Nester! Let's go!" Ralphie hollered up the stairs.

I grinned at him, gazing up to her door and feeling my insides simmer as she came out of it. She wasn't humming anymore, and I felt a boulder lodge in my throat when I caught her expression. She was wearing a long, black dress that wasn't her at all. It had a high collar and covered every inch of her body like a shapeless sack. It even had these sleeves that were so long, you couldn't even see her hands. She looked uncomfortable and out of place as she adjusted the dangling silver earring in her left ear and looked down at us with an awkward smile.

I hid my surprise at her outfit choice behind what I hoped was a friendly grin.

"You ready to go?" I came up the bottom two steps and held out my hand.

She drank me in, her eyes going wide with approval before dropping to the floor. She swallowed and smoothed down the back of her hair.

"Um." She shook her head. "You know what..."

She rubbed her temple and cringed. "I'm actually not gonna go. I just don't feel great today, so I'm gonna...yeah, I'm gonna stay."

She backed up the stairs, retreating to her room before I could reach her.

With a softly muttered curse, I looked back to the guys. "Just give me a minute."

"We'll wait for you in the car." Ralphie nodded, throwing me a sympathetic smile as he made for the door.

I took the stairs two at a time. I didn't knock, but strode into the room and wrapped my arms around Nessa's stiff torso. Resting my chin on her head, I whispered, "I need you there."

Her fingers brushed my arms locked around her waist. "I thought I could do it, but you guys all look so amazing and handsome and I just...I can't do this as my first public appearance. Everyone's going to want to ask how I'm doing, and they'll all be looking at me."

"I'm pretty sure they're going to be focused on Cole and Ella." I squeezed her back against my chest before letting her go and gently spinning her around. I held her shoulders lightly, gazing down at her with a look I hoped hid my frustration. Was this the way it was going to be from now on? I'd go out and live for the both of us while she hid away in her room?

"Ness, baby, you have nothing to worry about. You're perfect. You're—"

"Would you stop saying that!" She flicked me off her and stepped back. "I'm *not* perfect, Jimmy.

I'm a messed-up wreck who thought she could move forward, but then…" She shuddered, staring down at her draping dress sleeves before slashing a finger beneath her eyes. "I can't even look in the mirror without cringing. How am I supposed to stand next to the world's most gorgeous human being?"

Before she could talk any more shit, I grabbed her arm. Flipping back her sleeve, I pressed her stump to my lips, then gently brushed the scar with my thumb.

"Fuck the mirror." I held her arm against my beating heart. "I'm your mirror now, and every time you look at me, I want you to see that I love you just the way you are, right here, right now. I don't need you to change or be anything different. Whether you think you're perfect or not doesn't matter, because you're perfect for me."

Her eyes glassed over, tears brimming on her dark lashes. One broke free, trailing down her cheek and taking a smear of mascara with it. I skimmed it with my thumb, leaving a big black smudge across her cheek.

"Oh shit, sorry. I just…" I tried to rub the mark away again but only made it worse.

She smiled and dipped her head as another tear trailed down her cheek. "You are so incredibly sweet."

I kissed her forehead. I had a sinking feeling that although my speech had been epic, I wasn't going to be taking my girl to the wedding. "I meant what I said," I murmured into her hair.

She sniffed and nodded, gripping my shirt and mumbling, "I'm sorry I can't do this."

I clamped my teeth together and swallowed. "But you can. You're strong enough."

Her head started shaking before I'd even finished.

"I know you're afraid. I get it." I held her shoulders, forcing her to look at me. "I lay down every night scared shitless that I'm going to somehow turn into my dad again, and every morning when I wake up, I have to tell myself that I'm not. It's a choice. I am *choosing* to be the guy you need me to be, because I love you and I want to be with you."

Her smile was weak and watery.

"It's your turn to make a choice now. Who do you want to be? Who do you want to believe? Me? Or some chick from your past who never understood you? Rosie saw you for who you really are." I brushed the back of my finger down her damp, smeared cheek. "And so do I."

Her lips quivered open, her eyes flooding with even more tears.

"You have to overcome the bullshit so we can be together all the way. I am here, *waiting* for you, but I can't make this gap any smaller."

The words fell heavily into the room as we both warred with our own doubts. I'd laid mine bare, but I could tell by the dent in her forehead that hers were still on lockdown. I hated that there was nothing more I could do.

My throat swelled as I pictured our long-distance future. I didn't want to leave her, but I'd made commitments—to the band, Torrence Records...Ella and Cole.

"You sure you won't come?"

"I'm a mess, Jimmy." She swiped at her tears. "You have to go or you're going to be late."

Fresh tears streamed down her cheeks, but I didn't have time to brush them away. Pressing my lips together, I clenched my jaw then stroked my lips across her forehead.

"See you when I get back," I croaked and walked out of the room.

It was a lonely glide down the stairs and only brought home the fact that if I was going to stay true to my word and be a one-woman man, then come January, I had a lot of lonely, cold nights ahead of me. A thought like that would have sent me over the edge in the past; now, it just depressed me. I couldn't make her come to me. I couldn't make her sing.

I said I'd love her just the way she was, so that's what I had to do.

Running out to the van, I jumped in the back and slumped down next to Jace. The guys didn't say anything. Ralphie revved the engine, and we drove away from the guest house with the music blaring. The excited buzz that normally carried me through performances was a low, flickering murmur. Closing my eyes, I leaned my head back against the seat and had to wonder if I'd ever be able to adjust.

I didn't care how good we sounded; Chaos

without Nessa was soulless.

If only I could make her believe that.

FORTY-ONE

NESSA

The front door slammed shut, and I slumped onto my bed. The silence was thick and suffocating, but I'd left both remotes for the internal sound system downstairs. With a huff, I tromped down to the kitchen and pressed the 'play' button. I didn't even care what I listened to; I just couldn't have silence. Tears still trickled down my face, tickling my skin and tasting salty on my lips. I slashed at them, no doubt smearing even more mascara over my cheeks. I sniffed and clipped to the bathroom, tearing a wad of toilet paper free. I mopped at my tears, but they kept falling until my face was a smudged mess. I glanced in the mirror and froze.

Thick lines of mascara and eyeliner looked like war paint on my pale cheeks. My eyes were turning red and puffy as I roughly wiped the rest of the makeup off. Soon, I was looking at a blotchy, white complexion that reminded me of the defiant fourteen-year-old I once was.

I'd hated myself back then because my mother had.

I hated myself now because I couldn't move past everything she'd made me believe.

"How could he possibly think I'm beautiful?" I shook my head, staring at my reflection, wondering if it was a lie.

Pulling back my shoulders, I sniffed and looked myself in the eye. "You are amazing and beautiful," I mumbled. "Fucking perfect." My chin trembled as I heard Rosie's voice in my head. It'd taken her months of patient persistent to help me believe I was more than a devil-child. She'd taught me that I could be whatever I wanted. I'd bloomed under her care, discovered who I wanted to be...and then wilted when she died. Drumming had helped me mask my pain and cover my wounds with a fragile sticky tape that started popping free the morning Jimmy told me he couldn't love me. His rejection had unearthed a sleeping volcano of self-loathing that had been lying in wait to bubble and spew inside me until I couldn't hide it anymore. My confident veneer had crumbled around me, and I'd once again become the girl my mother had lost all hope in.

"Look at you." I glared at the glass, imitating my mother's disgusted tone. I held up my arm until the black fabric fell away to reveal an ugly stump. My face crumpled, and I squeaked, "You're ridiculous."

Jimmy's words nudged the back of my brain, like muffled shouting desperate to be heard.

I'm your mirror now. Whether you think you're perfect or not doesn't matter, because you're perfect for me.

Damn, that nearly made me melt on the spot. I wanted it to be true. I wanted to believe him. The look of searing disappointment as he left still burned. I was letting him down, and he was no doubt looking into the future and wondering if we could sustain a relationship like this.

Fear coiled in my belly like a python ready to strike. I gripped the edge of the vanity and started rocking as my mind threatened to shut down.

Shuffle play selected the next song and I stilled. I didn't recognize the opening piano riff. I had no memory of ever listening to the song or dragging it into my playlist, but I must have at some point, and I couldn't believe I'd never listened to it before.

"Mirror, mirror, on the wall…" I looked back at the mirror, my eyes transfixed to my ghostly reflection as the words soaked into me. My chest heaved as I listened to them. I couldn't be perfect. I'd never been able to be. The drumbeat kicked in for real and the music swelled around me, my breaths coming out fast through my nose.

The song was basically giving the mirror the

finger for trying to define the singer over the years, forcing her to be something she wasn't. I knew that feeling down to my very core. I'd fought my mother for as long as I could, but she'd left her poison inside and I'd allowed it to fester. I swore I'd never let her break me, but she had. She'd won.

My white-hot boyfriend was going to a wedding of people I cared about, *without me*, because I couldn't leave the damn house for fear people would look at me with that same pitiful, disgusted glare she always used to throw my way.

Jimmy had told me I was beautiful and practically begged me to join him, and I'd stood there like a stubborn ass, refusing to see things his way. I'd hurt him out of this sick belief that I wasn't good enough, and I'd most likely lose him for the same reason.

It was so incredibly fucked-up.

I'd wanted him for so long. Now I finally had this chance, but I couldn't see past my own shit to let him in.

Sobs jerked my belly as my face bunched with grief and fury.

"Damn you, Mother!" I screamed. "You did this to me!" I snatched Jimmy's cologne bottle off the vanity and hurled it at the glass. It smashed with a loud crack, scattering across the counter and releasing a pungent aroma that made my knees weak. The mirror was broken, five splinter lines forming where the corner of the bottle had hit the glass. Tears of perfume slid down the mirror and pooled along the metal frame. I gazed at my distorted reflection, my face chopped in half and displaced by the shards of glass. I looked like a Picasso painting. The drumbeat dropped away from the song, and a soulful piano riff filled the room as the singer spoke to the mirror.

I absorbed the words, softly repeating them to myself until the drums kicked back in, and I found the voice to shout, "I won't let you win. I may not be what you wanted, but I am perfect for him and that's enough. That's always been enough!"

I bent over on myself, sobs shaking my belly as I crumpled to the floor. I wrapped my hand around my stump, reliving the touch of Jimmy's soft lips pressed against it.

"It's enough," I whispered. "It has to be enough."

The song came to a finish, moving on to a heavy metal beat that I would usually bang my head and dance to. I scrambled off the floor and snatched the remote, pressing it until I was listening to "Mirror" again. I closed my eyes and let the words sink into my core. When the girls launched into the second chorus, my eyes snapped open. With a short sniff, I lifted my chin and made a terrifying decision.

FORTY-TWO

JIMMY

I adjusted the strap around my shoulders, running my finger under the leather so it didn't dig into my collar so much. So far, we'd played a little pre-reception music and then some quiet tunes while the guests ate. Our only big number had been when Ella and Cole entered the banquet hall. She'd been amazing as she glided across the wooden floor in this white dress that floated around her. The fabric was that soft, see-through kind—layers and layers of it that hugged her tiny frame before cascading to the floor. Cole's eyes were hungry and glowing and...damn, he was totally besotted with her. Their smiles were radiant, and they kept giving each other these goo-goo eyes. I would have thought it was kinda cute if it hadn't gotten on my nerves so much.

Troy watched me from a table at the side of the room. When he finally caught my eye, he gave me a quizzical frown. I rolled my eyes at him. If anyone could see behind my mask, it'd be him. I shook my head and made a concerted effort not to look at my brother for the rest of the night. He'd no doubt want to chat at break time, so I'd need to make myself scarce. I wasn't in the mood to talk.

Ella and Cole were blissfully happy, and I was standing on a stage without Nessa. It was hard to pull a smile when all I wanted to do was go back and wrap my arms around her. I felt like scum for leaving her crying. I felt like scum for knowing I wouldn't be around to help her with therapy. I hated the idea of leaving her alone while we were touring. I didn't care that Jace had offered to let her move in with his parents. I wanted to be the one who was there for her!

It killed me that she wouldn't step outside of herself to give us a fighting chance and I couldn't do a damn thing about it. Waiting for her to come to me was going to be fucking torture. What if she never made it?

I squeezed my eyes shut and gave them a rub.

No, damn it. I had to believe she would.

The microphone squeaked and I opened my eyes, forcing myself to focus as the speeches came to a finish.

Morgan cleared her throat and chuckled into the microphone as she stood from her seat. She looked a little nervous talking to the crowd, but she kept her eyes on the happy couple. I scanned the room and noted Jody slipping over to the door with a mic in her hand. We'd rehearsed just before we left for the ceremony. She would sing from the back of the room and walk forward with the mic. It gave the song extra flair, and people would get a kick out of it. Plus, it'd add to the surprise for Cole and Ella.

I tuned back into Morgan's voice, not wanting to miss my cue. "...and that is why we love you guys so much. You are an amazing couple. We are all so honored to know you, and we look forward to watching you grow old together over the years." She raised her champagne flute and said to the crowd, "Best friends make the best lovers—to Cole and Ella, may you have a long and happy life together."

People raised their champagne flutes with a cheer before taking a sip. I started playing "Lucky" before the glasses hit the tables, my pick skipping over the strings as I leaned into the mic and sang the first line. So not our style, but Nessa had been right. It was the perfect song.

The crowd let out a happy sigh while Ella and Cole looked at each other and grinned.

It was an effort to get out the words. I had to really concentrate as I sang about oceans and skies. My voice ended up croaking on my last word, and I was more than relieved to stop for a second so

Jody could sing her part.

But she didn't.

The voice coming through the mic wasn't Jody's. My chest restricted then pulled apart as Nessa's sweet melody filled the room. I froze still, my eyes locked on the path Jody had walked a few hours earlier. I held my breath, waiting, and then my girl appeared. Her cinnamon gaze hit me right in the heart, the playful way her lips formed the words nearly making me miss the chorus.

She winked at me and I lurched for the mic, coming in for the words 'best friend' and managing to find my harmony. I couldn't take my eyes off her as she swayed toward the stage. She was dressed in a tartan miniskirt that only just covered her cute butt and a pair of biker boots that zipped up to the knees. Her black tank top hugged her curves, the V so low you could just see the lacy edging of her black bra. She wore layers of muted silver necklaces and multiple rings on her fingers. She looked so…Nessa.

My rocker-chick was back. From the messy ponytail high on her head, to the dark eyeliner that made her eyes pop, to the cherry-red gloss on her luscious lips.

She held out her left arm and Ralphie gently took her stump, helping her onto the stage. She spun around and bumped her hip into mine. I turned to face her, singing into the mic and smiling so wide I could barely form the words.

Her smile lit the room as she faced the audience, tipping her head at Ella and Cole. They both waved at her while Ella wiped tears from under her lashes. I gazed around the rest of the room, watching people as they stared at my girl, completely enamored. She turned back to me and sang her lines with a flirty grin on her face. We finished off the rest of the song, performing like we were the only two people in the room.

I did my final strum and the audience started clapping. A loud cheer rose around the room, and I wrapped my arm around Nessa's neck and pulled her toward me. I kissed her hair and whispered into her ear.

"That cheering's for you, you know."

She leaned back and smiled up at me. "No, it's for us."

"Damn, I like loving you," I murmured.

"I like loving you, too, Jimmy Baker." She kissed my cheek then whispered into my ear, her hot breath making my insides sizzle. "You're fucking perfect for me."

I squeezed her shoulder and was about to lean her back and kiss her breathless, but Flick started playing "I'm Gonna Be" before I could. Raucous laughter went up around the room, and I quickly joined in to play the song Cole had serenaded Ella with in the middle of that college campus a few years ago. Cole let out a cheer and jumped up from his seat while I started singing into the mic.

Nessa giggled beside me when Cole lifted Ella out of her chair and carried her onto the dance floor. They twirled around the space, laughing together as he sang and wrapped his arms around her.

Nessa joined me on the chorus. I grinned like a lovesick fool as I watched her dance beside me. We hollered out the chorus like an anthem, and soon the entire room was joining us. People moved onto the dance floor and the party really got started.

As soon as one song finished, we kicked in with the next. The first set ran like a dream, Nessa slipping into the band like she'd been lead singer all along. We'd known each other long enough to work in perfect tandem. I guess that's what happens when you perform with your best friend.

EPILOGUE

NESSA

It was the first performance of our official tour. I was so nervous, I'd peed about fifty times already. I was going out of my mind until I discovered a drum kit, sitting empty in a back room. I raced off and told the guys where to find me, snatching my bag and leaving them all wondering what the hell was wrong with their crazy rocker-chick.

I adjusted the hook on my hand, slotting the stick into the attachment before popping my ear buds in. I pressed play and closed my eyes, the haunting tune swirling into my brain.

With a soft smile, I started singing "Fight Song"

along with Rachel Platten. My bass pedal kept a steady beat, and when the chorus kicked in, my hands got to work. It still felt weird drumming with a hook, but I was getting used to it. The beat flowed through me, and I dove into the song, swimming through the lyrics and making them my mantra.

The sticks felt good, sending vibrations up my arm every time I hit the skins. A smile spread across my face, wide and free, as the song came to a finish.

A soft clapping sounded from the other side of the room, and I opened my eyes to find Jimmy leaning against the doorframe, grinning at me. His blue gaze was electric, the way it always was before a performance.

He pushed off the frame and sauntered into the room. "I still believe in you." He gave me a cute smile and tapped his finger on the cymbal, making it rock and sway.

I caught it with my hand and chuckled. "I believe in you, too."

He appreciated the comment; I could tell by the whiff of pride that brushed over his lips whenever I said stuff like that to him. Now that I'd made my big leap of faith and presented myself to the world, there was no way in hell I was letting Jimmy turn back into his father. Every morning, we woke up beside each other and made a choice.

"You ready?" He tipped his head at me.

Nerves shot through my belly, but I nodded. "Yeah." Pulling my stick out of the hook, I placed them both down then stood.

Jimmy came around the kit to help me. His eyes roved my body, from my skintight leather pants to the sparkly, loose tank they had me wearing. I actually didn't mind it too much. It was silver and caught the light, making it shimmer as I danced around the stage. It'd looked pretty awesome in dress rehearsal.

"You look good enough to eat," Jimmy muttered, gripping my hip and pulling me against him.

I chuckled and winked. "You can taste me later."

He whined in his throat, lurching for my lips and hungrily kissing me. I threaded my fingers into his hair, sucking his tongue into my mouth.

"You guys better keep your clothes on!" Flick shouted from the door as he rushed past us.

Nerves always made him grumpy as sin.

I snickered and wiped my lips. "I don't have red smeared across my cheeks, do I?"

Jimmy tipped my head back and ran his thumb around my mouth. "No, you're perfect." He went to kiss me again, but I pulled back.

"I'll never be able to keep my clothes on if you keep kissing me like that, seriously."

He chuckled and reluctantly stepped back, but not so far that he couldn't reach forward and help me remove the hook. I pulled the sock off my stump and ran my finger over my latest tattoo. I'd gotten it for Christmas. It wrapped around my wrist like an ink bracelet.

Jimmy gently took my arm and kissed the swirling letters that created an endless sentence: *I am perfect for my true love.*

It was a permanent reminder that my mother could never touch me again.

"You guys nearly ready to go?" Marcus leaned against the doorframe. I peeked around Jimmy's torso and grinned at him. Our poor manager looked kind of tired and frazzled. The lead-up to the first big show had been huge and exhausting for him, not to mention some angst with a new secretary at Torrence. I didn't know all the details, but Marcus had been acting way weird since her arrival. I'd seen her once. She was stunning, with long, dark hair and perfect bone structure. Her body was all curves and she dressed so elegantly, it accentuated every single one of them perfectly. She was totally in the wrong vocation, if you asked me. Milan model would have suited her much better.

With a playful grin, I swaggered over to him.

"You're looking a little tired there, Marcus. That new girl Kelly's not giving you more grief, is she?" I asked the question innocently enough but got a low growl in reply.

Jimmy started laughing and slapped Marcus on the shoulder. "Don't worry, man. She'll see the light eventually."

Marcus scrubbed a hand over his face and mumbled, "Troublemaker." I had no idea what he was talking about, and I didn't have the chance to ask, because Ralphie came running to the door like an excited puppy and shouted, "Come on! Let's go show LA how to rock 'n' roll." He made the rock 'n' roll symbol with his hands and stuck out his tongue like a maniac before scampering off again.

"I don't know who I prefer less before a performance—Grumpy-Ass Flick or Hyper Ralphie." Jimmy grinned and kissed my lips before taking my hand and pulling me out the door.

I winked at Marcus, who looked as nervous as I felt. He gave me a breathy laugh and squeezed my shoulder, following us to the side curtain. We met up with the guys on the edge of the stage and stood there on jittery feet.

Although we couldn't see them, the energy buzzing from the crowd was an invisible electricity that lit the air. Anticipation and nerves sizzled through my veins as I bounced on my toes and smiled at my boys.

"You know, if we suck out there tonight, I'm still going to have the best time of my life."

They all grinned at me and Ralphie nodded. "Chaos forever."

"Damn right." A slow smile spread across Flick's face.

"Let's do this!" Jace whooped, and after a nod from Marcus, ran onto the stage, followed by Ralphie and Flick. The crowd went ballistic with an enchanting roar that filled the arena.

I turned to look at Jimmy, drinking in his sparkling, giddy gaze, and rose to my tiptoes.

He grabbed the back of my head, planting a hot, passionate kiss on my lips before letting me go and running onto the stage.

"Hey, hey, LA!" he shouted into the mic, pointing his finger into the sky. The chicks in the front row jumped up and down, screaming his name and swooning like giddy schoolgirls.

My man.

Ecstatic bubbles popped in my chest. Some days, I still couldn't believe it, but he was mine and I was his…forever. I couldn't help giggling as I ran onto the stage with my mic and shouted, "Are you ready to par-ty!"

The crowd surged with another cheer. I threw my head back and laughed, adrenaline pumping through me as Jace clicked his sticks and brought us in on a song Flick and I had written at the beginning of the year—before my life fell apart then got stitched back together again. I jumped on my toes and raised my left arm to the sky, letting out a loud whoop before singing the opening line of our epic rock anthem.

Another roar came up from the crowd, and I ran toward the front of the stage, bending low and singing as our enthusiastic fans joined us, hollering the lyrics.

I spun and skipped over to Jimmy when he hit his guitar solo. He looked so damn hot, biting his lip as he got into the song. I danced beside him then pulled the mic to my lips and sang my next line, throwing a sexy smirk at the crowd.

And you know what? I couldn't see my mother anywhere. All I saw was a crowd of kindred spirits who loved rock 'n' roll just as much as I did.

Standing there, performing with my guys, I

found perfect peace in Chaos, and I knew I'd be doing this for as long as I possibly could.

THE END

Thank you so much for reading *True Love*. If you've enjoyed it and would like to show me some support, please consider leaving a review on the site you purchased this book from.

KEEP READING TO FIND OUT ABOUT THE NEXT SONGBIRD NOVEL...

The next Songbird Novel belongs to:

Marcus & Kelly

TROUBLEMAKER

Is due for release early 2016

Kelly DeMarco is out of Marcus Chapman's league. When he met her in high school, he was besotted with the blue-eyed goddess, but she never gave him the time of day.

High school is now over, and the tide is turning.

Five years later, Kelly is looking for a job, and the best one she can find happens to be Marcus Chapman's personal assistant. He is thrilled by this second chance and determined to finally win the beauty's affections, but Kelly has no intention of falling for the 'class clown'.

What you're looking for can sometimes be hiding right in front of you.

In spite of her resolve, Marcus's playful charm begins to chip away at Kelly's protective veneer. She starts to realize that tall, dark, and handsome isn't always as fun and that sometimes Mr. I Don't Think So can actually be Mr. Perfect.

Will Kelly's obsession with keeping up appearances push Marcus away, or will he have enough drawing power to convince his favorite girl that honest love can outclass anything?

*****

If you'd like to stay up-to-date with the SONGBIRD NOVELS, please sign up for the newsletter, which includes a special offer, plus bonus features for newsletter subscribers only.

http://eepurl.com/1cqdj

You can find the other Songbird Novels on
Amazon.

FEVER
Ella & Cole's story

BULLETPROOF
Morgan & Sean's story

EVERYTHING
Jody & Leo's story

HOME
Rachel & Josh's story

.

ACKNOWLEDGEMENTS

I know I'm always thanking the same people each time I do my acknowledgements page, but their help is instrumental in making these books what they are, and they deserve all the praise they can get. ☺

Thank you so much to:

My advisors: Lisa and Pete. Your medical and technical advice carried through to this story and was so helpful in making the accident and recovery scenes plausible.

My critique readers: Cassie, Rae and Anna. Thank you so much for your thoughtful feedback. You've added so much depth to this story with your insights.

My editor: Laurie. You're the best. Love working with you.

My proofreaders: Kristin, Marcia, Lindsey and Karen. Love what you guys do for me. You're amazing.

My cover designer and photographer: Regina. Woohoo!!! This cover is so amazing. Thank you!

My publicity team: Mark My Words Publicity. Thanks for all your time and effort. You guys are the best.

My fellow writers: Inklings and Indie Inked. Thanks for your constant support and encouragement.

My Fan Club and readers: THANK YOU! I love you guys, you make this journey so much fun. ☺

My family: What would I do without you guys? Thank you for your constant love and support.

My savior: Thanks for teaching me how to look at my true self—*I am fearfully and wonderfully made.*

OTHER BOOKS BY MELISSA PEARL

THE SONGBIRD NOVELS

Fever—Bulletproof—Everything—Home

Coming in 2016: Troublemaker

THE FUGITIVE SERIES

I Know Lucy — Set Me Free

THE MASKS SERIES

True Colors—Two-Faced—Snake Eyes—Poker Face

THE TIME SPIRIT TRILOGY

Golden Blood — Black Blood — Pure Blood

THE ELEMENTS TRILOGY

Unknown — Unseen — Unleashed

THE MICA & LEXY SERIES

Forbidden Territory—Forbidden Waters

ABOUT MELISSA PEARL

Melissa Pearl is a kiwi at heart, but currently lives in Suzhou, China with her husband and two sons. She trained as an elementary school teacher, but has always had a passion for writing and finally completed her first manuscript in 2003. She has been writing ever since and the more she learns, the more she loves it.

She writes young adult and new adult fiction in a variety of romance genres - paranormal, fantasy, suspense, and contemporary. Her goal as a writer is to give readers the pleasure of escaping their everyday lives for a while and losing themselves in a journey…one that will make them laugh, cry and swoon.

MELISSA PEARL ONLINE

WEBSITE:

www.melissapearlauthor.com

YOUTUBE CHANNEL:

youtube.com / user / melissapearlauthor

FACEBOOK:

facebook.com / melissapearlauthor

TWITTER:

twitter.com / MelissaPearlG

PINTEREST:

pinterest.com / melissapearlg

INSTAGRAM:
instagram.com / melissapearlauthor

CPSIA information can be obtained
at www.ICGtesting.com
Printed in the USA
LVOW12s2224290916

506790LV00002B/143/P

9 781518 728747